THE ART OF DASH

Parker Rimes

Death is the golden key that opens the palace of eternity.

JOHN MILTON

CONTENTS

CHAPTER 1

The young black guy stepped away from the Chrysler and gestured to its open rear door.

"He wants to see you," he said. Wearing a dark suit; looked expensive, or Italian. Gold chains around his skinny neck and wrists, more sparkly minerals in his earlobes. The kind of guy who believed clothes maketh the man, instead of ignoring this ancient sales pitch.

"Who?" Zach asked. "Some jeweler offering discount specials? I'll pass, thanks. I don't wear trinkets." He moved to step around him.

Another guy, older, more mannish, climbed out of the front seat, spread his hands in a gesture that meant: let's not have any trouble here.

"He's no jeweler," the skinny one said. "Best not to piss him off if he wants a talk. We'll bring you back."

Both lightly built, no match for Zach in an arm wrestle, but probably strapped with some weapon.

"It would help if I knew the nature of this visit," he said. "Otherwise I'll feel testy and uncooperative."

The skinny one tilted his head. "You deal in news, right? He's got some, is all."

1

"How long will this take?" His curiosity piqued; some of his best stories came from unexpected sources, and he hadn't found a quality piece for months. Damn stupid to turn down a possible front pager.

"Takes as long as it takes."

"Sounds okay," he said agreeably, and climbed into the back of their car. The skinny guy took the space alongside him. The older one drove.

Zach's cell rang, and he reached for it.

"Leave it." The skinny guy put a hand on his arm. "Call back later."

The cell rang out, then pinged to advise of a message arriving. He ignored a second ping as well. His minders seemed relaxed, which reassured him. Best to assume they were doing what they said they were doing: fetching him for a meeting.

Nobody spoke while they sped south on North Michigan Avenue, pulling up outside a restaurant fifteen minutes later.

"Thai Style," proclaimed neon in red and blue in the window. "Closed," announced the sign on the door.

"Good choice, guys," he said, "but it's the wrong day."

"Private function." The skinny guy ushered him out of the car. He knocked on the door twice and as it opened, stood back to allow Zach to enter first.

Inside, a couple of bigger men, also black, sat at a table. No skinny aides-de-camp, they were bulky, with unbuttoned coats showing holsters and firearms. What the fuck was this about? One of them stood up and patted Zach down. The two who had brought him stayed behind him, blocking his exit.

"Careful now," Zach said. "I'm ticklish."

The guard removed his cell and his wallet. He took out Zach's driver's license and compared the photo to Zach's face.

"I know, I know, it was taken on a bad day," Zach told him. "The stylist was away."

Nobody spoke. The continued silence gnawed at his confidence; his normal assurance that he could cope with most anything the world threw his way. These guys were smart; they gave him nothing to work on, nothing to counter.

The skinny one took Zach to the back of the restaurant and along a corridor to a private room. Two knocks, and he eased the door open as if a wild animal was loose inside.

"Bring him in, Dash," somebody said.

Zach entered a small room dominated by a big black man at a table. In a corner sat another brute, the biggest Zach had ever seen off a football field. This one also wore his jacket undone, gun showing. These guys expecting gunplay any minute, or what?

Dash closed the door behind them and stood against it, hands clasped in front of him.

"Sit down, Mr. Zachary Bones," said the table man.

Zach sat, eyeing the Thai dishes arrayed on the table. Five different meals, steam rising from them, all for one diner. A lone beer complemented them. Nobody was offering him anything. Such manners.

"Do you know who I am?" the table man said.

He wasn't big like huge; he was big like Humpty-Dumpty. Normal-sized head, a wrecking ball for a body. Also favored gold chains, sparkling stones in his lobes, and a citrus-scented cologne.

"I can guess," Zach replied. The table man was Frankie Ritchie, a person of ongoing interest on the South Side. Famous in media and police circles for his involvement in street drugs despite not associating himself with either the Gangster Disciples or the Vice Lords. Both gangs had a big say, usually the final say, on who sold what in their streets, but Ritchie appeared to be trading without impediment. Trading successfully; his specialty: everything nasty.

From what Zach had picked up, the police, too, were baffled by Ritchie. He had one minor conviction from when he was a teen street runner, but he had never again soiled a charge sheet.

"I'm talking to Frankie Ritchie, the high-flying tycoon," Zach said.

Ritchie studied his face for a few seconds, probably figuring whether the remark held sarcasm, decided it didn't.

"You guessed right," he said. "And you are Zachary Bones, the corruption buster, the hotshot reporter for the *Chicago Post*."

"Modesty prevents me from agreeing with you."

"Like I care," Ritchie said. "I got news for you."

"You do?"

"You know of a guy called Jason Virgil?"

"Is he someone in your line of work?"

Ritchie's handsome face tightened. "You don't know me, and you sure know nothing about my work. Don't make rash judgments; I find them annoying."

"Sorry. What about this Virgil?" Best to ask questions, take control of the interview. Keep everybody smiling and reasonable, with all weapons staying in their holsters.

"He's a bad person. Sells drugs to kids. Needs to be brought to justice." Ritchie drained his beer.

4

A drug dealer complaining about somebody selling drugs? That was news, but not front page stuff. Not worth a free ride to the South Side.

"Not to black kids, which I know you don't care about, but to white kids," Ritchie said. "Up on the North Side. College kids, high school kids, elementary school kids for all I know."

"A bad person, as you say."

Ritchie pointed a fat finger at him. "You're a newspaper guy; you should publicize these crimes and stop that sort of thing."

"I'm sure the police are putting their shoulders to the task as we speak."

Ritchie grunted. "They fuckin' useless. They need help, and you are gonna to give it to them."

"Me? What do I know?"

"You gonna get vital evidence, and Virgil be put away for a couple of lifetimes."

Aah. This was why he was here. Another shape-the-story kind of situation. Just took him a while to spot it.

"Where will I find this evidence?" he asked, but he knew the answer.

"We give it to you."

"This is a stupid question, but why don't you give it to the cops?"

Ritchie regarded him for a second or two. "They told me you were a smart one, but now I think they was wrong." He leaned forward. "I can't trust the cops for nothing, but you have a journalistic creed, right?"

"A creed? Like, tell the truth?"

Ritchie laughed. A quick and dirty laugh. "Nobody tells the truth, my friend. I bet even Mother Teresa jived a few times."

My friend, he'd said. People who called him "friend" usually meant the opposite.

"You have certain privileges, right?" Ritchie asked.

"You mean journalistic privilege? Which we treasure, where we go to jail rather than reveal our sources?"

"Yeah, that's the one," Ritchie leaned back, smiling. "You got that, right?"

"We do. We think it's part of the First Amendment. Governments think it isn't."

"Skip the civics lesson. Here's what's happenin'. We gonna send you information regarding this Virgil. You gonna write a nice story, the police gonna come to you, you gonna hand over this information, and they gonna take Virgil off the streets."

"And if they ask how I came by this information, I'm gonna keep my mouth shut?"

Again Ritchie gave him the look, the one that said if you're dissing me, you're about to collect a train-load of grief. Again Ritchie decided Zach was innocent. "You won't have to," he said. "It'll come to you anonymously like, untraceable. What I'm saying, the information is genuine. You can check it yourself."

"And this meeting?"

"Today? It never happened. Nobody saw you here all day. And if they did, your journalistic privilege would stop you confirming it, right?"

"Possibly."

Ritchie leaned forward, unblinking. "Not possibly, definitely. Right?"

Zach said, "Can't say that. Have to see what we're talking about." Get it straight from the start. He wasn't a priest with confessional duties; he wasn't going to cover up a major crime anytime.

Behind him a chair creaked, floorboards groaned under heavy footsteps. His chair flew out from under him as the corner guard kicked it across the room. He fell to the floor, twisted around to a sitting position.

"What the fuck?" He looked up at his attacker.

"Oops," the guard said in a soft voice, like his bulk did all the loud talking necessary.

One massive hand bunched around Zach's collar and lifted him clear off the floor. The other gripped his waistband, and the giant threw him into the wall. He threw up a forearm to protect himself against the collision. It didn't work. He hit the wall like a rag doll; air exploded out of him, and he was back on the floor again.

"Melvin doesn't like those who be disrespecting," Ritchie said. "You notice that?"

Zach rose, his knees shaky, fighting back the panic that came with no air in the lungs. Waited for his breathing to restart. "We were having a discussion, I thought," he said finally. "I don't recall any insults." Melvin returned to his seat and grinned at him.

"A discussion?" Ritchie said. "Was no discussion. Was sayin' how things were, and you were listenin' and agreein'. Right?"

Zach hesitated, saw Melvin's grin spreading. "Right." Later, when this "evidence" arrived, he could decide whether or not it qualified as privileged information. Ritchie's information was almost certainly worthless and self-serving crap.

"Right," he said again.

Ritchie looked over at Dash. "He's done. Drop him back in the playground you found him."

As Zach moved to the door, Ritchie said, "Let's not meet again. People might talk."

"Wouldn't dream of it."

"One more thing," Ritchie said. "You walk that mouth around me again, and I'll remove its working parts forever."

They say spirit guides are here to help. Unless you have Bardo. His visible presence often signaled a major shift in Keera's life. New stuff crashing in, tricky stuff, bad stuff that tore the soul out of a body and left it scrabbling for a new home.

Not the best news, then, to walk into a room and find him comfortable in an easy chair, smiling an apology for his unexpected appearance.

She pushed the staffroom door shut, hoping no other faculty members entered and found her talking to thin air. An assistant professor in the Department of Anthropology at the University of Chicago couldn't explain Bardo.

"There's this man," he said without preamble or greeting, brushing imaginary crumbs off his monk's habit. "A powerful man, a large man, fond of eating." He leaned forward. "But that's not the problem." Bardo's size paid tribute to his own past interest in food, and his robe sported fat stains like campaign medals.

"He has plans," he said. "These plans will come to include you."

"In what way?" she asked.

"You'll become troublesome to him."

"Please explain."

"Your impulsiveness takes you to dark places, but doesn't get you out of them easily."

"Look," she said, with mounting anxiety, "You can't offer me aphorisms and leave me hanging." His previous life as a medieval monk in England had embedded in him an Anglo-Saxon preference for the understatement.

"You need to be careful. Just saying."

"Careful? Careful? A powerful man is coming, and you only tell me to be careful? I need more than that."

Bardo picked at a food stain with a fingernail. "You're a fighter. You always give a good account of yourself."

"What if I don't?"

"Then you'll pass over to spirit side."

No arguments could ever sway this man. Bardo considered death as another rite of passage that led to a spiritual peak. She, by contrast, figured a long and healthy physical life was also desirable.

She flopped into the easy chair opposite him, tried a new tack. "So what should I be doing?"

"Watch out for strangers."

"For God's sake, I've been doing that since grade school."

"And now's not the time to relax simple precautions."

"What kind of strangers?"

"Those who want you in their car."

Although Bardo was her best friend on both planes of existence, she still wanted to strangle him. Why was he pointing out the obvious? Freaking her out with homilies that carried dark undercurrents. "Get into their car?" she said. "Like I would anytime."

"You, yes, but your friend not so much."

"Zach? Zach? Is he in trouble?"

"He's stepping into a bear pit. What I said about strangers and cars? That goes for him, doubly so."

"He's a reporter, for God's sake. He's always dealing with strangers."

"These strangers he should avoid."

"I'll warn him tonight."

"I'd do it sooner. They're very close."

"Okay. When we're done."

"We're done," Bardo said. His outline shimmered before he faded from view.

Keera remained in the room and considered the previous five minutes. Bardo stayed mostly a voice in her head, guiding, chiding and explaining. He had entered her life when she was a teen and took over from the guiding spirits of her earlier years. He seldom volunteered information about the future; he needed to be asked, and even then he wouldn't elaborate or else answered obliquely. From his point of view, all earthly troubles were minor ones in the context of a vast and unknowable universe. Easy for him to see things that way: he didn't have a partner he would die for. For a start, he was already dead.

He'd had brought Zach to her, had insisted they were a perfect match although she ducked permanent relationships like young horses ducked bridles. Bardo had been right, though— she had been wrong. Now she couldn't bear a life without the man. She didn't understand why, just knew it.

She called Zach.

He didn't answer.

She tapped the keypad to send a text message: *don't get into cars with strangers.* As she pressed SEND she picked up on Zach laughing. Him assuming a joke, or some kind of touching-base thing, letting him know she had thought of him. She keyed out a new message. *I'm not joking, this is serious.* She sent it off to chase the previous one.

Keera settled herself and let her psychic self come into play. No images formed in her mind, no voice in her ear whispered soft words, just a hunch grew firm enough to become certain.

A black cloud was wrapping itself around Zach, and it would continue rolling and tumbling until it swallowed her as well.

CHAPTER 2

Dash led the reporter back to the Chrysler and popped the passenger side door for him. Just the two of them for the ride back. This Bones guy wasn't going to act crazy, wasn't the kind of fool to get in your face. No need for an extra hand to smack him around if shit happened. Melvin had seen to that. Bones no longer the struttin' rooster like before.

The guy paused with his hand on the door handle. "I ride up front now?" he said. "I get a promotion or something?"

"You get a free trip back is what you get." Dash hoped he didn't yap yap all the way. He swung the car away from the curb and headed for North Michigan.

"How come they call you Dash?"

The dude might have shaky legs but his yapper still worked. He gave him a look that said shut the fuck up.

"Is it because you're a lively person? Always running around?"

Fool couldn't read sign language. "It's my name," he answered, deliberately showing irritation. "Got a problem with that?"

"No need to get huffy. Your given name? Dash? Sounds to me like there's a story there. Or is it a street name?"

"It's short for Dashiell."

"You're named after Dashiell Hammett? The crime writer? Hell of a thing. You got a bookworm in the family?"

Dash threw another look at him. "You dissin' me?"

"It's no disrespect to suggest your ma was a book reader. She read Hammett? The guy's been dead for fifty years. Stopped writing years before that. She must have been dedicated to track him down."

Dedicated, shit. She was dedicated. Whacked his skinny ass with any magazine she holding at the time. Never wanted to be disturbed. Not for shit like him hungry for a snack, needing a new game, bored with his own company. She got her face into some celebrity shit and she gone from the world.

"Yeah," he said. "She was dedicated."

"So, she gave you his name, an unusual name for a kid these days."

Dash didn't answer. Truth was, he liked the name. Sounded like a badass king pin, knew his ancestors, right down to their middle names.

"You got a middle and a last name?"

The guy reading his mind.

"But Dash became your regular name?"

Fuck, this guy was persistent. Gave him a bit more to shut him up. "Got shortened to Dash. Suited me, see. I always had style, looking good, talking good." He glanced at the reporter's jeans and shirt. "See you ain't reached that level yet."

Bones grinned. "You read any of him, Dash? Sounds like you got reading genes. Hammett was a top crime writer. You could pick up some neat ideas if you and your colleagues ever run out of ways to rob and steal."

"Don't see the need to read. I got movies, YouTube. They faster."

"What's faster? The telling of the story? That's like saying sex is best when it's over quickest. Some stories, you need to slow down, love the words a little."

Dash laughed. "You telling me about sex? A white boy. We all know you not rated in that department."

Bones laughed also and looked out the window. "That's just urban legends to make you guys feel good. I rate way up there."

"Yeah? You've been rating yourself, I'm thinking."

Bones shut up for a while, then asked another question, his tone no longer easy. "You often pick up strangers on the street like you did me? Like, just stand there and say 'come along bro'?"

"You're the first of the day," Dash answered, keeping it light.

"Just saying, I don't appreciate it." Bones looking out the window.

"Didn't hear you putting up a fuss when you had the chance."

"I'm lodging a complaint now. Tell your fat, fearless leader it's no way to operate if he wants to deal with me."

"You want me to use your exact words?"

"Just use words he'll understand. One letter at a time if you have to."

Dash said, "Big man waits 'til he down the road apiece before talking smack." Smiling at him, letting him know how chickenshit he was when Melvin fixed his attitude.

Bones still looking out the window. "The story comes first. I had to listen to what Ritchie had to say. Didn't get a chance to set out the terms of the relationship."

14

"Relationship? Shit, it's easy. He talks, you listen, you do what he say."

"That your way of life, Dash? You listen to his garbage, then rush around like a trained dog fetching and carrying?"

Bones working himself up. Probably feeling less of a man than he did an hour ago. Ritchie had that effect on people. Bones trying to get him riled up, say something stupid.

"What kind of shit your outfit's selling?" he asked.

The fucker wasn't going to stop; would keep huffing and puffing until he got a whack around the chops.

"Let me guess," Bones said. "Rocks, blow, ice. All the traditional stuff."

Dash kept his eyes ahead, acting like he had no ears.

"Prescription drugs? Oxycontin, hydrocodone, Percocet? Ritchie got a copy machine out the back of the Thai joint, rolling out thousands of fake prescriptions? Or has he got you running a crack house somewhere?"

They stopped at a red light.

"I forgot some old favorites," Bones continued like he was counting shit off his fingers. "Methadone, Xanax, Dilaudid and Valium." Waited a while, then, "Maybe X and roofies, too."

Dash broke out a laugh. "Roofies? You got the wrong handle on that one. No bro I know needs roofies to get a bitch to lay down with him. That's a white boy's toy, that is. Shit, drop a pill into a drink, and your idea of a good time is giving it to someone who don't even know you're there?"

He open-palmed Bones's shoulder, shoving him against the passenger door.

"When I'm down and digging it with a woman," he said, "I

want her to know who's taking her to heaven and back. Shit."
Moved the car forward on green. Bones hadn't reacted to the
contact. He felt good for a whole five seconds until the fucker
started up again.

"What about the other stuff, then? You feel good about selling
that shit to kids, in school, just out of school, too stupid to
know there's little difference between trying shit and needing
it?"

"You not from here, you don't understand," Dash said, wanting
to shut him down. "People take what they need to get by. Got
it?"

"Oh, I get it. You're part of a public health service. Nice to
know. You a patient, Dash? You take stuff to get by?"

"I got no pain. In fact, I'm so happy that at night I hit myself
with a brick to stop from singing out loud and keeping the
neighbors awake." He smiled at Bones to let him know it was
okay to smile back, to let him know who was in charge here.

"The business you're in," Bones said. "What kind of career path
you planning on?"

Fucker had no laughs in him. Dash drew a long breath. "You
gonna shut up, or do I put earplugs in?"

"Only asking," Bones said. "It's not my area of specialty, just
curious. I mean, you don't see many dealers who reach a nice
old age where they can look back on all the good works they
did, and get all warm and fuzzy inside."

Dash gave up. Bones kept coming with the questions, slipping
in the knife at the same time, thinking it wouldn't be noticed.

"I mean, most of you guys don't make it past your mid-twen-
ties," Bones said. "You're found shot up, spilling your insides
onto a dirty street, and the next fool steps up to take your
place. You got a plan to avoid that fate?" He stopped like he'd

run out of shit to say. Then a new thing came to his busy mind. "How many birthdays you had, Dash? Twenty or so? Keep 'em in your memory bank, Dash, 'cause you won't get a lot more."

Dash pulled over to the curb. Pointed to the passenger door. "Your ride stops here, bitch ass white fucker. I'm done with you and your questions."

"I have a few more. I should do a piece on you, showing your rise and likely fall. A shining example to your peers. What it's like to live a short life as a street rat."

Bones way out of control now, running off like a loose hose spraying water everywhere. Dash locked eyes with him. "A piece? I got a piece I'm gonna lay across your face a dozen times you talk anymore."

Bones held his gaze for a couple more seconds then opened his door. "I felt like stretching my legs anyway." He got out. Held the door open and stuck his head back in.

"You ever want to talk about shit, call me," he said, sincere as a preacher now, dropped his card on the seat. "You'll find I'm a good listener. I protect my sources." Pushed the door shut and stepped away.

Career fucking path, Dash thought as he drove off. He already made more in a day than that lippy fucker made in a week; that be certain.

CHAPTER 3

Ritchie's promised proof arrived as Zach returned to his desk at the Post. An anonymous email, the same way Zach received most of his leaks from disgruntled government employees. Dozens of attachments; all jpegs, no text. The pictures showed a tall blond man in most of them. A sequence of stills, shot from ten yards away, showing men coming into view around a shoulder-high stack of olive-oil cans. At least, that's how the cans were labeled.

The blond flanked by two white guys. Some images showed them watching the blond's face; Zach guessed this was Virgil. Three other men, all black, stood in a separate group. One clear plastic bag of white substance lay on a table. Could be heroin, but could be flour; if people stood around a single packet of flour in warehouses.

Interesting images, but not proof of anything. He hadn't read the subject line of the email. An address in Andersonville. He knew the area. On the North Side, once predominantly Swedish, now a fissionable mix of many ethnic groups.

None of the pics showed the faces of the blacks. Like they knew of the camera's existence. He sorted through the shots again. Six men, but only three of them identifiable, the whites, the fall guys.

Ritchie had promised indictable and provable stuff, but this wasn't enough to get the cops interested. It looked exactly like the set-up it was. Zach was the wrong person to bring them evidence that wasn't solid. He was a corrupt cop exposer, not popular, to be ignored. These photos were a dead end. He would tell Ritchie's hired hands, if they came around again, the shots were nixed by his editor as being too inconclusive. Sorry fellas, he would say, out of my hands, I can't do anything about it.

Zach enlarged another shot to fill his screen. Mrs. Ed strolled by and stopped. Edwina Moss, City Editor. Her droll exterior masked her inner Attila the Hun.

"What's that?" she asked. "A movie still?"

"A bunch of these came in anonymously." He pointed to the thumbnails across the bottom of his monitor. "Maybe a dealer making a big deal. Not sure what to do with them." He'd decided to keep the meeting with Ritchie from her, for now. The more editors knew the more they tried to angle the story their way.

"Show me the rest." Edwina bent down and peered at the screen while Zach scrolled through them. "A new shot every few seconds. Who's the photographer?"

"Don't know. I'm guessing, but I expect it's a remote camera operated by one of the three guys who don't show their faces."

"You think this was some kind of trap for the others?"

"It looks that way. If we publish these shots, then the white guys are identifiable and would attract police attention, to say the least."

She straightened. "We're not publishing anything, yet. I want provenance and a believable account of what those shots portray."

"There goes the front page then." Zach looked up. "Nobody's going to admit sending these in."

Her gray eyes shone with a bright idea. "You know those nice police officers you love to write about?"

"I only write about the bad cops."

"And you've written about so many of them, there can't be any left. Let's assume the rest are nice people."

"And?" What tormented task was she about to lay on him?

"You show them your pictures. Ask them who these people are. They might give you some leads."

"They might. They're more likely to laugh their heads off when I ask for their help."

"You'll be helping them too, Zach. They won't like it, but if you have this photographic collection, they'll be required to act on it."

That Ritchie was so clever; now he had Mrs. Ed on his side.

"The thing is, Edwina, these pics have to be a hoax. They sure look it. It's all too neat and tidy. We don't know who sent them, we don't know their motives. Let's file 'em and forget 'em." Fuck Ritchie. He didn't want to be his errand boy, the white boy they had on a string. Best to dump this and deal with the consequences later.

Edwina perched herself on Zach's desk. "You sure you want to be in the news business?" Gently. As if she was worried about his career health. "This could be something big, or a waste of time. Most reporters would gallop off to check it out at least. You, you sit there like you're too good for the basics. Remember them? The research, the asking of questions, the spotting of the telling detail."

Unbelievable. Ritchie was about to get him fired. Had him

where he wanted. Zach surrendered.

"Okay, it's worth a shot. I wasn't thinking."

"It's definitely worth taking further. A front page in the making. Sort of thing that gives circulation a lift."

All newsprint media were hemorrhaging readers, and almost every month Zach attended a farewell drinks party for a staff member culled from the editorial herd to reduce costs. She had a point: he had to give this tidbit active attention. It might be his own job he was saving.

"I'll print a couple of these off, and pay the good guys a visit," he said.

"It's not your normal beat, though, is it?" She gave him a quizzical look. "You're a local corruption specialist, not a crime watch person."

"Sure, but if stories cross my desk, they come for a reason."

"What's that?"

"I am meant to do them."

She smiled. "That's a bit karmic for you. Why don't we pass these on to Jeremy? He's the one with contacts and can dig up stuff quickly. He doesn't carry the baggage you do with the police."

"That's the thanks I get for keeping this city a decent place for decent folk?"

She stood, patted his shoulder. "You know I hate to be effusive."

Zach kept his voice even. "Jeremy Brackett does social commentary that he passes off for news pieces. Picks on a string of burglaries, a pattern of liquor store holdups, tries to make social points along the way. Most of his background stuff he gets because he feeds nickels and dimes to street people who tell him what he wants to hear. He's out of his depth if he snoops around major drug people."

"I think you might be biased, Zach."

"And you aren't?"

His comeback was too quick, too ill considered, too likely to be taken as an insult. He waited for the return firestorm. It didn't happen.

Edwina held his gaze for a while. "We'll talk when you come back." Her tone noncommittal, her departure slow and regretful. Like a priest giving up on an unrepentant sinner.

"You have a wonderful talent with people, Zach," said a voice behind him.

Zach swung around to face Howard Hossack, the other reporter who covered government affairs. He was a tall red-blond, with freckles spattered across his face like a painter's accident. His desk almost joined Zach's, making a private conversation impossible. Now his enjoyment of Zach's exchange with Edwina plainly evident.

"I have a distaste for being led by the nose," Zach said. He indicated the image on his screen with a jerk of his head. "That rubbish just arrived. It's an obvious set-up, but Edwina sees a story in it."

"What's it about?" Howard rolled his chair over and glanced at the shadowy figures on the screen.

"I've been sent these images of guys buying heroin, and I'm supposed to show this fantasy to Narcotics."

"So what's the problem? You show them these images, and they laugh, and you come back with a story about cops ignoring evidence."

"You trying to make me more unpopular than I am already? I don't write those cheap shots. You know that."

Howard rolled his chair back again. "Just trying to get Edwina liking you again. You know she goes with anything that sells papers nowadays. Lofty standards, dear boy, are for those who can afford them."

Zach looked over the image again. "What do you know about heroin use in the suburbs?" Howard, the office Wikipedia. It was easier to fire a question at him and get a quick summary than to wade through pages of unreliable Internet sources, and end up with unsubstantiated fluff.

"We're number one in the charts. We live in a place that has more heroin use than anywhere else in the USA. It's cheap, in some areas so cheap, it's a bargain buy compared to a Bud six-pack. It's become a party drug for many."

"Not crack?"

"Not popular among the middle class. They've seen the before and after pics, and they value their looks."

"Some party when you doze off in a corner for the night. You telling me that jabbing a needle in your arm is no longer confined to aging musicians, and those stuck in hellish neighborhoods?"

"The quality is so pure you can snort it, and pretend you're a rock god."

"So there's an emerging market for the stuff in new areas? The traditional dealers must be jostling to get in there."

"They would be," Howard said. "But their networks were built up during the Vietnam years when a lot of returning soldiers came back with the habit. Most of those guys stayed inner city, and the networks did, too. How they cash in on the new boom isn't obvious. They won't have easy access to suburban kids. There are racial and cultural barriers."

Zach leaned back in his chair and contemplated the images on his screen. "This shows, or is supposed to show, black guys trading with white guys. Seems they have no problem with barriers where money's involved."

"What it shows is unclear." Howard pulled his keyboard toward him. "I'll be interested in what your investigation uncovers."

Okay, maybe Edwina was right. The cops just might give him something. Like enough information to push and pull like playdough until he could see a shape forming.

He remembered a message arriving earlier, and pulled out his cell. Don't get into cars with strangers. Nice one, Keera. Helpful, but late. And he would have ignored it anyway. Keera was psychic, and a clever academic, but she had no idea of newsgathering techniques. He'd explain that to her later tonight.

He saw another message: I am not joking, this is serious. Okay, so she had forecast the little exchange with Melvin. He still would have ignored the text. News is news; the lumps that come your way are part of it. He'd explain that also.

CHAPTER 4

Ritchie was almost done with his lunch when Dash returned though that didn't mean so much. Ritchie ate whenever his belly told him to, and his belly and his brain exchanged signals often.

Dash didn't take a seat, hadn't been asked to. He leaned against the doorframe like he was tired of sitting down. Tyrell sat at the table with Ritchie; Melvin had a chair where he could watch the door easy.

"That fool say anything interesting on the way back?" Ritchie stabbed his chopsticks towards Dash.

Dash said, "He huffy about being delivered here, like he was a grocery sack, that's all."

"You explain things to him?"

"S'plained how things work; how to listen when you speak."

"Oh, he's gonna do that, all right. He's a paperboy. He wants a tale to tell that no one else has." Ritchie turned to Tyrell. "I gotta admit, I didn't think the photo job would come off. Those guys gonna stay quiet about it?"

"You kidding?" Tyrell laughed softly. "We gave 'em a lotta slam for the gram, hardly cut it, made their eyes bug out. All they had to do was keep an itty bitty remote hidden in they hand and snap coupla happy snaps. I told 'em not to look in a certain direction. They'll be eating and whoring their profits for a long time. They know, cause I told 'em to keep they mouths shut they wanna live a long and joyful life."

"You saying silence is gonna be golden, right?'

"Right. I know these two. Been corner traders for a while, made it plain they wanted to move higher up, had some cash put away."

"Their cash or mine?"

Tyrell laughed again. "They not that stupid. They don't use, not much, they have money—"

Melvin broke in. "They know about consequences. I explained the idea to them once. Just the once. They got it. I thought they little heads would fall off the way they be bobbin' them up and down so fast."

"You're so good at those kind of explanations," Ritchie said. He speared the last dumpling on his plate and waved it in Melvin's direction. "A teacher is what you are. A damn fine teacher."

"I still think we should just waste Virgil," Melvin said.

The man had no subtle moves in him, Dash knew, but some of his ideas were real stupid.

Ritchie gave Melvin an irritated glare. "One shot, just one fuckin' shot and we have retaliation, maybe a gang war. Then what happens? The press get on they high horse and make the politicians look stupid, the politicians get onto the cops, and soon we're all being flicked out our beds and our cribs are tossed for evidence. Fuck that. Me, I want the quiet life. This way easier, trust me."

Like anybody could find Ritchie in a hurry. The man kept moving round faster than a rabbit with a choice of burrows. Never in the same place two days running, never went outside during daylight hours.

"He don't have no army," Melvin persisted. 'We got the Disciples."

Ritchie pointed a finger at him. "Get this into your fuzzy head. They not on our side. We pay them taxes because right now it suits them. This does not mean they step up when heat arrives. They be more likely to help themselves to our thing. That's why I don't want no trouble."

He looked over at Dash as if including him in his remarks. "The whole reason we are doing this," he said, "the only fuckin' reason we doing this, 'cause the Disciples will one day move in on our operation. And sooner, not later. They see how well we doing, they'll want more of it for themselves. We have to move our business."

"Why we have to bring a white boy into this?" Melvin asked, like the dumb shit he was.

"Because he's white, dummy. He's useful to us now and might be more useful later on."

Ritchie's hands were restless now. Moving to his face then back to the table. Dash knew what that meant.

Ritchie put both hands on the table. "Dash," he said, "get me a thong yip."

Dash straightened and left the room. Made his face blank, like no feelings reached there. Gave the order to the chef and came back with a plate of the sweet egg yolks scented with jasmine, and a plastic cocktail fork wrapped in a paper napkin. Smelt like temple incense, but it was Ritchie's favorite.

He set it down and Ritchie speared a yolk ball and dropped it into his mouth.

Tyrell's cell chirped and cheeped. Some dumb shit ringtone of the week. Tyrell said, "Yo?" then listened. "You done yourself a favor," he said. "I won't forget." Tyrell disconnected. Took a long breath. "One of our people in the photograph? He's telling everyone who's listening about it. As if he gonna be famous or something."

Ritchie stopped chewing. "He what?" He swallowed what he had chewed, and fixed the coldest eye on Tyrell. "This one of the guys you knew so well? One of the guys you promised me would stay zipped up?"

"Turned out I was wrong, Frankie." Tyrell hurrying his answer. "He musta been cranked up when I told him the importance of silence. Didn't take it all in. I can go see him now, make him get the message proper."

Ritchie ignored his offer. "Fuckin' knew it," he said. "Life was too easy to last. Who that you talking to?"

"One of our street guys. I give him extra, and he tells me who's doing what with whom. Fills me in what people are saying."

"How good is this dirt?"

"It's solid. This dog don't lie. At least I ain't caught him at it, yet."

Ritchie poked at an egg ball. "The big-mouthed kid, he connected to anybody we should know about?"

"No. He got no big bro watching over him. Never heard of any family from around here."

Ritchie pointed the bare fork at Melvin. "Tell Melvin where to find this kid," he said to Tyrell. "Melvin, you visit a consequence on him, shut his face forever. Dash, you take him."

"I should go," Tyrell said. "I know him."

"That's why you don't go. You been seen with him before, Mel-

28

vin hasn't. You didn't make him see things straight. Ain't taking a second chance you do this right either. Tell Melvin what he needs to know, and you stay here."

"I could talk sense into him." Tyrell, worried face, persisting. "He's only a kid, being foolish."

"He's only opening a gate to hell for us, is what he's doin'. He don't get to play extra time."

* * *

Dash drove Melvin to the address Tyrell gave them.

"Go 'round the corner and wait," Melvin said. "Leave the motor running."

He watched Melvin walk away in the rearview mirror, hoped whatever Melvin did, he did it in the apartment. Out of sight. He sipped from a soda can in the cup holder, made a face. Damn thing, warm already.

Melvin returned not five minutes later. His arm around a skinny bro, maybe eighteen years old. In the brief glimpse Dash caught of his face, he wasn't too scared, just twitchy nervous.

Melvin ushered the kid into the back seat and climbed in after him. "Take us back," he said to Dash. "Young Elon here is very excited to be honored with a meet at the highest level. Take the Eisenhower, we're in a hurry."

The Eisenhower. That wasn't going anywhere near their destination. The kid getting a short ride at a long freeway for the last few minutes of his life.

"Found Elon all alone, just watching TV. Dr. Phil, would you believe? Told him the boss had big plans for him." Melvin letting Dash know nobody saw Washington leave. The kid sat silent, thinking what?

Dash took the on-ramp and merged with the afternoon traffic. His tinted windows were beyond-legal black. Nobody saw inside.

Seconds after Dash settled in his lane, he heard a choking. Feet kicked wildly against the back of the passenger's seat. A faint crack told him a bone had broken, the kicking stopped. The smell of urine filled the car.

"Fuck you, Melvin," he yelled. "If I knew you were going to do him in my ride I woulda gotta piece of junk for the job."

"Isn't that what you have? Oh, my bad." Melvin laughed. "I didn't know this was your treasure. Take us to Sonny's." He snapped the screen off Elon's cruddy flip cell and threw it out the window. The battery followed a few seconds later. Dash heard the snap and crackle of the casing breaking open. Melvin leaned forward and dropped the SIM card into Dash's soda.

"You see what that shit does to the SIM, you never, ever drink any more of it," Melvin said.

Dash drove to Riverdale, to a car wreck joint. A massive yard, dirt alleys lined with old cars piled on each other. If you had a mind to, and a good wrench and a screwdriver, you could detach the part you wanted for your own heap. Much lower cost than asking for it at the shop out the front.

At this time of day, nobody drove down the aisles staring at the cars, hoping to find a match for theirs. They would arrive after their scrubby-ass jobs were finished. He drove up and across a few aisles until he was sure they had minutes alone. Made sure that no camera could see them. Helped Melvin drag the kid out of the back, lifted the trunk lid of a Chevy Nova and stuck the body inside.

Back at the main gate, he stopped as a clerk came out of a shack supposed to be a store. "You find anything?" the clerk asked.

"Looking for some sweet trim for the wheels," he said. "Nothing there."

The clerk dropped his eyes to the Chrysler's wheels. "You got fine babies already."

"Yeah, but me, I'm the restless kind. Want something different all the time."

"Wheel trims we keep inside. Wanna come in?"

"Right out of time, bro."

The clerk gestured to the trunk. "Company policy."

Dash popped the trunk and the clerk took two seconds to peep inside and close it again.

"You two don't look like the mechanical type," the clerk said. "I wondered why you drove through. Nothing out there but body panels, fenders and tires."

"Was a thought, that's all." Making it sound like it was no big thing. "Times are tough, no need to spend money for no reason."

The clerk stepped closer to Dash's window, sniffed. "What's that smell?"

"Your neighborhood," he replied, letting the car roll forward.

"Got that right," the clerk said and returned to the shop.

"Drop me downtown," Melvin said. "Ain't no sweet bed of roses in here no more."

"Got any more breaking news?" Dash shot back. "I gotta find a valet joint right now.

Melvin laughed and Dash got it. The man got more out of messing his ride than icing the kid.

CHAPTER 5

Zach pulled up outside Keera's town house in Old Town and wondered how much to keep from her. The situation could become major serious, and Keera would want to help. Which would make her a target for Ritchie. How do you keep secrets from a psychic? How many other reporters had this problem?

"How was your day?" Keera asked him when he walked in the door.

The way she asked, she knew everything already. He enveloped her in a tight hug, wondered if close physical contact made it easier for her to read him. Didn't care if it did. It had been a day of defeats, and the quicker she picked up on that and gave him room to recalibrate the better.

"Met some interesting characters, got in a car with them," he said, leading her to the kitchen, opening the fridge and pulling out a beer. Her herbal tea already on the table. "Thanks for the warning, though, but it arrived a couple of seconds late."

"And?"

"I was taken to meet a fat man, Frankie Ritchie, a middling-to-large dealer on the South Side." He threw down some beer. She didn't touch her tea.

"And?"

"He wanted me to help shaft another dealer. Said he'd give me evidence."

"That's it?" Her eyes searched his for unspoken thoughts.

"When I got back, an email arrived with an image of this other guy, Jason Virgil, in what appeared to be a deal going down."

"Nothing happened to you?"

She knew.

"They pushed me around to make their point. Nothing serious. Had worse moments in college football."

She reached out and touched him. "You OK?" Probably examining his chakras for wear and tear.

"Sure, it's all part of a reporter's daily round."

"What happens next?"

You're the psychic, he wanted to say, you tell me. But he knew better than to tease her when he was already tense.

"I'm sensing bad energy here," she said. "You should stay away from those people."

"Stay away? You think I have a choice?" he said. "I've been given orders to proceed with this email like it's an important leak. Tomorrow I'll contact the cops. Right off, they'll be on my case about the email's source. They might do nothing about the photos because there's not much they can do. Inspect an empty warehouse?"

"Well, that's not a bad result for you, is it?"

"If that's the result, but it won't be. It'll get worse. After a few weeks, Mr. Circumference and his boys will wonder how things are going. They'll drop by to chat. It's not a conversation I want to have because they're going to talk with the hands, not the face."

Keera blinked a few times at that news. Must have found the idea unsettling, changed the subject.

"Why did they come and fetch you like that?" she asked. "Why couldn't they simply send the email?"

An academic like her could be slow to grasp life's realities. "They made sure I knew it was important. That I wouldn't ignore it, treat it as a dumb joke sent in by a kid."

"Why not come clean and tell the police what happened?" she said. "You were kidnapped, after all."

Tell the police. Good idea, Keera. He had first heard Ritchie's name when covering corrupt baggage handlers at O'Hare. A few had taken the dirty dollar to bypass security on certain packages and were caught. When he interviewed other handlers, Ritchie's name was mentioned. The way people mention the Black Death.

"Yeah, sure, good move," he said. "Ritchie would deny ever seeing me, and then punish me. I'm stuck."

She gazed at him as if there was more he should tell her. "I find it astonishing that these people can order you about as if you were one of the gang."

"When you have money and power and you are the whole of the law, you can do what you want." He drained his beer.

"But you're being used. How do you feel about that?"

"I feel I'm being used, what else? It feels shitty. I'm a tiny piece that gets moved so that kingdoms fall."

"So, who is this Virgil person?"

"I assume he's a rival. Can't see how. They work different sides of the city. I haven't researched him yet. That's for tomorrow before I talk to the cops."

He reached for her laptop sitting on the table. Powered it up and logged into his email. Brought the images up on screen and turned the laptop around, so she could see.

"He's the tall white guy in these shots," he said.

Keera skimmed over the thumbnails, calling each up in turn until she'd seen them all. "His energy comes through," she murmured.

"You kidding me? You get that from a fuzzy image?"

"Sure, images convey energy in a powerful manner. Try browsing an art gallery sometime, tell me you're not affected." She pushed the laptop aside. "You think Ritchie wants this Virgil out of the way?"

"Well, obviously. I just don't understand why."

"So if you somehow get Virgil arrested, then the job's done? Ritchie will leave you alone?"

"He won't need me anymore, will he?" That was a lie. No mob let anybody go once they had a hold on them.

"I don't like it, Zach. You're in a dangerous place. It won't be as clear-cut as you think."

"Nothing ever is." He rocked the empty bottle on its base. "I'll figure a way through this; I'll be fine."

"Of course you will. Together we can do anything."

"I'm not so sure you should get involved."

"You. Are. Kidding."

"I'm not." This was it. She would push to get involved, and he had to push back. For both their sakes.

She tried again. "What's wrong? You need help, that's all. I can do stuff you can't." Her face tightened. "Are you saying you don't need me?"

He reached for her hand, but she drew it away. "You don't get how nasty these people are," he said. "If they figure out you're part of me, it gives them an extra hold on me. I can't have that, not going to have that."

"Really?" Her face stony, a sure sign she was bottling up stuff up.

"Really."

"How will they know anything about me? I don't need a physical presence to be somewhere, and watch and listen and learn."

"It doesn't feel right. I'll be reacting to everything you find out, and people will ask how I got this knowledge and that knowledge, and I won't be able to explain."

"It's better than working in the dark."

"You think?"

She finally snapped.

"As you know," she said tautly, "I've never given myself to just any cute-ass that walked into my life. You're the first I've decided it was worthwhile to cultivate a relationship with."

"You ended a sentence with a preposition; careless grammatical construction." She wasn't grasping what he was saying. Best to distract her before she drew the big sword. The one with words engraved on its blade: I am rethinking this relationship.

She paused, clearly pondering whether his remark was worth attacking. Decided it wasn't. "I've committed to you," she said. Her chest heaving.

"I'm so honored." Stupid thing to say, fucking provocative thing to say, but his accumulated resentment forced inflammatory words to the surface. Pushed around by Ritchie, thrown around by Melvin, ordered around by Edwina, and now, even Keera was taking over.

She stopped again. Calmed herself. "I'm ignoring that remark before I take it seriously." She took another moment to tamp down her fire. When she resumed, her voice was softer. "It's not about me helping, is it, Zach? It's about you thinking you'll lose control. Am I right?"

"Wrong." But she was right.

"Here's what you forget," Keera said. "You, the most difficult person I've ever met, and the most compelling." Her hand smoothed an imaginary table cloth between them. "There's two of us; there'll always be two of us. What hurts you, hurts me. If we don't fight this together, we don't exist together: we'll be solitary stars orbiting each other."

She'd outmaneuvered him again; made him feel like an unthinking fool for trying to shield her. And she was right. They had to face everything as one, or this togetherness, this whole glorious thing, would evaporate.

There was no other way.

Keera waited until Zach fell asleep before moving to the living room where she could shift onto the astral plane without the distraction of his presence.

She pulled two cushions off a couch, dropped them on the floor. Adjusted one under her head, and the other under her knees; her arms lay alongside her, her eyes closed. She drew long, deep breaths, visualizing her chakras one by one, working through them, accepting the lightness, holding at the edge of sleep, not letting go. A rumble, growing to a roaring in her head, a wrenching sensation and she floated free.

Ritchie, she said, take me to Ritchie.

This deliberate thought triggered a whirling through the darkness of space, destination unknown except that it would contain Ritchie. Minutes later, maybe seconds, it was impossible to measure time in this state, the emptiness around her coalesced into matter. She hovered in a barroom, three feet off the ground. A fat man at a table with another man opposite. Two others, one of them a boy, really, and the other the size of three boys, lined the bar counter and watched them.

Meet Ritchie and his team.

Bardo had joined her.

Ritchie wasn't talking, but inspecting a wine bottle, reading the label, his fingers reaching for cheese chunks on a platter.

The other man, slim and relaxed, asked, "This Bones, how long before he takes what we gave him to the narcs?"

Ritchie pushed cheese around the platter before he selected one. "He's in the news business; those people chase stories for a living. He be talking to the cops tomorrow if he ain't already run over there today."

"And then?"

"We wait a week or more for Virgil to find out just how fine my product is. Then we tell him there's more available, same excellent price, but he has to buy large this time. Organize eight keys and cut them as much as you can. We're gonna lose this shipment, and I don't need to take a bigger cash hit than necessary."

Ritchie lapsed into reflective silence. Keera understood now,

Virgil was being set up. Zach's role to make sure the police knew about Virgil, and to prime them for the main event: the next drug deal between Virgil and Ritchie's organization. Clever. Clever and evil.

Keera glanced at the men at the bar, startled to see one staring right back at her. His slightly open mouth told her everything. She floated higher and dropped over to the other side of the booth. The man's eyes followed her.

Yes, he can see you.

What do I do? she asked him.

Nothing. He sees only a shape for now.

Who is he?

His name is Dash. He brought Zach to Ritchie.

Is he dangerous?

All of them are. Let me show you something else.

The scene in front of her faded, and she whipped away into darkness.

When the light returned, it showed a hotel room. A tall blond man in his mid-thirties was dressing. Jason Virgil, she knew instantly. He pulled on chinos, tucked in a salmon-colored polo shirt, and slipped into loafers. Anonymous preppy. A rugged face crossed with a hint of petulance. The bed rumpled from use.

A woman came out of the bathroom. Young, a child not long ago. Thin and blonde, tank top, mini skirt tight and short.

"You said two hundred, right?" she said to Virgil. Her eyes anxious.

He glanced over at her, his mind on something else. "I don't recall that. I don't pay for sex, ever. The door's over there."

The girl blinking at this, but making another attempt to get her money. "You said two hundred."

"Who cares? What I'm saying is leave through that door. Your moment's over."

The girl drew herself up. "You cheap bastard. I still have to pay my pimp. You've cost me—"

Virgil took two strides and slammed his hand against her face, knocking her to the floor. He stood over her. "Do you want to keep a normal face, or do you want to do tricks wearing a mask?"

The girl didn't press, just scrambled to her feet, grabbed her bag, headed for the door holding a hand to her face.

A tug told Keera she was returning to her body. She left the room, flying back to hers.

She opened her eyes and sat up, figured Bardo had stayed close by and spoke aloud. "He rips off hookers? I thought he had piles of money." She took a few breaths to calm herself after the unsettling vision.

He has money. He also has the urge to dominate.

"I bet he once pulled the wings off flies."

He did, actually.

"And Zach's going to get mixed up with an animal like that?"

Alas.

"Can't Zach walk away?"

He's made the decision. He won't walk. It's hard for him to explain but he welcomes the challenge.

"You're kidding. He just told me he was trapped, couldn't get out."

He doesn't want out.

"Is that wise? Isn't Zach out of his league with these people?"

It's his choice. Wisdom has little to do with it.

"Well, thanks for that," she said. "I need to know much more, though—"

You have enough Bardo said, and left.

Keera returned to the kitchen and another herbal tea. Chamomile this time, for de-stressing. Impressions of Virgil still zipped through her head. A glimpse of him shooting a man in a garage. Another glimpse of him taunting an associate. She shook her head to stop the images. Sure, Virgil had to be taken off the streets, but did Zach have to be involved? Ritchie would stay out of the limelight and Zach, if he published the photos, would be the one held responsible by Virgil.

Zach sought trouble, Bardo had said. He was wrong. Zach didn't seek trouble—he inhaled it.

CHAPTER 6

In the morning, Zach left Keera sleeping and slipped out, heading for the Post. He printed off two of the Virgil images, collected his '66 Mustang from the parking garage and drove to South Michigan Avenue, the home of the Chicago Police Department. Spent the whole time wondering how much better sex was anytime after he and Keera inched closer to breaking up.

"I'd like to talk to somebody in Narcotics," he told the female uniform at the reception counter.

The woman looked him over for several speculative seconds. "You can speak to Detective Warren if he's in. Give me your name and take a seat." She hadn't figured out who he was; that's why the unexpected civility.

Since his exposé of a few precinct cops pocketing bribes from pimps last year, he hadn't been a pinup boy in Copland. Not that it proved a problem, except when he needed police help. Then, it came grudgingly, if at all. He understood the reaction. Every bad cop he, and others like him, exposed brought all police another inch lower in the public esteem. The good guys suffered through no fault of their own. It was collateral damage he didn't want to think about. Damage the cops never forgot.

Detective Warren was a solid forty-year-old, with close-cropped hair and clipped efficiency.

"What's the nature of your visit?" he asked when he arrived in the reception area.

"I'm Zachary Bones from the Chicago Post. I've come into possession of these," Zach said. He pulled the two paper prints from his pocket, unfolded them and offered them up.

The detective didn't take them. Didn't look at them. "Bones. From the Post? Ke-rist."

"This isn't an interview, Detective. I have something you might be interested in, and you might have information I need in return."

"Might? You think we deal in mights? You came here to shoot the hypothetical breeze, like a cozy coffee morning with an old pal?"

"Nothing like that."

"Good. 'Cos pals is something you're short of around here."

Warren held his stare for another second then took the photocopies. "Who took these?"

"Don't know. They arrived anonymously."

"What do you want from us?"

"Any names you can give me. I have more images."

Zach looked around. The desk woman had overheard the exchange. She fixed him with her own stare, probably trying to connect the loose dots in her head.

"Come upstairs," Warren said, walking to the elevator.

Zach followed him past desks in cramped cubicles, pizza boxes jostling with stacks of hefty folders. Post-It Notes framed most monitors.

Warren's desk sat in a space more suitable for a child than any waisty cop. Even Zach's trim figure was a mismatch here. He took a metal chair opposite.

"What's your interest in these guys?" Warren asked. "Drugs not your usual thing, is it? No more bent cops to flush out?"

"If these shots are genuine then I have a front page," Zach said. "I need to know who the others are—"

"You think I care about your front page?"

"You might care about evidence of a major deal going down."

"I'll decide what I care about," Warren said, but his eyes strayed back to the pictures in his hand.

"I think that Jason Virgil is in that shot," Zach said, making it sound he knew heaps about Virgil.

"Jason who?" Warren with the blank face. "He a friend of yours?"

The casual indifference was a giveaway. Warren was interested. Time to dangle more bait. "I hear he's got something happening."

He took it. "Who told you that?"

"Sources, you know, the kind I can't reveal."

The detective almost grinned. "You're a tricky piece of shit, aren't you?" He tapped the copies with the back of his fingers. "This could be Photoshopped. The tall guy's head is Jason Virgil's, probably pasted in. A packet of white stuff on a table? A pre-law student would tear this to bits." He dropped the prints on his desk. "What do the rest look like?"

"Give me Internet access and you can have them."

Warren shifted his chair over, and Zach dragged his chair around to face the monitor. The detective punched a few keys, clicked his mouse and shoved the keyboard and mouse over to Zach, who brought up his Gmail page.

"No peeking," he said as he tapped in his password. "I back up a few things to my private mailbox." He opened the Ritchie email and clicked on "View All Images." As the photographs filled the screen, he said, "These came with the address in the subject line."

"Forward me this," Warren said, holding up his card with a contact number and email. When Zach's email arrived, he opened the other images. "Same damn thing over and over. Who are the black guys?"

"What can you tell me about Jason Virgil?"

Warren swiveled around to glare at him. "I ask the questions here."

"I don't do interrogations, Detective. But I do trade with the right people. Friendly types."

Warren flexed his fingers. "Virgil's a dealer. North Side," he said heavily. "Who are the black guys?"

Zach moved his chair back around the desk again. Tried to spread some warmth, to get Warren away from unhelpful answers.

"Look," he said. "I don't know what I've got here. It could be nothing. It could be the start of something. I'll tell you what I know about the black guys: zip. I'm not good at recognizing faces from the back, and even if they looked at the camera, I'm not sure it would help." Was Warren interested enough to give up more information? "My turn. How big is Virgil's operation?"

"Wait a minute. You've told me nothing except that you know

nothing. What kind of trade is that?"

"If you help out, I can lever that info to find out more. I'll keep you in the loop."

The detective responded nicely. "He's got a growing organization as far as we can tell, sticks to the affluent areas. Known for dealing ninety-five-percent pure."

"Doesn't that level of purity kill?"

"Depends. People die from heroin overdose because they buy stuff that's heavily cut, and they figure out the dose needed to get out of their heads. One day they unknowingly get a load that's not so cut. They nod out, don't come back." Warren staying on safe ground, telling Zach what everybody knew.

"So why doesn't this happen with Virgil's customers?"

"It does, but not to the same extent. With that kind of purity, the kids don't need a needle. They can snort it like coke. Makes them feel like a rock star or something, but it's cheaper than coke. About the cost of a six-pack for a hit." Warren shook his head as if he couldn't believe this.

"You have college kids getting addicted, right?" Zach asked. "Wouldn't that mean prompt police action? The wealthy don't hesitate when it comes to shaking the police tree if one of their kids—"

"They can and do behave in the manner you're suggesting, but without strong evidence we have nothing." Warren practically sighed with frustration. "We're not going to court with a brain-damaged junkie as our only witness."

"Apart from Virgil," Zach asked, "who else do you recognize in those shots?"

"My turn to ask a question. Who do you figure sent you these, and why?"

"I have suspicions I can't share with you right now."

"Of course not." Warren's tone sneery as shit.

"But, like I said, I'll keep you informed as much as I can."

"Sure you will."

Zach pressed on. "It would help me if I knew which of the others you recognized."

Warren made a show of dragging his eyes back to the screen. "That guy," he said, touching the glass, "on Virgil's left, is Charlie Hostler. Virgil's closest associate. Has a clean sheet. The guy facing him, looks like Shrek, is Eric Tanner. He's linked to a Colombian mob. We think he's the guy sourcing much of Virgil's product. Probably gets a cut of the action. Which is why he's there, to count the take. He might have introduced the sellers to the buyers. Otherwise, he'd stay away. I don't know the other people."

"So who took the photos?" Zach pressed while Warren was in a giving mood.

"If they're genuine, it's somebody wanting to put a banana peel under Virgil's foot. All the black dudes never face the camera. That pretty much points the finger at the likely source of the snaps."

"A rival?"

"Or somebody with a grievance."

Warren scrolled through the shots again. "The camera's about four feet above their heads, around ten yards away, on a shelf. Maybe hidden in a box with a hole cut out. Had to run silently, none of that fake shutter noise they put in digital cameras. Operated by remote, I assume."

He slid the mouse over and clicked. "The 'Properties' gives the date, time and exposure details ... a Pentax." Warren was in detective mode, his dislike of Zach temporarily overlooked.

"Taken three weeks ago. Ten thirty-nine a.m." Warren slouched back in his chair. "I think the black guys knew the camera was there. It makes no sense to record your presence at a crime scene. Which is why we can't see their faces."

"Are these images any good to you or not?"

"If we could prove that white powder is an illegal substance, which we can't, we might have something here."

"You have an address in the subject line," Zach said. "You have a place where heroin and money has changed hands. Just wait for Virgil to turn up again, rush in and bust him."

"You oughta run this department with bright ideas like that." Warren turned to him, eyes dark with suspicion. "Why would you receive these and not us?"

"I guess you were meant to get them via me. I'm the insurance that you won't ignore them."

"You thinking of publishing any of these?"

"Only if we're willing to wear a zillion-dollar lawsuit from Virgil. We can't prove any of this is what it seems."

"So that's a no. You're going to wait for us to move, and then front page this stuff. Scoop pictures, right?"

"I don't know how this will pan out. But if these images are genuine, they're hot. The question is: what are you going to do with this information?"

"The first thing I'm going to do is not talk to the press about plans." Warren stood. "We'll work from this, and I hope our trade was to our mutual benefit, although it was damned one-sided. You find out more, you tell me more." Warren backed out of the cubicle. "What are you going to do?"

Zach followed him. "I'll wait. If you guys do nothing, I expect I'll hear from whoever sent me these."

Warren lifted an arm in the direction of the exit. "And I expect you'll call me. The elevator's still where we left it."

Zach left, sorting out what he had gained from the exchange. Warren was hooked on the images. He hadn't said why, but his interest was obvious. The other thing was that the sellers were black, not Mexican or Asian. That indicated a financial shift was taking place.

A black group, a local group offering a better deal than Mexicans? That was news.

CHAPTER 7

Zach killed the engine outside Keera's townhouse. Her father, a top-level oil executive, had bought it for her. He also gave her access to a trust fund while he spent his time negotiating maintenance contracts abroad.

"He was never home, my mother rarely sober," she said once in a rare peek into her early years. Her freakish abilities alienated her school friends, so she grew up reliant on nobody but herself. And her guide, Bardo. Zach wondered if Bardo suffered the same exasperation when dealing with Keera's stubbornness.

She wasn't initially comfortable with a close relationship; Zach had seen that at once. She'd veered from the possessive to the detached. But, as she had emphasized last night, she'd surrendered to the powerful attraction between them, difficult as that had been. However, surrender didn't mean compliance. Well, he knew that from the start, and somehow had forgotten it last night. Wouldn't make that mistake again.

A dim light in the pane above the front door announced she was home, and expecting him. Its absence would have been a signal that she was out of her body again: visitors not welcome. He'd learned that message early, too.

She insisted they live apart even as their feelings for each other engulfed both of them. "Most evenings, if I'm doing stuff, someone else's presence is distracting." She meant psychic stuff, astral travel stuff.

"I'll stay extra quiet," he offered. "Your breathing will be the loudest sound in the house."

"I'd still know you're there."

"It seems silly to live apart." He couldn't believe his own words, even as he said them. He, Zach, solitary man, who thought a three-week relationship was two weeks too long, now wanting, needing to be with someone—constantly. Keera electrified his life like nobody before her.

"It's not silly," she'd said. "I need time alone." She wouldn't budge on the issue, and then delivered the killing point: "I want to be always glad to see you."

Now, he realized she had been right. A year together and his heart still flapped like a flag when he saw her.

He couldn't explain the attraction between them: the daughter of a wealthy oil executive, born to privilege, and he the son of Berkeley radicals, whose contempt of capitalism found them scrabbling all their lives to put a filling meal on the table. Luckily, he had inherited intelligence genes and a strong work ethic. Scholarships took him to college; student loans completed his formal education; the streets of Chicago did the rest. After a few years of covering local crime—the street kind and the paper-shuffling kind—he grew familiar with the underbelly of this town.

He opened the car door and stood upright, taking in the cool air, the distant traffic sounds. The other thing about her? It was like having the world's best radar system right beside you. A major plus. A radar system that loved you. Unbelievable.

"I observed Ritchie last night," Keera said as they broke apart from their greeting embrace.

"Now you tell me? You're such a spy camera. What did you see that I should know?"

"They're planning something."

"No shit."

Her face hardened. "You want the rest or not?"

"Sure," he said quickly. Together for only seconds, and he'd already crossed a tension line. The steam from their scrap the night before hadn't quite evaporated.

She led him to the kitchen and made him wait while she brewed her tea in silence. After she sat at the table and took her first sip, she said, "Ritchie is setting this Virgil up for a bust."

"Nice to have my gut feelings confirmed. Anything else?"

"He likes to eat, doesn't he?"

Zach laughed, hoping she had recovered her mood. "You noticed, huh? He carries a year's supply of Oreos around his waist. When's this bust taking place?"

"They didn't say exactly. They're waiting for you to visit the police, and then they'll organize a new sale with Virgil. Ritchie suggested a week or so from now."

"And they drop the cops right in on this one? And lose a few of their guys in the process?" What weird shit was Ritchie planning? "That doesn't make sense. He's got to have a more sophisticated plan than that."

"He's not planning to use his people but hasn't made any solid decisions. But I understood he would keep his men out of it."

Zach pulled a beer out of the fridge, popped the top and drained half of it. "Another piece of the puzzle drops into place," he said. "If Virgil's dumb enough to attend a pickup and he gets arrested, Ritchie deals with Virgil's number two. He might grow so close to this guy that when Virgil's released, he finds he's got no organization left."

"What will he do?"

"Not a lot. He'll be alone, no soldiers working for him. He'll creep away quietly."

Keera shook her head. "Virgil's not that type. I sensed strongly that he never lets go, he'll fight until he's dead."

"You get all that from those photographs?"

"No."

Zach sat down again. "You have been busy. Tell me everything."

"I had to see for myself what this Virgil was like. It wasn't a warm and cuddly scene."

"You were expecting to find him leading Boy Scouts in a campfire sing-a-long?"

"Zach, I was worried about you. I wanted a closer look at the guy." She sipped her tea. "You can save the sarcasm for others. He beat on a hooker rather than pay her. He's ... arrogant."

"Sounds like a psychopath."

"What do you think the police will do?" she asked, changing the subject. "Did you take the photographs to them?"

"Yep. A Detective Warren was unhelpful as he could be, but he couldn't hide his interest. Gave me some names: an Eric Tanner is the guy who probably set up the deal with Ritchie."

"I'll keep a look out for him."

"You going back out there tonight?"

"I'll go whenever I feel I should. I have no script."

How did she function like this? No logic, no working out of complex scenarios, just reacting from pure instinct and feelings. "I reckon I'll get a visit from one of his goons after a while," he said. "They'll ask what I did with the images."

"When will this be?"

"I'm not the future expert here, you are. You tell me."

Her face was unreadable while she regarded him in silence. Another verbalization he should have kept to himself. Had he provoked her again? Of course he had.

"Ah, fuck it. I'll just muddle through like I did before we hooked up."

"If you need to know something, and I know the answer, I'll pass it on," she said evenly. "Until then, I'd prefer it if you stopped being such a schoolboy. I find it irksome."

Now they were both pissed off with each other. How did this happen so fast? Put it down to stress. Go back to his apartment and let both their nerves untangle themselves overnight.

Keera rose. Must have read his mind.

"I better go, need to chill and get some perspective on all this," he said, rising also.

She walked him to the front door and opened it, accepted his kiss on her cheek but didn't speak. Closed the door behind him with a soft click.

Dash sat up as Bones left the girl's house. He'd been expecting a long wait, until morning, if necessary, to intercept the man. "Find out what he done so far," Ritchie had ordered, and Dash wasn't going back with no answer.

Bones started up a cherry-red Mustang, a sweet color for a clunky old ride. Dash followed for twenty minutes until he turned into a ramp leading down to the parking garage of an apartment building.

He pulled up close and watched Bones wave a pass card in front of the boom control unit. As Bones passed under the boom, Dash accelerated to within a thin inch of his rear bumper and followed him down the ramp. The boom stayed up, the sensor reading only that a long car had passed.

Bones, staring in his rearview now, had to be wondering what the fuck. He stayed on his tail until he pulled into a space, then drew his Chrysler across the rear of the Mustang and climbed out.

The fool was already out and waiting.

"See you got home safely," Dash said.

"Homing instinct," Bones replied. "I'm good with it." He gripped his keys like they be weapons. Had enough muscles to cause pain with any little thing.

"Boss man wants to know how you getting along with investigating that Virgil trash." Made it sound like a simple request. Giving him time to feel the steel behind the soft words.

"That why you following me? Got no meth head customers today? They suddenly all wise up and stop buying death by the bag?"

The guy was buggin', wanting to get physical. Musta had an argument with his bitch. "Aw man, just because your girl ain't thirsty for you tonight, that's no way to be talking."

"What do you know about any girl? If I've got one."

Another car crept down the ramp and approached Dash still standing in the way. Gave a timid beep. He replied with the deadeye for ten seconds before stepping aside and letting the car pass. An older woman steered the car, eyes fixed straight ahead.

Dash said, "So, where were we? Oh yeah. The information you received, what did the cops say?"

"Why don't you call and ask them?" Bones took a step as if to walk off.

Dash drew his Glock and held it along his thigh.

Bones stopped.

"Before we continue with this fascinating topic, you gimme your parking pass," Dash said.

"Why?"

"Got my reasons."

"If I don't?"

"I put a bunch of holes in that scrubby ass ride of yours, then I take the card out your trembling hands anyway."

Bones had to think about it. Shook his head. "My hands won't be trembling. They'll be crushing your windpipe."

The reporter was angry enough to get real stupid. Time to switch targets. "You know what's gonna happen if I break off this here entertaining moment? I'm driving back to where you just came from and putting a whole bunch of lead through the front door of your friend." He extended his left hand. "Now gimme the fuckin' card."

Bones pulled the card from his side pocket, handed it over.

Dash slipped it into his pants. "I'm gonna have to keep this item," he said. "Sorry to inconvenience you, ask the concierge for a new one. They be happy to oblige."

Bones wasn't looking at him anymore; he was walking off.

"Hey, Bones," Dash said. "I haven't finished yet."

Bones kept walking toward the elevators.

He racked the slide on the Glock, knowing the sound carried.

The fucker disappeared from view around the elevator shaft.

Oughta blast a few holes in the Mustang anyway. That be soothing.

Another car came down the ramp, and he tucked his weapon into his waistband. He took his car through the exit, using Bones's card and smiling at the memory of getting it. Eased the Chrysler out into the street and drove south.

Thought of what to tell Ritchie. Should have followed Bones to his apartment; they still didn't know which one was his. Would have been a tasty morsel to return with. But the pass card was good; gave them access to the building anytime.

But Ritchie needed more, something cheery. A lie be good. A lie be necessary.

Like yeah, Bones saw the cops, and they bought it, said they would check it out. He wasn't real helpful at first, so I took his pass card off him, made him see straight. That sounded good, sounded right.

Sounded like he took care of shit.

◆ ◆ ◆

Zach closed the door to his apartment and leaned back against it. Blew out some air. Let his shoulders drop. No bullet lodged between them. He'd taken a risk walking away like that, but he'd figured Dash wouldn't shoot at him without a direct say-so from Ritchie. They still needed him alive and pressing the cops to take action on Virgil, not in a hospital bed hooked up to life-support, and too doped up on morphine to talk.

If he'd stood his ground, Dash might have found a way to make him spill the information he wanted. The guy was quick with believable threats. The walking away was also a good move; once out of earshot he couldn't hear the next threat. But he didn't want to try it again; it was murder on his nerves.

Keera.

They knew about her and, as Dash had made plain, wouldn't hesitate to use her against him. How much they knew wasn't clear. It might have been the first time he'd been followed to her door. Better be more careful for a while. Not drop by so often. Make like she wasn't a permanent fixture in his life. Easy to do. Like pretending you don't need to breathe.

He opened his fridge then closed it. No fun to drink alone. Something else came to mind. He shouldn't have handed over the pass card so fast. That was solid confirmation to Dash how important Keera was. Dropped onto the sofa, put his cell on the coffee table. It buzzed. Picked it up again. Keera.

"You're safe then," she said.

"It was dicey for a minute, but I survived. How do you know stuff happened?" Stupid question.

"I sensed danger soon as you left. If you hadn't irritated me, I would've picked it up sooner. I had a vision. A man, young, boyish, one of Ritchie's, following you and asking you questions. You walking away, slowly, but your heart beating fast."

"It sure was," he said. "He had a gun in his hand."

"I saw that too." A pause. "You home now?"

"Home alone. Wanna come over?"

She laughed softly, the earlier frostiness between them

melted. "A girl needs her beauty sleep."

Some girls needed beauty sleep, twenty-three hours a day. Not Keera.

She asked, "What did he want?"

"He wanted to know what I'd done with the images. I wasn't in a good mood, as you might recall, didn't tell him a thing."

"That's why he had a gun in his hand?"

"Sort of. Listen, he followed me here when I left you. The little shit threatened to shoot up your place if I didn't give him my pass card to the parking garage. Keep your senses switched on, all right? This guy's itching to take action."

"I'm not without resources, Zach. But thanks for the warning."

"This is exactly what worried me from the start. They know about you—how much, I don't know—but they'll use you against me if they have to."

"They'll have to get close first." She sounded confident.

"Meaning you'll hire bodyguards?"

"In a way. I can ask for more help."

More help. She meant spook stuff: visions, astral sneaking around, guide voices in her head. Made him feel real secure, that did.

"What about something more practical, like moving somewhere else, somewhere safer? Until this thing is done?"

"I'm not moving because of some lowlifes, Zach." Her scorn crackled down the line. "We can stand up to them, remove them from our lives."

"Yeah, I know," he said, "but it'll take time, and they play to their rules, not ours. And they make up the rules as they go along. They're predators, Keera. They see money and move instinctively to it."

"Like I said. I'm not without resources."

"You're gifted, Keera, but even you can't stop a speeding bullet."

She laughed again. "No. But I can make sure the situation doesn't arise in the first place. If I give this problem my full attention, I'll know what they intend before they do."

Her faith in achieving successful outcomes was unshakable. Partly the result of her keen intelligence, coupled with psychic powers that gave her a head start on everybody else. The rest because of her privileged upbringing. The wealthy were insured against failure, never tasted it like other mortals. Never expected to encounter it in their lives.

But Keera had stepped into a different world here. She would no longer be above normal troubles but a target for the ruthless. She was on the periphery for the moment but who knew how the situation would change? What if Ritchie found out Keera came with wealth? He'd turn his attention to her: wouldn't, couldn't, pass up luscious prey like that.

"Keera, please," he said. "Don't worry me so much. Move to a secure apartment for a few months. Your place is as safe as a doll's house."

"It's got a strong door and good window locks. I'm not moving. Anyway, I'll still have to conduct classes every day. High walls won't work, being aware of danger will."

He couldn't think of another argument but knew it wouldn't matter. Keera did what she wanted when she wanted. That's what he liked about her. Her strong independent streak had been a major draw for him when they first met. It still was.

"Okay," he said. "Do what you think best, but please check in with me twice a day. I want to be sure you're safe."

"Aye, aye, sir." She laughed and closed the connection.

Good to know she was taking this seriously.

CHAPTER 8

For twelve days, Ritchie didn't exist. No Dash came by; no cold-eyed gunmen asked him to ride with them, no startling emails with attachments appeared in the inbox. Keera tutored her daily classes and came home safely each night. Most nights they spent together, their conversations moving away from Ritchie toward more personal stuff. Non-life-threatening stuff.

Until that Monday morning.

When Zach arrived at the Post, Edwina waved him into her glassed cage. Jeremy Brackett was already there; absolute proof some shit was heading his way.

Edwina held up a tabloid-sized printout of the next front page and Zach's face tightened. "Preppy Gangsta Arrested" the headline shouted. One of the Ritchie images was the top half of the page; the article took up the rest. A slow burn worked its way up from his neck to his hairline.

Zach put his hand out for the sheet and Edwina passed it over. He scanned the copy. Virgil and three others arrested with four kilos of high-grade heroin worth over half a million dollars at street level. The drug haul was discovered after police noticed suspicious activity outside a warehouse in Andersonville.

"Andersonville?" He raised an eyebrow at Edwina. "This seems familiar. Wasn't that where those pictures were taken?"

Edwina nodded but didn't elaborate. He resumed reading.

Two men were observed taking a parcel from an unlocked car and dropping it into the trunk of their own car. Suspecting theft, the officers apprehended the men. Further investigation revealed the parcel to contain heroin. The police discovered that the car's GPS was set to an address in affluent Kenilworth. A backup team rushed there and waited for the delivery to arrive. The vehicle was driven to the destination with police officers concealed in the back seat. Jason Virgil was observed emerging from the house as the car pulled up in the driveway. He approached the vehicle and tapped on the trunk lid, indicating that it be opened.

The police swooped, and Virgil was detained. A narcotics squad searched his house, where small amounts of illegal drugs and several unregistered handguns were discovered. Virgil was arrested along with the two men in the car and a fourth man in the house.

Zach scanned the rest but found no mention of Charlie Hostler or Eric Tanner. A mention that Virgil graduated from the Dorchester Academy, a top-rated college.

The worse thing about the whole story: Brackett's by-line on top.

Instead of his.

He said, "How the fuck did my story get on the front page without me writing it?"

Edwina's face darkened. "The PD contacted Jeremy when they made the bust. They gave us an hour's start before they called a press conference. By then, Jeremy had grabbed quotes from the arresting officers. We have the best cover; the story's on our website now, the other online media are playing catch-up."

Zach looked over at Brackett, the smirking fuck, swung back to Edwina. "Why wasn't I called in for this?"

"The police wanted Jeremy. We weren't in a position to say it was your story. It was their call."

Brackett had been at the Post less than six months and had a front-page already. Zach hadn't got closer than page three. He didn't want to look at Brackett again, didn't trust himself not to punch the guy's face.

"The cops knew I was nosing around with that story. I gave them that image to follow up. I was promised—"

"Promised?" Brackett cut in. "That's not what I heard. Your name only came up joined to negative descriptions. Like slime ball, prick and asshole. I don't think they promised you anything, buddy boy."

Zach ignored the jabs, as hard as it was. "What about Warren? You speak to him?"

"Not at all. It wasn't his bust; there's a Detective Carbone in charge of it."

"This looks like payback to me," Zach said to Edwina. "They gave us the first bite of the cherry because we gave them the lead that delivered the bust. They have to keep us on the side for future information. But they shafted me because of my bent cops stories."

"You're right, Zach, and we can't control what they release to whom." At least she sounded sympathetic. "We always go with the best story we get each time. I understand your feelings."

Zach looked at the photo again. "How does it happen that this, which you deemed too risky to publish before, is now front and center?"

"Legal gave us a way around it. Check the caption."

"Jason Virgil, third from left, meeting with associates" read the caption. No mention of what the white stuff, clearly visible, might be. Letting the readers draw their own conclusion, like there could be any other.

"Clever, in a sneaky way," Zach said. "But any poolroom lawyer will get a lot of mileage claiming his client is being defamed with this."

"We thought the chance of Virgil going to court on this was slim, given as how we might be able to produce evidence about his activities. Evidence he wouldn't want made public before the trial."

What was she talking about? "We knew nothing about this guy except that he photographs nicely, and now we have evidence?"

Brackett said, "The police let me have a look at Virgil's file."

"You reporting on them, or working for them?"

Brackett colored. "I didn't burn down the bridge I needed to cross the moat. I'm in and getting material. You're on the outside, pressing your face to the window."

Zach rose so quickly Brackett reared back, expecting a punch. "I gotta go, get some fresh air and an attitude I can live with," Zach said.

Edwina didn't stop him.

◆ ◆ ◆

Warren picked up after one ring. Zach started before Warren

even identified himself. "I gave you the photo that gave you Virgil, and you hand the story to Brackett? What's with that?"

"Sorry, pal." Warren sounded genuine. "It wasn't my collar, and I had no idea Brackett was called in."

"You not only called him in, you gave him favorable treatment. The kind of treatment I would never get. If anybody there wanted to shove my face in it, they did a great job."

"Funny about that. There's a lot of resentment about you here. You won't snuff it out anytime soon."

Warren was placating, taking the punches, not swinging back, waiting for Zach's fire to burn down a notch. Zach wasn't ready.

"Who let Brackett look at the files?"

A pause. "Didn't know about that."

"Bullshit."

"It's true," Warren said, sounding exasperated. "It's not something I'd do after I had the suspect collared. Before, maybe, to help speed up inquiries. But not after we have the guy."

"Who was it?"

"Can't say."

"Won't say."

Warren said, "I just told you I didn't know about Brackett looking at the file."

Warren's responses rang true. No discordant notes to catch his attention. He poked the possum one more time to see which way it scuttled. "When I gave you the photos, you sounded like the investigating officer. You knew about Virgil. Why wasn't it your bust? Aren't you senior enough?"

Warren chuckled. "That low blow didn't connect, Bones. Virgil's a peripheral figure to me. I don't do the North Side. The South Side is my watch."

"You spend your time gathering evidence on the Gangsta Disciples, then. Not white boys."

"Among other things."

"What does Virgil have to do with the Disciples? How does he even come into your frame?"

"I don't only watch the Disciples."

"You watch the Latins?"

"Nope, that's another squad."

Ritchie. Warren was on Ritchie's ass. He poked again. "What about that Ritchie guy?" Tried to make it sound like a guess.

A longer pause from Warren. "What do you know about him? You got a story you're working on?"

It was Ritchie. "If I did, after the way I was treated by your department, do you think I'd come rushing over to show you?"

"I know you're mad and with good cause, Bones. But seriously, if you have information on Ritchie I want it."

"Sure you do. And you'd pass it on to some jackass to humiliate me."

"For God's sake." Warren almost shouting now. "It wasn't me who did that. I can't say it over and over. I'm not stupid enough to alienate somebody who came in with a useful lead on Virgil."

"I didn't get any call during to warn me either."

"It was out of my hands like I said. I figured you'd give me a heap of grief over this, and I wasn't going to spoil my day by calling you. We're not such close friends I'd do that." Warren calming down as he spoke. "What do you know about Ritchie?".

"Not as much as you."

"You got something, I can tell. You didn't bring up his name by chance. Help me out, and I'll see how to square things with you."

"Not sure you've got the clout to square anything," Zach said, not wanting to stop gnawing this particular bone.

Warren said, "Okay, I see how this is panning out. Let's talk soon, when we're both feeling sunny. Gotta go, catch you soon." He hung up.

Well, that cleared the air. Zach dropped the handset back in the cradle. Most of his anger dwindling to a small flickering flame now. Wouldn't flare up again unless somebody stupid tossed more fuel on it. You can't change the past, he reminded himself, and immediately recalled the time he and Keera had done just that. Fuck, even homilies weren't true.

He guessed Edwina ignored his outburst and the flouncing-out stuff. Reporters loved their stories like they were newborn kittens. Editors drowned them at their peril, and she knew this. Still, he'd been stupid. Now he'd have to face the water cooler jibes, the snarky asides, the snickering in the background after a remark he didn't quite catch.

Fuck 'em. He had discovered something mighty. Warren, his only contact in the CPD, knew about Ritchie. He had stuff that Warren would kill to know. Getting dumped from the Virgil story could rankle a long time. Getting the Ritchie story would erase that moment instantly.

He checked the time; Keera would have finished her morning lecture. Called her.

"Virgil's busted," he said when she responded.

"When?"

"Last night. He's being held, for now, won't get bail. Not after they caught him with two million bucks worth of product."

"My God, he's a major player, isn't he?"

"I guess. The economics of heroin isn't my specialty. But it's normal for cops to exaggerate the size of a haul. Nor did Virgil pay anything like that wholesale. But it's big. Pretty big."

"I'm getting you're not happy about this." Keera didn't have to be a mind reader to detect the anger in his voice. He knew it still washed over him, coloring everything.

"The story was handed to Brackett, another reporter, a prick. The cops preferred him over me even when it was my story."

"It's still your story," she said. "I'm picking that up."

"You're wrong. Brackett will be assigned to it until Virgil is sent—"

"I'm picking up something else," she said. "Virgil's arrest, it isn't the end of the story. It's the beginning."

CHAPTER 9

Dash found Ritchie in the private room upstairs of the bar with Melvin and Tyrell. All three of them warm and huggy after pulling off the set-up. The set-up planned for some future date, but somehow Ritchie got the urge to go right ahead with it while Dash was still talking to the reporter. Like he was only the errand boy, not part of the inner circle.

"You step those keys like I said?" Ritchie asked Tyrell as he paced the floor, excited as Dash had ever seen.

Tyrell grinned, lazy and wide. "Mostly baking soda. He was never gonna test it before it was took off him."

Ritchie said, "The whole thing came out cheaper than I hoped. And that business with the GPS was gold. Pure gold, Tyrell. Pure fuckin' gold."

He turned to Dash. "After our snitch woke up the cops to what was going down I figured they'd watch and follow the car. Didn't expect them to jump out and collar the mules."

Nice to be included in the conversation. Dash shook his head, agreeing with Ritchie on the stupidity of mules.

Ritchie tapped a newspaper on the table. "Says here the fool driver had his GPS on. Gave it all away. It worked out fine, super fine."

Tyrell beamed some more. "The surveillance was shit. Two white guys in a car, watching the warehouse. Just two guys, cheap operation. Me and Melvin spotted them easy. They in a Camry, pretending what? They stopped for a heart to heart? Shit."

Dash wondered how the cops be so dumb. Rule number one for undercover shit: look like you belong.

Tyrell continued, explaining more for Dash's benefit. "One of our street guys left the deal in this ride, this Honda, parked close to the surveillance guys. Left the car unlocked. Made it real clear to the cops. Once Virgil's guys handed over the cash, back up the street a ways, I told them to take the Honda up ahead. Weight in the trunk, keys in the ignition, the usual."

"Right," Dash said. "They were supposed to take the Honda."

"Yeah, but they didn't. Me and Melvin zipped out of there, but them ignorant fuckers didn't trust us or something. Grabbed the bag instead, the papers said. Got grabbed in return." Tyrell grinned like he'd stolen the cat's milk and eaten the cat as well.

Dash said, "How did they agree to this delivery without testing? Kinda unusual."

"Listen and you learn," Melvin said.

"Simple marketing techniques, Dash," Ritchie said. "Tyrell told that Tanner guy if they didn't like the quality, they could return the unopened bags for a full refund. They knew I wanted a long-term deal, that I wasn't about to pull a quality scam on them. It was an itty bit of risk, not a big thing. They trusted Tanner; he trusts me."

"Virgil gonna see we shafted him."

"It'll cross his mind, Dash. But I'll contact Tanner, lay sorrowful shit on him, tell him the bust was unfortunate, tell him we'll give back half the money, take half the pain, if he sets up a new deal. Tell him we still want a long-term relationship and we're willing to help out now, as a sign of good faith. He'll figure that since we're so generous, we ain't connected to the bust. It'll look like a snitch was at work."

That could work, Tanner figuring Ritchie being helpful and all. Ritchie was good at cutting deals: cross deals, side deals, backup deals until you were so dizzy you didn't notice your pants were missing. Ritchie happy to wait for a profit too; nobody else Dash knew had that patience or the confidence that everything would fall their way.

"We gotta move quietly on this," Dash said. "Like you said, it's not a good time to make more noise."

Melvin swung around to him. "The fuck you know? You just stay with the fetch and carry shit."

Dash's face burned, but he held a cool stare back. Melvin liked to get physical if he got lip he didn't like; best let the insult slide. He said to Ritchie. "What happens now?"

Ritchie settled himself in his chair. "The wheel of fortune is gonna stop on our number, Dash. Just wait and see."

For Zach the worst thing about Virgil's bust was reading Brackett's follow-up stories. Virgil refused bail due to flight concerns; trial not scheduled for nine months; speculation in the Post and other media about Virgil's deadly grip on the North Side. Made him sound like a vampire sucking the lifeblood out of nice college kids. Which he was.

The best thing was that Brackett had to ask Zach about the

photograph.

"Sorry how things worked out," Brackett said the next day. He'd stopped by Zach's desk. "I didn't know about the pic or your briefing with Warren. Edwina told me later. I got a call from the cops and took off without checking with you or her."

Zach leaned back in his chair, looking up at him. "You ever ask yourself why me? You're not the senior reporter in this section."

"True, I haven't been around as long as you. No big stories coming my way and this was a good start. I had to grab it. You're right, I should have given it more thought, but I didn't. I'm sorry if I tangled your wires on this."

Brackett looked about as sorry as a kid caught sneaking a chocolate bar from the kitchen cupboard. Zach gave him all the magnanimity he could muster. "Fuck off," he said.

"Seriously. I have to follow up on this. That photograph. Who do you reckon sent it to you?"

The guy had no pride. "You gone deaf now? God punish you for stealing my story."

"Ha ha. Don't you think it was weird that you got the pic and not the cops?"

Zach stood. Brackett backed off. "Okay, okay," he said. "This isn't a good time. We'll talk again." He moved away.

"I'm not planning to make a good time," Zach said to his back. Brackett didn't respond.

Zach sat down again. Felt much better. The only pleasing thing about Brackett having the Virgil story was that he was now stuck with it. Had to find new material all the time to fill pages. Then, when the trial started, he would have to attend court every day. He could be tied to this story for months, and the highlight—the actual bust—was over. From now on, there would be a gradual decline in reader interest as the trial ground on to the day of sentencing. Unless something sensational turned up. And that only happened in the movies.

Meanwhile, Zach was free to follow any story he liked, and he liked the Ritchie one most.

Ritchie ran a drug operation in a Gangsta Disciples area. But he wasn't one of them. So he paid street taxes. But why would the Disciples organize things that way? To stay at arm's length of the drugs? A possibility.

Maybe the Disciples were cleaning themselves up, becoming a force for good. At least, they could portray it that way. Some already ran community programs, even got federal funding. It made sense. The Disciples could become a kind of cultural organization, looking out for members and financing community activities with street taxes. That would leave them in control of their patch. The police would only be an irritant, not the real body that administered the laws.

If they wanted to, they could remove Ritchie quicker than slapping a mosquito. See? they could say to the mayor, we don't tolerate drugs here. Ritchie would know that. To survive, he had to move out of the Disciples' reach, move his operation north. That's why Virgil was in jail.

He caught Howard settling down with coffee. Leaned toward his desk, asked, "How easy is it for community groups to get funding from City Hall?"

"If they don't want much, quite easy. But we're talking a couple of grand here and there." Howard sipped from his paper cup. "You forming one?"

"Thinking of the Gangsta Disciples. They got funding for some project or other. That true?"

"The feds gave a group known to be associated with the Disciples about thirty grand to help fund a war vets home. Plenty of Disciples in the army, you know."

Zach considered this. "How tough are the auditing procedures for those kinds of funds?"

Howard smiled. "Depends on the sensitivity of the government to race relations."

"Meaning?"

"Meaning, some government bodies won't look too hard if there's a possibility that the people being investigated can complain about being picked on because they're black or Hispanic or Calathumpian."

"Calathumpian?"

"Just joking."

Howard had plenty of preppy jokes like that. Zach moved on before he thought of another one. "So, there's room to pad the books and slide a few dollars out of the project into private purses."

"You have encapsulated the situation perfectly." Howard drained his coffee. "You got something on the Disciples?"

"Related to them. I'm interested in Frankie Ritchie, a South Side dealer. Trying to figure out why they let Ritchie ply his trade on their patch. Maybe they're thinking of getting out of the street-drug business, going legit in some way. By that, I mean getting a stream of funding and siphoning off healthy amounts: like decent folk."

"You're so cynical, Zach, but so wrong. How would they get regular funding? You have to network for that, network with the guys you went to college with. How many gang members are college graduates? How many of them have risen to powerful positions in government? How many fingers do I need for this exercise?"

Zach swiveled back to his screen. "Okay, it was a thought, that's all. Thanks for your help."

"Anytime, Zach. You know I love to talk." Howard tossed his cup into the wastebasket, sat down and asked, "You over being shafted on that Virgil story?"

"Yeah, but scars will remain," Zach said, "until they're covered up by newer ones."

"That's a shame. When I saw that Virgil went to Dorchester, I asked around."

"What's so important about his school?"

"It's also my old school."

Zach stared at him, stunned. "What?"

Howard held up his hands. "Hey, I didn't know him, he attended after me. I asked around. Some of my friends had younger brothers and sisters who also attended. And they knew him."

"I could have used that info. I might have gotten close to him by using your contacts. Would've worked up a much better story than just a drug bust."

"Well, Zach, you just keep that fanciful idea in your head. The only way you'd have gotten close to him was when he was standing over your dead body. He was, is, pretty rough."

"They knew he had a drug operation going?"

"There's such a thing as the old boy network. They found out things."

Zach sank back in his chair. "Anything else you can tell me about Jason Virgil?"

Howard crossed an ankle over his knee, looked like he would have sucked on a pipe if he had one. "He was a bully. Probably a kind of sociopath—no empathy for his victims. If he decided to beat someone up, the beating would last until the intervention of his ghastly but slightly more sensible companions."

"What would set him off?"

"Nothing. Anything. He liked to torment people until they snapped back, which apparently gave him license to kill."

"What was he good at academically?"

Howard laughed. "Biology. That's funny. I couldn't imagine him as a doctor unless it was as an understudy to Dr. Mengele. Maybe he saw a future in South America somewhere, torturing for dictators."

"What happened to him after he left college?"

"He was suspended before graduation for physically intimidating a staffer. He disappeared for a couple of years. They say he was back in town last year. Word filtered through that he was dealing to high school seniors. Nobody realized how much. Two million. Gosh."

Zach leaned forward. "This I don't get. If Virgil came from money, why did he move into the drug business? I know the profits are colossal, but if his parents could afford his level of education, he must have had money coming to him anyway."

"Sure. But if he was counting on a trust fund, it's possible it wouldn't pay out before he was thirty, or be enough for his wants. Virgil's an impatient guy by accounts."

"Any girlfriends? Long-term partners?"

"Hell, no." Howard shook his head. "The girls who met him hated him, thought he was creepy, detached, not of the human race. They'd heard he could get physical, and that's hardly acceptable behavior in those circles. No female from his background would put up with a beater."

"He sounds delightful company."

Howard asked, "Why so interested in Virgil? He's incarcerated, not likely to see daylight for a while."

"Virgil's connected to my story on the Disciples," Zach said. "Something funny happening there."

Howard raised a melodramatic eyebrow. "You chasing them for a story? If so, may I point out it might be your last story ever?"

"I'm not going anywhere without a solid contact to introduce me. You go to school with any of these Disciples?"

CHAPTER 10

The next morning, Zach spent a couple of fruitless hours in front of his monitor gathering background on Virgil.

Then he didn't need to anymore.

The news flashed on his screen: Jason Virgil dead.

Jailhouse knifing.

"Ah, Jesus." He clicked rapidly through the rest of the story.

Howard looked up from the adjacent workstation. "What's happened?"

"Check your newsfeed, Virgil's dead."

Zach ran through the brief report again. Virgil knifed to death with an improvised weapon by an inmate in the recreation room. An unnamed inmate being questioned further. It was believed an argument broke out, leading to Virgil's death.

"That just saved the city a pile of money," Howard said, scrolling through the story.

"Hardly. If it was a simple argument gone wrong, then we get a murder trial instead of a drug trial. If it wasn't, we get a conspiracy investigation as well."

"You implying something here, Zach? You think there's something else behind this?"

"I have learned to take nothing at face value." He leaned back, his mind firing up assumptions and outcomes.

His cell beeped. Detective Warren.

"Those photos you gave me?" he said without any hello-how-are-yous. "They've dropped you into a murder investigation."

"I was just coming to the same conclusion," Zach replied. "What do you know about Virgil's death?"

"That your photos were instrumental in Virgil's arrest and incarceration."

"Who got to him? You know that?"

"We're good, but not always fast. We'll find out soon enough. Who sent you those photos?"

That's how it started. The cops pounding him for information until he let something slip. "I told you, I don't know."

"Something in my weary cop bones that tells me you're lying." Tone flat, uncompromising.

"Get a doc to check you over. I'm not lying."

"But you got yourself a problem," Warren said.

"How? I'm trying to help out here."

"Not with me, not yet. Your problem comes from elsewhere. Virgil's investigation team will ask questions about your photo. Same questions I'm asking now. Guess who's going to get a visit from them sometime soon?"

"You going to reveal your sources?"

"Of course," Warren said. "I'm not a sainted journalist."

"You told everyone?"

"Virgil wasn't my watch. I passed your photos on to the right man."

"Who is?"

"Detective Carbone."

"Never had the pleasure."

"Lucky man. Don't think you two would hit it off."

Warren sounded pleased about that. "You saying he's spreading the word about me?"

"No, I'm not. I'm saying that if he needs help from you, he won't hesitate to get right in your face if you clam up. He's like a hyena tearing at a carcass. In fact, he's more like a whole pack."

"I can't reveal what I don't know."

"Yeah, sure."

Warren's mocking told Zach to move to new ground.

"This Ritchie guy we talked about before, I'm thinking of paying him a visit."

A short pause from Warren. Then: "Do me a favor. Before you go, leave instructions with your lawyer that in the event of your probable death, he's to reveal to me the source of those photos. I'll be expecting a call real soon."

"Why would I be in danger? I'm only going to ask Ritchie how he's changed his life around since his only bust. A cute little follow-up story about teenage delinquents waking up to reality as they matured."

Warren barked laughter.

"You're fucking crazy. Ritchie's a stone killer. If he thinks you're dissing him, there'll be nothing left of you except a pencil and notepad on the ground."

"What else can you tell me about him? Where does he live, for a start?"

"His home address? We don't have it. It might not exist; he likes to move around."

"Where does he hang during the day?"

Warren laughed again. "If we knew the stuff you think we should, we could keep an easy watch on the guy. He's survived so far because he's not sloppy."

His tone changed. Brisk, verging on dismissive.

"Anyway, nothing I know is for your ears."

"Well, let's not ruin our exciting relationship. After I talk to Ritchie, I'll pass on what I can. You notice how much nicer a person I am than you? In exchange, keep Carbone in the zoo and away from me."

"It doesn't work like that," Warren said. "Talk to me soon." He hung up.

Zach ran through the scenario again, seeing it from a new perspective. Ritchie had used him to get Virgil picked up and held in jail, where his men would have access to him. It had Ritchie's cologne all over it, and a reporter had been the chump who assisted the whole project.

His future was seriously unpromising. Ritchie had made sure this one dumb journalist was part of a murder conspiracy. If the cops ever nailed Ritchie for it, he would plea bargain, give up Zachary Bones as an accessory. I gave him the photographs, Ritchie would say. He agreed to hand them to the police, Ritchie would add.

He was in on it.

All the way.

The Thai restaurant was open with a small pre-lunch crowd attacking noodles with snaffling relish. The Asian waitress, middle-aged and smiling, asked, "How many in the party, sir?"

"I want to speak to Frankie Ritchie," Zach said. "As soon as possible."

Her smile vanished. "Him no here. Only Thai chefs."

"He was here a few weeks ago. You closed the restaurant for him. Know where he is?"

"No person like that here. You go now." She glanced back over the counter to the kitchen area. A small guy stopped tossing noodles and picked up a cleaver, waited for more instructions.

"Okay," Zach said. "I'm going. Just tell Ritchie I have to see him. My name is Bones." He turned and left. Tensed his shoulders for a cleaver strike.

The word would get to Ritchie; he was sure of that. The method wasn't as sophisticated as using a phone; it was more like scratching a message on a subway wall and waiting. But it would work. It worked so well that Dash was leaning on his Chrysler outside the Post building when he returned.

"He wants to see you," he said. He was alone this time. Ritchie must have figured he wasn't dealing with a violent type.

"Not so, Dash, I want to see him." Better get it straight who's in charge here.

Dash made with the sneering. "Whatever; let's go, huh?"

He climbed in the front of his car. Dash held out a hand. "Your cell."

"Yours run out of charge?" Zach asked as he drew his cell out. "You need to check in with your mom?"

"You so funny. Can't wait to hear your audition tape for Jimmy Fallon." Dash switched the cell off and handed it back. Then passed him a black hood.

"It's Halloween already? Time flies, huh? I don't see any eye holes."

"Ain't none. Put it on."

He slipped the hood over his face. It was thick, coarse and impenetrable. "It's scratchy, so let's get going."

The car made a few turns and he guessed they were heading back south again. His initial anger had ebbed as he realized this meeting with Ritchie wouldn't be a cosy fireside chat. But he couldn't afford to show his anxiety. Ritchie was a bully, guys like that fed on fear. Kept telling himself that.

Dash pulled to a stop maybe fifteen minutes later. "Don't move until someone takes your arm. Act nice, they wiggin' today."

Zach's door opened and somebody gripped his elbow like a spot-weld, and led him inside a building. Hands pulled Zach's jacket off, he heard his recorder, wallet and cell clank and thud on a table.

"Take your shirt off," a voice said in front of him. His voice a lot softer than his grip.

"This a hot tub party? Nobody told me." He unbuttoned his shirt, shrugged it off and kept it in his hand.

"Drop your pants," the voice said.

"Excuse me?"

"Drop your pants. We not faggots, we looking for a wire."

"Glad that's sorted." Zach unbuttoned his jeans and let them fall. Somebody walked around him and stopped. Fingers grasped the elastic band of his shorts and pulled it out, snapped the band back.

"Pull 'em up," the voice said. "You better hide that miserable thing quick as you can."

"Nobody's complained yet," Zach said, dragging his jeans over his hips.

"You must be talking white girls. Some bitches I know, be laughing so hard they see your junk, they wouldn't be in the mood for weeks. Put your shirt back on. Don't want to see any more sorry-looking flab than we have to."

"Hey, I work out."

"Sure you do. Tap tap tap on the keyboard all day. Must be exhausting. I can tell by your fine body. Such a six-pack you got."

"You got one? How did you get it? Slapping pimply teens around when they don't buy what you're selling?"

A large hand wrapped around his jaw and squeezed. Shards of pain torched muscle and bone.

"You ignorant, need your horizons broadened. Keep that mouth working and it'll happen before you know it."

The hand released him. The pain melted away, but it was a couple of beats before Zach could manage a reply.

"I'm ready," he said, making a deliberate effort not to touch his aching jaw. "Always ready to broaden a horizon or two."

A familiar grip resettled on his elbow and took him a few steps.

"Stairs," the gripper said. He put Zach's right hand on a bannister. "Take them to the top. No rushing, makes people nervous.

Say hello to the man waiting for you up there." Gave Zach's elbow a piercing squeeze before releasing it.

"A regular pass-the-parcel kind of day, isn't it?" Zach said as he took the first step. "You must do a lot of kiddie parties to get this good at it."

A guard at the top of the stairs removed the hood. "Keep sassin' that man," he said, "he gonna make you eat your words with the one tooth he leaves you."

"Yeah, whatever," he said. "We done with this tough-guy stuff? Where's Ritchie?"

The stair guard knocked twice on a door and opened it.

Inside the room, Ritchie sat at a table by himself. In front of him lay a plate of frosted cupcakes, a coffee pot and a dainty cup and saucer. Two more guards flanked him on chairs against the walls. Ritchie pointed to the empty chair opposite him. Zach took it.

"You really fucked me over," Zach started. "You've set me up on a conspiracy-to-murder charge."

"Whoa, racehorse," Ritchie said. "What you talking about?"

"You had Virgil killed and made it look like I was helping you."

Ritchie smiled, high-wattage stuff, supposed to make him relax. "You notice the obvious? Me out here, Virgil in there? His death, pleasant news as it was, had nothing to do with me."

"You know the guy who killed him?"

"I see no names in the paper, so I can't say. But you know, people around here are steady, hardworking folk. Wouldn't be like them to do any murdering."

"How did you know the killer was from around here?"

"I didn't say that, I just said—" Ritchie straightened. Blinked a couple of times. "The fuck you doin' here?"

"The police told me it was a gang-related hit. I believe your name was in the air." True enough supposition. Every gang leader was suspect now.

"What did you tell them?" Ritchie's tone silky.

"Nothing to tell."

"Yeah. The creed. Never reveal your sources. It still working, huh?"

"Still working."

"Good to hear it."

"Those photos you sent me—"

"Whoa, boy, what photos? I sent you nothing." Ritchie picked up the cup and sipped, his eyes watching Zach over the rim.

"The photos that showed Virgil doing a deal."

"Those ones? Oh, I saw that in your paper. Not mine, but congratulations on getting such a scoop shot." Ritchie lowered his cup. "I read the story, too. How come your name wasn't on it? Somebody I never heard of wrote it. You been demoted or something?"

"The cops gave the bust story to another guy."

"What a shame. You being so good at exposing crime. You annoy people over at the police department? Can't see how, you being such a nice person."

One of the goons along the wall snickered. Zach shot him a look. That made the other one snicker as well.

"You know what's going to happen next?" he asked Ritchie.

Ritchie kept his face blank as marble. "You tell me."

"Virgil's men will want to know how that photo popped up at just the right time."

"Some people are like that. Always wondering about things they can't understand. Should leave that stuff to their betters."

"I have this feeling they're not those sort of people. They'll ask around, find me and ask me questions. What do I tell them?"

"Tell them what you like, but leave my name out of every conversation."

Ritchie was pretty comfortable about the whole conversation. The fucker had figured out the whole game plan ahead of him. Whatever idea Zach came up with now, Ritchie would have a counter ready. But there had to be a weakness somewhere, and if he kept probing, he might expose it.

"Leave your name out of it?" he said. "How is that possible, since you're the beginning and the end of the photo story

"You a newspaper man. You know how to twist truth to make it sound like lies. Use your talents to stay healthy."

"You saying my health's in jeopardy? From you?"

Ritchie spread out his arms. "Who knows who you gonna annoy when you start talking?"

"Good thing I got insurance against an early death then."

Ritchie waited, not blinking.

"What kind of insurance?" he asked finally.

"You know, the usual stuff. Depositions, information in the custody of my lawyer to be handed to police on my death." Better get around to that on the way back to the Post.

Ritchie relaxed. "Oh, those things. Can't see how they help you. Might even bring unfortunate events upon your girlfriend."

Keera. They knew about Keera. The fucker had checked him out before Dash appeared with the first summons.

Ritchie knew what he was thinking, the happy grin spreading across his face proved it. "So, we done now, Zach?" he asked, reaching for another cupcake. "I hate to rush you, but you're not the only one I have to help today."

Zach rose. "Thanks for explaining the situation so well."

"Glad to assist. Say hello to Miz Keera for me. She look like a fun thing. A bit on the skinny side for me, but every man has his own taste, yo?" Ritchie waved his cupcake at the door. "We can discuss her, the next time we meet."

The next time? The next time? Then he got it. Any time Ritchie called, he had to listen.

Ritchie now owned him.

Forever.

CHAPTER 11

Zach headed straight to Keera's home after his humiliation. One thing he'd had done, just one thing: open an email from Ritchie, and he was instantly enmeshed with his organization. With no clear escape, and no friends on the right side of the law. Keera had a different way of seeing things; she might provide a fresh slant on this. A way forward. A way out.

"This is a nightmare," He said to her when he arrived. "He knows you exist, knows your name even. They must have followed me, saw you, checked your mailbox to get your name." He sprawled on her kitchen chair. "I'm screwed both ways. If the cops find out the photos came from Ritchie, they'll collar me. If Ritchie finds out the cops know about the connection, he'll lever my head off."

Keera sat across the table and regarded him with steady blue eyes, like he was explaining how to operate a new microwave. "Why are you so anxious," she said. "Wouldn't one event rule out the other?"

"You mean if I'm dead, the cops won't arrest me? Yep, you got that right."

"Don't be difficult. I mean, if the police work out the photo came from Ritchie, won't they move on him?"

"That's only a link; not proof of anything. If the cops shake up Ritchie for information on the photos, I'm a dead man typing."

"Nobody's going to kill you," she said with a sudden intensity. "Not while I'm around."

That was practically a declaration of love coming from her, she who hated to reveal herself.

"Gee, thanks." He grinned at her unexpected show of feelings. "How do you plan to protect me?"

"I'll keep a closer eye on this Ritchie, that's for sure." She avoided eye contact, visibly embarrassed at her outburst. "What you know in advance could save you," she added.

"Hell, yes. I'd know when to start packing to leave town."

She lifted her head. "There's no running away from this, is there? If he doesn't get you, he gets me."

"You're so good at summing up."

Her eyes glinted. "I'll put down your tiresome sarcasm to stress."

"Thanks."

She waited for more, but he wasn't going to give her any more. He'd run through the scenarios a dozen times, and all possible outcomes looked shitty every which way. She would come to the same conclusion: Ritchie held him–and her–in a tightly clenched fist.

She spoke again. "You said you thought Ritchie knew Virgil's killer. How did he react?"

"I pushed a touchy button. He was evasive. I'm sure he ordered the hit."

"Won't the police figure the same?"

"They'll need something stronger than a hunch."

"So, if they question Ritchie because they found a link between him and the killer, won't that take the heat off you?"

"In what way?"

"The police won't need the photos to link the two events. So, Ritchie will think somebody else gave him up, not you."

He weighed up her logic. Fetched a Peroni from the fridge to help. She was right. The cops only needed to find the link. The origin of the photos wouldn't be important after that. Keera had applied commonsense while he was still venting his frustrations.

"Of course, the police might never find the link," she said.

"I was feeling better until you said that."

"Unless we help." She was no longer seeing him. She was in a place he couldn't share.

He waited for her to come back. It wouldn't take long, maybe a minute. He had learned to accept her ability to switch from this reality to one he would never understand. Had no choice in the matter, especially when her psychic abilities pulled him out of tight places.

She blinked and refocused on him.

"Sorry," she said, rubbing her face with her hands. "Bardo interrupted there. He came and showed me something."

"Oh, him? Any old time he feels like it, he snatches you away from a conversation with normal people. It's not very mannerly, is it?"

She shot him a look that said I know you're trying to be funny, but this is not the time.

"It doesn't happen often. He must've felt he could … hurry

matters along."

Zach took a hit from the bottle. "Anything relevant to our discussion?"

"I got a vision. Saw Virgil's killer in his cell. Solitary. I guess the guards don't want him dead either."

"Was he feeling any remorse before he gets another zillion years?"

"No, he's resigned to staying inside for life. He was thinking of the money he was promised. It seemed like a lot."

"If they open a K-Mart store inside, he'll spend big."

"He was also thinking of his woman. And a child. Not his, but he doesn't know that. She's getting the money."

"Not his?" Zach finished the bottle. "The poor fucker, everybody's screwing the guy. Anything else?"

"That's all."

"You see where the money came from?"

"No. His thoughts were mostly of his woman. Later, I'll see if I can locate her." She brightened. "We now have a plan. We find her, show she received money from Ritchie, and you're a free man."

She had figured out a way forward, and a way out of Ritchie's hands while he was feeling sorry for himself and sucking on a beer.

"You make it sound easy, but at least we got something to start on. You're a fucking marvel."

"You're pretty nice, too." She waited.

He waited, too.

"It's late," he said finally. "You sleepy soon?"

"Not tonight, Zach," she said, her smile manufactured. "I've stuff to do, and I need to be alone."

"Right, I understand." Zach stood and unhooked his jacket from the back of a chair, slipped it on. "Good to see you ready to stand by your man when he's down and needs company." He sounded childish and ungrateful and wanted to take the words back. Didn't get a chance; Keera knew how to raise his mood.

She moved to him, slid her hands under his jacket and around his waist. "You know what I mean; don't be sulky." She rose on tiptoes to kiss him. "Tomorrow night, it's a date, right?"

He pulled her closer to him, savoring her scent, half perfume, half narcotic. He wanted to hold her until the middle of the next week, but he broke away before she did. "It's a date," he said, his voice husky.

The Mustang took him home, the exhaust bubbling with happy vigor, the 1966 classic asking to be let loose somewhere, please, just for a minute. What made him buy a car like this when he never got to have fun in it? A few seconds tearing up a stretch of freeway didn't really do it for him. Maybe he could talk Keera into a picnic on top of a mountain, at the end of a fast twisting road.

Afterward. After they pried Ritchie from their throats and cast him back to his slime pit. They could do it; they'd overcome worse odds before.

He approached his apartment building. Five years old, with steel gates to pass through before the car was in its slot. He waved his new card in front of the sensor and the gates clanked apart. Lost or stolen pass cards were common enough for the concierge desk to keep a box of replacements handy. If Dash were already inside and waiting, the new card wouldn't have worked. The security system knew when his car came in, and refused access to another one on the same card ID. Dash thought he was smart grabbing the card, but if he used it, Zach would know. He would know Dash was already inside and waiting. And there would be steel gates between them. The dumb fuck.

A passkey-operated elevator took him up five floors to his one-bedroom apartment. He unlocked his door, slipped off his jacket in the entry and stopped.

Paper crunched under his feet.

He switched on the light. Book pages lay on the floor. Pages and pages and pages. Scattered from one side of the hallway to the other. Ankle deep in places. Cut precisely at one edge. His pages, his books: he recognized them. Paperback fiction, hardcover political biographies, large-format reference book pages. His last ten years scattered in front of him.

He froze. Heard nothing unusual, felt no presence. He shuffled through the pages, past the bedroom, glanced in and stopped. The furniture had changed. He switched on the light.

The bed was no longer in the middle of the room. It stood on its head, hard up against the wall, the mattress and bedding stuffed behind it. Both bedside tables jammed between the bed and the ceiling. The window, which only partly opened, had the room's area rug rolled up and crammed into the twelve-inch gap.

"Holy God." He steeled himself to move on.

The paper trail stopped at the end of the hall. He peered into the living room. That too was different. In the semi-darkness, the difference was unclear. He flicked a light switch, and a frozen frenzy lay in front of him. A madman had stacked the furniture. The sofa, the coffee table, the dining table and four chairs, all crammed into a corner, piled up, reaching to the ceiling—a picture of violent geometry.

At the far end of the room, the kitchen end, the cupboards hung open, their contents on the floor. Smashed glass and china mingled with broken food containers and utensils.

No footprints in the debris.

No human had done this.

His bookshelves, two tall cases against the wall behind his sofa, were empty, apart from book covers piled at each shelf end. He picked up a couple to find all the pages missing. Flicked through a few more, same thing: no pages. He knew where they were—he had waded through them.

No human could have done this.

Not the kitchen trashing, not the furniture stacking and definitely not the deliberate and careful cutting of pages from over six hundred books.

He pulled his cell from his back pocket and punched Keera's number with unsteady fingers. No answer. She would have switched off by now, getting into her astral stuff. Not to be disturbed until morning. He killed the cell.

The fridge door still closed.

Didn't want to open it.

Had to.

He crunched through the glass shards, wrenched open the door. Nothing disturbed. Ground beef still in plastic wrapping, drained, not crushed. Everything as before.

Except for one thing.

Wedged between the milk carton and the orange juice bottle: a single piece of copy paper.

He reached in and pulled it out, turned it face up.

The image of Virgil buying heroin in the warehouse.

The front-page photograph.

"This happened too fast," Ritchie said, restless and pacing the room. "It looks obvious, Little League, know what I mean?"

What he meant, Dash knew, it looked like he'd lost his edge.

"This way," Ritchie said, "it looks exactly like a set-up. Emmett was to wait. Virgil was gonna sit there for weeks before the trial."

"Maybe he took the first chance he got," Dash said. "Virgil had enough muscle to get special protection. He might've been moved soon." Had to stop Ritchie going on some dopey train of thought or he'd have them all running around on useless errands.

"Could be so, Dash, could be so, but it makes the operation a lot more hazardous." Ritchie stopped pacing and sat down. But his fingers kept marching, drumming on the table in front of him.

"Nothing we can't handle," Melvin said, butting in like he could make a major contribution. Melvin, who figured a smack to the head solved every problem.

Ritchie stopped drumming, looked over at Melvin. "Ever read Sun Tzu, The Art of War?"

"It got pictures?" he said. "Otherwise, I'll wait for the movie."

"There's drawings of Chinese guys but they not important. He was a famous general, long time ago. And one of the smart things he says is that it's best to take over a territory intact."

"What's that all mean, then?" Melvin asked.

Ritchie drew a breath as if explaining stuff that should be obvious was a heavy chore. "It means that we wanna have a big finger in Virgil's operation, not wreck it. We have to make a deal with the guy who runs it now. And if this guy figures we had Virgil wasted, well, guess what, Melvin? We don't get to party on their turf, and we can't build a new game in their area cause we ain't from there. Got it?"

"Yeah, makes sense," Melvin said. "Was thinking more of trouble coming our way. Right now."

"It'll come first from the cops, and that kind you don't handle by getting in they face. You lay still and quiet until they go away."

Telling Melvin to back off, Dash thought, was like telling a hurricane to calm down.

Ritchie said, "It'll take a while for Virgil's crew to work out a link between us and his unfortunate demise. In the meantime, we can contact them with a special introductory offer."

"You want me to bring one of 'em to you?" Melvin asked. Behind him, Tyrell laughed.

"Uh, no," Ritchie said. "You spook people."

He turned to Dash. "You know Emmett better than any of us, what's on his mind right now?"

"Emmett's not one for deep thoughts, know what I mean. He be happy he done the job like we asked, and now he'll wait to hear from us."

"No chance the cops will turn him over?"

"No chance."

Ritchie leaned back, clasped his fingers behind his head. "Yeah, we move ahead. Dash, get Tanner in for exploratory talks, as they say."

CHAPTER 12

Keera waited until she heard Zach's car drive away before climbing the stairs to her bedroom. She prepared for bed, wishing Zach were with her but knowing he couldn't be. All night she had sensed he was in deeper trouble than he thought. Accessing the astral plane would clarify the situation.

She settled, asked for Bardo to make himself known. He didn't respond. What does he do when not with me? I should ask him next time. She drew in slow breaths and immersed herself in the tingling, the rush as she swept out of her body and floated free.

She pictured Ritchie and found herself standing beside him. He sat opposite another, familiar man in a booth. The place was a neighborhood bar, the kind of place where nobody wants to know your name. She brushed Ritchie as she moved past, and he moved a hand back to scratch where she had touched him.

"You know she's not gonna stay around when she sees this much money," the man said to Ritchie, who eyed a plate of cheese cubes in front of him.

"Twenty thousand, not enough to start a new life." Ritchie popped a cube into his mouth.

"Shit, this bitch never seen more than a hundred at one time. She's gonna think heaven arrived at her door in a Chrysler. She'll wrap that kid in traveling clothes and be gone."

"Just give her what I promised Emmett. I always keep a promise. People expect it."

"Frankie, you not thinking straight. When that bitch blows, Emmett's gonna be hit hard. He crazy about her."

"Dash, you want me to find him another woman?"

Dash. Keera recognized him: the one who had spotted her last time.

"I know him," Dash said. "He'll get down on himself for a while, then he'll look to blame someone else." He leaned forward. "He might think you didn't do enough to stop her. Who knows what will happen after that? The guy's in a jail cell; only one thing he can do if he's in a mind to—talk to somebody."

Ritchie didn't answer, rotated the wine glass between his fingers. Zach was right. Ritchie had paid someone to eliminate Virgil, that someone being this Emmett.

Dash looked away from Ritchie and saw her. His expression didn't change but their eyes locked and she knew. The way he gazed at her, then turned his head this way and that way to see if peripheral vision helped his view. It did, he was seeing more than a shadow this time. She floated behind him. He didn't follow.

"Got a sore neck?" Ritchie asked Dash. "What you twisting your head around like that?"

"Didn't sleep right last night. Got some kinda kink there."

"You young, shouldn't be having physical problems. You not eating right?"

That's because there's no food left after you done eating, Dash thought, and Keera laughed. He twisted his head to find her. He had heard her; she didn't expect that. She levitated higher, closer to the ceiling, hoping he didn't look up.

"Dash, Dash," Ritchie said. "You got the money, go and give it to her. Maybe your neck get better on the way. The way you twisting your head around, it's putting me off my cheese here."

Dash rose out of his seat and looked around. Keera positioned herself to stay out of his direct vision. He walked out of the bar, nodded to the guard outside the door. Dropped into the driver's seat of a parked car. She settled into the back seat, the easy way to maintain contact with him.

He was still aware of her presence, the way he fidgeted in his seat before he put the car in gear. Like something was bothering him, but he couldn't figure out what. Dash took it slow, cruising through streets, a freeway on-ramp in the distance. He checked his mirror as he changed lanes.

He saw her.

"Hey," he yelled and slammed his foot on the brake. The car slewed, coming to rest with a bump as a wheel mounted the curb. He was out of the car and jerking the rear door open before the car stopped rocking.

Keera was gone. Suspended above him in the blackness of the night. Too hard for him to see her now. Shadow in shadow.

This was unexpected. She'd often seen spirits in mirrors but hadn't thought it could happen to her, a live person just visiting the next plane.

Below, Dash ran his hands over the rear seats trying to locate her, feeling around for something that was invisible but might be solid. He had guts, she gave him that. Most others would have been either paralyzed by what they'd seen or wouldn't stop running until daylight.

She retreated further into the darkness, to prevent him from seeing her clearly. She'd come back to Ritchie, locate more of his bases, and most important, his plans for Zach. If Dash saw her every time, she would be severely hampered.

Dash gave up on the interior and looked around the streets. No cars passed at first, but when one did, it slowed, and the four occupants took a long look at him. She picked up their intentions: hostile, figuring the lone driver for a tourist type, loaded with cash and credit cards. They weren't so wrong. Dash had Emmett's twenty thousand in the car.

His car looked like the aftermath of a slight accident, the driver waiting for a tow. The scene was irresistible to the hostiles. They stopped further along and made a U-turn, coming back and stopping behind the Chrysler.

The driver sat, three youths emerged, leaving three doors wide open. They were black and lanky like Dash. They moved apart to flank him, their hands visible, hanging loose at their sides. One of them limped. Keera saw a switchblade knife in his back pocket. A deadly weapon, once it was close enough.

Dash's hands didn't hang loose. One of them held his gun down by his side, and the other was in his pants. He spoke first.

"Got permission to be out here tonight?"

The three stopped, hearing his words and seeing his gun hand at the same time.

"From who?" one asked.

"Disciples."

"You not a Disciple," the limper said.

"Private business going on here," Dash said. His tone suggesting he had an army to back him up, just out of view.

"Saw a bro in trouble, that's all," he said, sounding helpful but not backing off.

"Nobody in trouble here, my friend. Best you all go back to your Nintendos."

"Why your ride parked like that?" asked another of them. He moved forward as if to get a better look.

Dash leveled his gun and shot at one of the open car doors. The blast of gunfire, the clang of metal on metal ripped the night apart. The three men now stock still.

The driver's door opened and Dash pointed his gun at it. "This gonna be a shootout? 'Cause if it is, I already got my weapon, and you boys got nothing in your hands except a bunch of fingers."

The driver halted, but his hands remained hidden by the door.

"Hafta make my point more obvious?" Dash asked and aimed at the leading youth's legs.

"Awright now," the driver yelled. "We going." He turned to the others. "Chill."

He slid back into his seat and the others walked backward to theirs, not taking their eyes off Dash. The car reversed, swung around and sped away, Dash's gun covering until it was out of range.

He holstered his gun and looked around. "I know you still here, pretty woman," he said. "I know you watching me. I can feel the tingling. Soon, I'm going to catch you and find out who you are."

Guess that ruled out hitching a ride with him. She'd have to follow him the hard way, keeping her distance.

Dash drove off, taking the on-ramp, and she followed, staying high above him. She recognized none of the neighborhoods below her, never needing to come here before.

Dash came off the freeway and nosed into narrow streets that looked the same as the ones he'd left. He pulled up outside a house with wood siding, all the lights on inside like it was seven p.m., not past midnight.

Keera put the car between her and Dash and waited.

An old man sat on the porch stoop, regarding Dash with mild curiosity. "You come up in the world since we seen you last," he said to Dash. "Looks like your suit cost more than this house."

"Reckon a Happy Meal cost more than this."

The old man cracked a smile in return but she picked up a residual animosity towards Dash.

"Rhiannon inside?" Dash asked.

"Inside, but not for long. She been waiting for you, musta heard you arrive."

The screen door flew open, and a young woman in her twenties rattled down the steps into Dash's arms. Golden honey poured into a flower-print dress.

"Dash," she said holding him around the waist but tilting her face back to look into his. "I hear you brought me a present."

"It's not a present, babe, it's a payment that belongs to Emmett. He asked for you to hold it." Dash tried to stay serious, but Rhiannon's infectious joy destroyed all chance of that. He grinned as if he was the one getting the present.

"Show me, show me,' she said, excited, working around him and peering into the car. He detached himself and opened the trunk, pulled out a thick buff envelope.

Rhiannon squealed, clapping her hands.

"Hush," Dash said, alarmed and looking about. "You crazy or what? You still want to have this in the morning?"

She stilled immediately. "Shit, Dash. I got no way of being really secure, you know what I mean?" Real security didn't include a collapsing house guarded by a solitary old man.

"You mean you don't want it right now?"

She glanced over at the porch. "Maybe you give me a coupla thousand now. Right? Hold the rest until I got a safe place to put it."

Keera saw Dash torn, picked up on his thoughts. If he didn't deliver all the money, Ritchie might suspect he stole some. It wasn't a good look for Dash to be holding cash he was supposed to pay out.

Dash opened the rear car door. "Get in for a second." Inside, he slit the envelope with his finger and took out a bundle. "This is two grand in twenties," he said as he passed it to her. Her eyes widened as she riffled the notes. "You gotta sign something," he added.

He reached into his jacket and pulled out a small notebook. He wrote on it, "I took $2,000 today as part of the $20,000 owed." He wrote a date under it and gave his pen to her. "Sign over the date."

Rhiannon signed in a hurry; Dash pocketed the notebook.

"How long before you got a good place for the rest?" he asked.

"A day or two, I'll get a deposit box at the bank or some such."

"Good thinking. Gotta go, Rhiannon."

She touched his arm. "Gonna help me spend some of this?" Her smile promised a good time over and above the spending part.

Dash shook his head. "You know I can't. I'd be thinking of Emmett all the time."

"Me too, baby," she said. "I'd be thinking my Emmett don't want me sitting home all sad and blue. He'd want me to live my life, know what I'm saying? That guy's a saint."

He grinned. "He wouldn't stay saintly if the word got around his woman was spending his cash on skinny-ass guys like me."

She made a face. "You wanna think about it, Dash? You're not the only cake on the plate, some just itching to be eaten. You weren't so backward comin' forward last few times, as I recall."

"I ain't backward, baby, just some moments ain't the right ones for playin'."

She tightened her lips and scrambled out, clutching her payment as if it was freshly fallen manna.

"Bye," she called and scooted back up the stairs.

Dash lifted a hand to the old man and moved to the driver's door. Stopped. Stared back at the porch.

Keera followed his gaze.

Another man stood behind the old one on the porch. Blond hair, salmon polo shirt and chinos.

And dead.

Jason Virgil.

CHAPTER 13

"You found Ritchie, and then?" Zach asked Keera over lunch the next day.

"He was talking to Dash when I arrived."

"The errand boy?"

"You might change your mind in a minute. Dash was to deliver money to a woman."

"Like I said, the errand boy."

"He's more than that. He shot at a car load of muggers."

"What! What the fuck for?" The news startled him. The guy was a driver, a messenger. "He didn't strike me as a gunslinger." She filled him in. Dash spotting her, other guys arriving, Dash shooting through the door.

"He can see you?" This was bad news.

"He's catching glimpses. He'll get better with time." She didn't seem concerned. "He delivered the money to a woman called Rhiannon, Emmett's partner. I don't know his last name; they didn't say it, and it didn't come to me in another way. The money was payment for Virgil's killing."

"Ah."

"Someone else saw this transaction: Virgil."

Keera was full of surprises today.

"Like how? Just standing around, curious? Angry? He see you?"

"I took off right away. I'd been out of the body for a long time. I wouldn't have much energy left to deal with Virgil if he got cranky. He wasn't looking at me. He probably didn't register I wasn't dead."

"Not dead?"

"At his stage, barely passed over, and staying close to his earthly surroundings, he's seeing a lot of people around. Some dead like him, but he also sees the live ones moving around the same spaces. He can't tell them apart easily. There'll be a lot of confusion in his mind."

The death plane was pretty crowded, it seemed. The dead and the living all jostling for space and ignoring each other. Just like your average mall.

Zach's Danish and coffee, her salad and tea, arrived. Your basic American diner, a place where sensible folk came for fats, sugars, carbs and coffee, and she still ordered leaves on a plate and more leaves in hot water. Lunch for an insect.

She took a sip and made a face. "People who serve tea should know it requires boiling water to brew; it's not coffee—"

"Keera, I'll start a blog on the topic, okay?" Get her going on anything she was passionate about, and he'd be facing an hour-long lecture. "You think he was there to cause trouble?"

"Maybe, but his presence is ominous."

"Meaning what?"

"Meaning, he hasn't gone to any white light. He's a stayer."

"Staying for a reason, I guess. Revenge?"

"He passed unexpectedly, loads of unfinished business I assume."

Zach swallowed the last of his coffee and signaled for another. "I think part of his unfinished business was with me. Last night."

Her fork hovered above a cherry tomato. "What do you mean?"

"Something trashed my place last night. Piled up my furniture in a freaky way. Not a normal burglary. Nothing taken, a couple of things broken."

"You didn't call me?"

"You didn't want to be disturbed."

She glared at him, annoyed. "Tell me more. Tell me about the furniture."

"It was heaped up; everything perched on everything else. It would have taken me hours to do that, even if I could figure out how to. Such a weird balancing act, with stuff jammed in under the ceiling. I would've needed a ladder, and I don't have one."

He paused to visualize the scene again. "It was as if a giant madman dropped in and amused himself with my stuff like it was building blocks. Took me an hour just to reorganize my bed. The rest can wait until I get back. And my books ... shit, my books. Every single page ripped out and thrown across the hallway. Not torn out, cut out. Like somebody used a guillotine."

She put down her fork, leaned back in the booth. "That has to be Virgil. Furniture moving, that's typical angry poltergeist activity. Smashing stuff proves it. Why is he mad at you, though? You weren't in on the plan; you were used. It doesn't make sense." She picked up her fork, guided more garden produce onto it. "The worse thing is if he continues to target you. He could cause major damage when he figures out how to."

"Major damage? What the fuck do you call what he did to my place last night: left it a little untidy?"

"I meant that he hasn't tried to do you physical harm, yet. Furniture shuffling is him sending you a message he's around."

"He's around all right; he left a very specific message."

She waited, didn't press. Like she knew already.

"I found a paper print in the fridge," he said. "A copy of the front-page photograph. The one that nailed Virgil in the warehouse with packets of white powder."

She drew the cooling cup of tea toward her. Drained it. "He's not one for ambiguity, is he?"

"He made it clear why we're not friends."

"Virgil's developed a surprising amount of power in such a short time. And he gets stronger by grabbing your attention."

"You saying we're dealing with a monster that feeds off earthling energy?"

"Something like that. The more you acknowledge these kinds of spirits, the stronger they get. He's making sure you can't help but acknowledge him. He's already smart enough to do that."

The waitress brought the coffee pot over and reloaded his cup. Zach waited until she left. "I was the innocent patsy in the middle of all this. He wants to play crazy chairs, why doesn't he redecorate Ritchie's crib?"

"He might have, although Ritchie was calm enough last night. Virgil has sent you a message; he'll do the same to him. He'll know by now that it was Ritchie who had him killed." She moved more leaves around on the plate. "That's why he was at Rhiannon's place last night. He's putting the pieces together, figuring out what else went on."

"Why don't you go back to see him, explain things? Tell him that lil' ol' me never meant to hurt Mr. Jason Virgil. Tell him Ritchie's the source of his problem." Never thought he would describe death as a problem before. "Maybe you could lay some of your powerful suggestions on him and banish him. I liked my furniture the way it was."

She gave him her pained expression. "I'm quite limited while on his plane. He has the power; I'm only a psychic. I'm not Gandalf."

A long counter ran along part of the diner, catering for those who wanted to perch and munch. Behind it, a gray-haired man pushed burger patties around the grill, making sure they lined up orderly. Near him, a girl placed a chocolate shake on the countertop.

Stayed staring at it.

The glass wobbled, then shook. It lifted free of the counter and smashed into the wall next to Zach's head.

The girl screamed.

Zach dived out of the booth, tense and ready for another attack. Thick glass shards littered the tabletop and floor.

The whole diner fell silent. Everybody watched him, confused.

Nothing else happened.

He grabbed paper napkins to wipe chocolate off himself, but Keera took his arm.

"Let's go," she said. "It's worse than I thought."

◆ ◆ ◆

Dash couldn't figure out how to break the news but every minute he didn't bring up the shooting would cost him Ritchie's trust. Decided just to bust out with it and hope.

"Had to shoot at bros last night," he said to Ritchie in the back of the Thai joint. "They musta smelt the money on me."

Ritchie halted the beer partway to his mouth and replaced it on the table. "Say again?" Tyrell, sitting beside Ritchie, got busy inspecting his belt buckle.

Dash took a breath. "These bros came onto me when I was stopped on the road. Looking to score anything I had. Four of them, one of me. I put a hole in their ride. They took off again."

"What were you doing stopped on the road?" Ritchie was calm in questioning, but could get mad if he saw stupidity.

"I braked to miss a cat and hit the curb. No damage, though." Keep that witchy woman out of it for now.

"The fuck I care about your ride, Dash. Who were these guys? Please say they weren't Disciples?"

"Didn't see no tatts, no marks. They were young, riding a ten-year-old Lincoln. I asked them if the Disciples knew they were out bothering people. They didn't say they were connected."

"They connected all right. Not members maybe, but they'll have friends and kin who are." Ritchie sipped his beer. "The question is, did they connect you to me?"

"Your name didn't come into it."

"Doesn't matter. You put yourself in the neighborhood in that car, those clothes; people will remember you. Some will know you're with me." Ritchie paused. "You used the Disciples name like you were allowed to. That's real bad. They hear about this, they'll want to explain to you how bad that idea was." Ritchie figuring stuff out loud.

"Shit, Frankie, I was only delivering the money to Rhiannon, like you said. I had to take care of it." The way Ritchie was talking it could be he'd give him up to the Disciples.

"Okay, okay, chill. We might have to pay a fee for that incident, that's all, and there ain't no accident insurance in your contract with me."

"What you saying?"

"I'm saying if I have to pay them to go away, I'll use your dime, not mine."

"But I didn't go looking for them, they found me."

"'Cause you stopped. Next time, run over the little kitty and stay wealthier."

"Aw, boss," Tyrell said, smiling. "You putting a bad picture in my head."

Ritchie ignored him, spoke to Dash. "The girl get the money OK, then?"

"It's done. All good. She happy."

"She say what she's going to do with it?"

"Thinking of having a good time, that's the feeling I got. Pretty excited to see the cash."

Ritchie rubbed his chin. "You tell her to keep quiet about it?"

"Shit, she squeal so much when she saw it, she might as well grabbed a mike and made with a long thank-you speech. I calmed her down, Frankie. Got her worried about what'd happen if the wrong kind found out. She took that in, I know it. She quiet and thoughtful after that."

"You have a sweet way with women." Ritchie grinning now. "If I ever plan to have a female branch of the organization I'm gonna put you in charge."

"If you did that, it would be the best-performing part of our business." Dash going along with the joke but letting Ritchie know he was up for anything.

"It would have to be, Dash. These bros you annoyed won't just be asking for bodywork money. Probably want to do shit to you that'll bring tears to your eyes."

"We ain't having that. Our reputation will be damaged, handing over a loyal member of the organization."

"Loyal, but stupid." Ritchie stroked his glass with a forefinger. He looked up at Dash. "Relax, I can hear your asshole squeaking from here. We won't hand you over; we'll push for compensation, apologize for our big mistake."

"That'd be the way to go," Dash said. "It's like when the Air Force bomb the wrong towel-heads, they say sorry and hand out a few Hershey Bars. Works every time."

Ritchie flicked a fingernail against the glass as if the pinging helped him think. "We not dealing with the government here, Dash. Those bros got rules we never heard of." He drained the last of the beer. "The reason we never heard of'em is they don't make them up until they arrive at our doorstep. Depends on their frame of mind as to what happens next." He rolled back in his chair, grinned.

"All the same, Dash, you better get yourself a bunch of Hershey Bars."

CHAPTER 14

E dwina Moss looked up from her paperwork when Zach knocked and entered her office. "Most people wait to be called in," she said.

"I saw you alone. Figured you'd be cool for a two-minute chat."

"Do the two minutes include a tantrum?"

Zach slipped into the visitor's chair. "Sorry for that. I was pissed about losing my story. And I did apologize later."

"Your thoughtful gesture noted. What can I do for you now?"

"I'm working a possible story on Frankie Ritchie, a dealer on the South Side. Could be linked to the death of Jason Virgil."

Edwina tapped a pen under her chin, not that it was sagging and needed help. "How strong is it?"

He thought of Keera and her astral spying. Rotated a hand this way and that. "I wouldn't want to go to print with it yet, but I think I can confirm it."

"And you want Jeremy off the Virgil story and you back on?"

"There is no Virgil story, is there? It died with him."

"Jeremy has now progressed to the death-of-Virgil story. Your information would be helpful to him."

115

"Let him work his side of the street. I'm coming from a different direction."

"It doesn't look that way from here." She scanned her paper pile and withdrew a sheet. "The person who killed Virgil has been identified as Emmett Hurtle. Been charged with robbery and assault, trial due in a week. No bail, considered a flight risk. Made no statement, yet." She looked up. "Does this gel with what you know?"

"It doesn't contradict it."

"I like it when you're so forthcoming."

"Edwina, I could have a top story here, and I don't want it trampled on by that oaf."

"Fine way to talk about fellow scribes." She put the sheet down. "You go ahead, but keep me in the loop. If I think the story works better with both of you on it, then both of you will be on it."

"Please, no."

"Your two minutes are up. Talk to me soon." She picked up the phone and waited for him to leave.

Zach left and found an interview booth for privacy. Called Keera.

"I got a name for Virgil's killer," he said when she answered.

"It's Emmett, I already told you."

"It's Emmett Hurtle. You going to see him soon?"

"Not sure. Not sure whether it will tell me anything." She paused. "It's Virgil that worries me, and I'm not keen to meet him if he's in a raging temper."

"Sounds like he's going to stay that way for a while. What can we do?"

"Normally somebody would tell him about the white light."

Meaning, he guessed, that it wasn't happening this time.

"That somebody would be you?" he said.

"Uh-uh. I don't have the training to deal with a force like this."

"You think I'm going home to find that another spooky tsunami came through my apartment?"

"I think you're going to stay with me more often."

She laughed, but he wasn't sure if it was because the idea was preposterous. At least she was considering the possibility. He tried to sort out the scenario in his mind. "I still don't get why Virgil went for me. If Emmett was the actual killer, wouldn't Virgil take revenge on him first?"

"It depends on his state of mind at death. When he passed over, he might have been brooding about the photograph that caused his arrest. Once dead, when he knew you were the facilitator, he made you his priority. I'm sure he'll turn on Ritchie and Emmett in due course."

"Somehow I don't feel like warning them. I hope Virgil tosses the sloppiest food over the fat fucker."

"I know it's not funny to you, but you did look a scream with chocolate shake dripping off you."

More laughs coming down the line. Thanks, Keera.

"I love it when you're supportive. I cleaned up fine; you can stop laughing now."

"Okay, but it's an image that will never leave me," she said. "One of my most treasured memories." She switched to serious. "Maybe you're right. I should check on Emmett and get a grasp of his condition. If his girlfriend dumps him like Dash suggested, I want to know if he'll talk. He might try for a reduced sentence. If that puts Ritchie away, Virgil might disappear."

"I'll cross my fingers while I wait," Zach said.

"It's worth trying anyway. I'll go for it tonight. Don't come over; it might take a while. Bye."

He stared at the dead cell in his hand. You'll be staying with me more often she'd said. Don't come over, she'd also said. That's what he adored about her: the clarity, the precision.

Keera didn't get to Emmett; she was rerouted to Ritchie again. Bardo, in his usual way, suggesting this was a better idea.

Ritchie in a restaurant, a bowl of laksa soup in front of him. A white man across the table from Ritchie. Two of his lieutenants sat in chairs to one side. One of them was Dash. She immediately swung high up to a corner where he couldn't easily spot her.

Ritchie said, "It's a bad business all round, Tanner."

Tanner. Zach had mentioned him. Virgil's supply source. He was why Bardo had brought her here.

Tanner nodded back at Ritchie and waited. Ritchie moved shrimp around the bowl. "Your man loses his investment, then loses his life in a stupid jailhouse fight."

"The word's coming through it wasn't a fight," Tanner said.

"It were a fight for sure. People get mighty prickly jammed up together. Maybe Mr. Virgil ignored the rules set up to keep people acting right."

Virgil. Don't say his name. It pulls him here.

"It wasn't a place he'd been before, I can safely say that."

"That's the truth." Ritchie pushed the bowl to one side. "Here's how nice we are. First, we gonna split the loss due to the bust." He held his hand up as if to stop Tanner's protest though he hadn't reacted. "We're good people like that. It's a gesture of goodwill. Continuing goodwill."

"Continuing goodwill?"

"Absolutely, my friend. We wish to maintain and develop the association we have started."

"It wasn't a good start."

"No, it wasn't. But things will get better."

Tanner leaned forward. "The thing is, with the loss of the product and Virgil dead, nobody's itching to go that way again real soon."

Virgil again.

"You people getting out of the business?" Ritchie sounding like it was a terrible idea. "You found something better?"

"Nobody thinks it's a smart move to deal with you again. They're not happy with me either, for leading them into this."

"You a good friend of this Charlie guy I've heard about?" Ritchie asked.

Tanner showed no outward sign, but Keera picked up his sudden dismay.

"Charlie Hostler?" Tanner asked.

"Yeah, him."

"Not friends. We work together on some things." Tanner, she saw, knew instantly where Ritchie was heading.

"I've heard he's a fine, upstanding member of his community. Is that right?"

"Can't say I've heard that, but Charlie's well respected. Has a head for figures."

"That's what I mean." Ritchie leaned back, satisfied. "A head for figures is all it takes to get ahead, be respected, right?"

Tanner shrugged.

"Isn't that right?" Ritchie insisting that Tanner agree with him.

"It's right enough," Tanner said.

"It's damn right enough. A man with a head for figures knows a profitable situation when it's put to him, right?"

"Right." Tanner reluctantly accepting the role of yes-man.

"If," Ritchie asked, locking onto Tanner, "if this Charlie were presented with an agreeable situation, he would see the sense in it, wouldn't he?"

"Yes, he would."

"So if I were to have a polite conversation with fine, upstanding Charlie, I wouldn't be disappointed in the outcome, would I?"

Tanner hesitated. Keera read his thoughts like they were billboards. Ritchie preparing the ground for talks with Charlie Hostler, that was fine. Holding him, Tanner, responsible if the result wasn't to Ritchie's liking, wasn't so fine.

"I can't predict what Charlie will say in any kind of situation," Tanner said. "He's got all the smarts; I'm not in his league in that department."

Ritchie busied himself with the bowl until it was empty. He pushed it to one side. Dash tensing, she saw, waiting for the command to clear it away, but it didn't come.

"Charlie's got smarts, that I know for myself," Ritchie said.

"You don't get to be number two by being stupid. That's why I want to talk. You arrange it. Dash will give you his number; you call him when your man is ready. We come and get you and Charlie."

"I don't know, Frankie. I wasn't at the pickup like you suggested. And I wasn't at the house later either. The more people talk about this possible hit on Virgil, the trickier things look for me."

It's getting worse. They're not only mentioning his name, they're making him the subject of the conversation.

Ritchie snorted. "Hostler wasn't at the collection. Wasn't at the house either. Forget it. It's just your nerves making you twitchy. Tell him we have to talk."

Tanner straightened. "You can't be serious. If I bring him a message from you, I won't live long enough to change my underwear. It'll be obvious that I knew something about the set-up on Virgil."

His name again. For God's sake, why don't you just send him a written invitation?

"Virgil, Virgil," Ritchie snorted. "I bet Charlie's real glad Virgil's gone, and he's now the head honcho. He's the number-one man now, isn't he?"

Tanner nodded.

"He likely to stay in charge, do you think?"

"No other prospect."

"So, we have to meet. Strangers-who-should-be-friends sort of thing, right?"

"Right," Tanner said. "But I shouldn't be part of the meeting."

Ritchie wiped his mouth with a napkin. "Okay, we do it this

way. You call Dash when you and Charlie are going to be together somewhere public, like in a restaurant. Dash comes
along, says 'Hi' to Charlie and hands him a note—"

"He won't get that close."

"Okay, okay." Ritchie outwardly irritated now. "We get the
waiter to hand him the note. Suggesting a meeting. How does
that sound?"

"Charlie won't come to the South Side, and you'll be visible on
his turf."

"Do I look stupid to you? We meet at a classy hotel, downtown, middle of the tourist area."

"Why do I have to be there when he gets the note?" Tanner
searching for a way out of the whole thing.

"So I know for sure Charlie got the note, and you can tell me
how he feels about a meet. If he's agreeable, you can suggest
yourself as the go-between. Better still, make sure one of his
people goes with you to report back. That'll take the heat off
you."

Tanner thought about Ritchie's suggestion, then asked,
"What's in the note? Instructions on how to meet?"

Ritchie laughed. "You sure slow for an educated white boy.
It'll have a cell number, and a suggestion we meet, that's all.
Charlie and me talk, figure each other out, agree to meet. The
details come later. Let's get going on this."

Ritchie glanced at Dash, who opened the door. Tanner stood.

"I'll try," he said to Ritchie.

"You'll succeed," Ritchie said, with emphasis, and Tanner left,
Dash following him and closing the door behind them.

In the opposite corner: a new figure formed.

Virgil.

Angry.

His hate energy was phosphorescent. It blazed through the electric circuits and blew out all the bulbs in the room. Ritchie jumped up, his form visible to her, not to Tyrell.

"Hey," Ritchie snapped. "Open the door, get some light in here. Get a new bulb while you're at it."

Tyrell shuffled to the door, his arms outstretched to protect himself from banging into a wall. He reached the door and ran his hand down it, searching for the handle. When he found it, he couldn't turn it. More of Virgil's unseen work.

"The door's locked, Frankie." Tyrell wrenched at the handle repeatedly.

"Shit." Ritchie scrambled away from the table and pressed his body against the wall. "Get away from the fuckin' door; it's trouble."

Tyrell slid to the other side of the door, both men with drawn guns. They stood quiet, listening for footsteps, waiting for the door to open. Keera picked up jumbled images from both of them, Ritchie visualizing a spray of bullets from a machine gun, Tyrell seeing a hand throw a grenade in the room.

Footsteps approached, the handle turned down. The door opened a fraction and stopped.

"Frankie?" Dash called into the darkness. "Tyrell? What's with the light?"

"Open wide, Dash," Ritchie commanded. "Let's get a look at you." He moved silently away from where his last words came from. Tyrell too, stepped back.

Dash pushed the door wide open. Light from the hallway spread over the floor, illuminating the interior dimly. His eyes widened at the guns. Aimed at him.

"Shit, Frankie," he said. "What I do wrong?"

Ritchie lowered his gun. "Nothing, Dash, nothing. We got a little spooked when the light went out, that's all. The door was locked, too. Least the handle didn't move."

Dash jerked on the handle, pushing it down, letting it come up. "Handle's fine. Weren't locked when I came back."

"It was stuck," Tyrell said and bustled past him, came back with a light bulb, stood on a chair and screwed it in. The new light showed three faces strained in tension.

Virgil watching them.

Until he saw her.

"You're not part of this," he said. "You can leave." His eyes black and implacable.

"I leave whenever I want," she said. "I don't need your permission." Their conversation on this plane undetected by the others in the room. The antagonism came off him in waves, but he didn't reply.

"You're evil," she said. "Evil before your death and evil after it. You're supposed to see yourself more clearly now, make amends for what you did."

He still didn't respond, staring like he was burning her image into his memory for future use. He cast another look at the three confused men, then vanished.

"Seriously weird shit," Ritchie said to the others. "The light going, the door jamming up like that."

"Fuckin' weird, spooky shit," Tyrell added.

"Spooky? It was a spook hanging around?" Ritchie swept his hand over the room.

Dash followed his hand and spotted her in the corner. She stayed still, waiting for his reaction.

Ritchie said to Dash, "That voodoo woman you told me about once? You better get her. We need a special team for this kind of game."

"Voodoo woman?" Dash echoed, keeping his gaze on her. "I think she already here."

CHAPTER 15

R itchie caught onto Dash's remark too fast. "You saying a woman did this?" He waved his arms at the door.

Dash looked around for the woman but couldn't see anything, not even a wisp like the first time.

"I thought I saw one, is all," he said. "I didn't say she done it."

"How long you been seeing this woman, any woman?" Ritchie getting curious. "You one of those creepy guys who see dead people?"

"Not me." He knew Ritchie would be wary if one of his guys were into ghost shit' n' all. "It must have been a trick of the lights. I was jumpy when I came in, all that dark 'n' shit. Didn't know what was happening, ready to fire at shadows, you know what I mean?"

"Dash, you see women everywhere, and I've seen them look back at you."

"They can look all they want, but I be choosy when it comes to the vital moment. I like 'em with some style, you know? A woman who don't set off her finest points with the right apparel isn't right for me." Get him off the topic; that be best.

Ritchie sat at the table. "Get some beers, Tyrell," he said.

Tyrell stuck his head out the door and called for two beers, resumed his place beside the door.

"'Apparel'," Ritchie said. "You wanna run a little boutique somewhere, Dash? You making me nervous. Pretty soon you won't clip a guy because it'll wreck his fine suit, you know what I mean?"

"That's not gonna happen. Business is business."

Tyrell let in a waitress with two beers on a tray. She set them down, avoiding eye contact, and left as softly as she'd come. Ritchie picked up a glass and motioned to the other.

"Sit with me, Dash; we gotta have a think-tank-thing going here."

Dash sat and drew the beer to him, not yet drinking.

Ritchie said, "Where this spook come from all of a sudden? Can your voodoo woman tell us that?"

The voodoo woman was not a voodoo child at all, just a storefront psychic, but he'd once referred to her as voodoo and Ritchie had hung onto that idea. There was no good way to tell him different. "I say she can. We should go first thing, not waste our time. She can tell us why they came as well."

"You been to her often?" Ritchie watched him over the rim of the glass.

"Now and then."

"What questions you ask her?"

He kept his answer light. "The usual shit. Love, money, health."

Ritchie cracked a laugh. "And what she tell you? You gonna be rich, gonna have twenty-four-hour pussy and live to the end of time? That's what she tell all the po' boys who come 'round."

She tells me a lot more than that, Dash thought. "She helps me get my thinking straight sometimes. What she can do is find out who did this to us."

Ritchie wasn't listening. "I've heard about these active-type spooks. Poltergeists, right? They inhabit buildings, usually old places. This here joint is old, right? Like 1950s built. This thing that came today, it's from that time. Maybe a customer who died and wants to hang in his favorite room." Ritchie leaned back, satisfied with his reasoning. "It's not gonna be anybody significant, is it? Probably some spook who don't want his favorite crib to be a Thai joint. Wanting to drive customers away."

"Why didn't it come before?" Dash impatient, wanting to get a quick answer from his woman, not shoot the shit about what could be. "We use this room a lot."

"Fuck knows." Ritchie was over the attack, figured it out, ready to move on.

"We have to know who it was." Dash persisted.

"Sure we do. That's your job." Ritchie drained his beer, eyed Dash's untouched glass. "You on antibiotics or something?" When Dash shook his head, Ritchie reached over for the full glass and pulled it toward him, sank half the contents down his throat. Looked over at Tyrell.

"Tyrell, get the car. All this excitement has put me off eating." Ritchie turned back to Dash as Tyrell pulled out his cell. "You tell me as soon as Tanner calls you."

Ritchie finished Dash's beer and left with Tyrell. Dash checked his cell for any missed calls, found none. Scrolled through his contacts list, found the voodoo woman.

"Li'l Marie," Dash said when she picked up, "we had an spooky shit happen today."

"Ooh, Dash," she said, "Good to hear your voice. Come over and tell me about it."

"I thought you could save me a ride, tell me the significance of it now."

Li'l Marie laughed, soft and warm. She wasn't going to go with that idea.

"I got a nice place here," she said. "Just right for translating the spirit world. My daughter's coming over soon, you recall her, Letitia. She like to see you, Dash, as we all do. Come over and I'll sort your troubles out, quick as lightning."

Shit, Dash thought, she's not gonna sort my troubles out, she's gonna try to sort her kid out with a cashed-up husband, is what she intends.

"Can't you tell me stuff over the phone? It's late, and I don't want to drive over," Dash wondered if she could read his secret thoughts while he was talking to her.

"Dash," Li'l Marie purred. "I do my best work face to face, as you know. Your guide talks to my guide, and we get a resolution. You know what I'm saying? A resolution. You wanna chat over the phone, well, I can't guarantee results. Guides don't like phones."

Dash tried a last time. "We had a spook here that locked the boys in a room, blew the lights out. What do you make of that?"

She stayed quiet for a half minute like she was thinking, or talking to her own spooks, then she replied. "There were two of them; that's all I'm getting for now."

"Two? I thought I saw one."

"Two, for sure. Not friends of yours, either."

"Li'l Marie, people make enemies in business, it's only natural.

I didn't know they stayed pissed after they die."

She laughed down the line. "You pissed off one of them for sure: a real bad mutha, this one."

Keera returned to her body and sat up, curling her legs under in a yoga pose. Allowed time to settle her soul as the sky darkened through the window and thoughts of Virgil ran through her head. He wasn't going away anytime soon, and his power was growing. There was something else. He could move objects easily, but hadn't caused major harm. Just inflicted pain and fear—a warning shot rather than an attack. Must be the tormenting type. He could get worse, she knew.

She rose to her feet in a single motion, located her cell on the coffee table and called Zach.

"We should talk," she said when he answered. "You coming over?"

"You said not to." His answer laced with irritation.

"That was then, here is now. When can you get here?"

"If I stop moving my furniture, twenty minutes. Should I bring a nightcap?"

"You might need something for yourself, I'm fine." She killed the call.

Zach could stay tonight, and she welcomed it. He never completely understood the demands on her. The nights on the astral plane, the constant psychic input during the day. It must be so peaceful to have moments where nothing grabbed your attention. She needed time to explore her world, and time to recover afterward. Her life forced her to push him away more than she wanted. Tonight, her work was done early, a chance to chill. She stepped into the shower and washed the day off.

Zach brought Chablis, one of the few wines she liked, a Roquefort cheese and a warm baguette. He assumed she needed the wine to loosen up before bedtime. Keera took the proffered glass and sipped. Chablis always reminded her of their first time, an experience that caught her by surprise when she found she desired him. After that, she'd kept him at arm's length for months, while she considered the ramifications. She still did this sometimes, more out of reflex than design.

"I was taken to Ritchie tonight, not Emmett," she told Zach. "Virgil turned up."

"Hey, that's news. Ritchie get food all over him?"

"Virgil blew his lights out, trapped him a dark room. Didn't hurt him. I think he's just toying with his intended victims for now."

He cut off a chunk of cheese and squashed it onto a torn hunk of bread. "How did Ritchie react?"

"He's smart enough to rule nothing out. He's wondering if a spook was involved. Didn't connect it to Virgil, though."

"Didn't connect to you, then."

"Sort of. Dash came in later and saw me."

"Uh-oh." Zach put his bread and cheese down. "What happened?"

"Ritchie told Dash to get a voodoo woman for protection. Dash said there was already one in the room."

"Dash thinks a woman attacked them?"

"I believe so. Me." Dash, she now knew, was one of those people who stumble into your life and make it worse.

"Does Dash know what you look like?"

131

She shrugged. "You said they knew about me. Does that mean they watched me?"

His turn to shrug. "They might have only checked your mail. Or maybe caught a glimpse of you."

"In any case, I won't appear the same to them on the astral plane as I do on the physical. I might only be a female shape. Certainly Dash didn't recognize me when he spotted me the first time."

"Let's assume they're thinking it's a dead person messing with them. They won't connect to you in a hurry. If they do, they'll be mighty confused."

"They'll connect to me as soon as they get a decent medium." As if they would. Hard guys like them rarely consulted mediums. It made them look weak.

Zach said, "In that case, we ought to let Ritchie know it's Virgil giving him a hard time before he finds good help."

"Nice idea, but how do you explain me?"

"I won't. I'll contact Ritchie, bitch about Virgil messing with my apartment. Tell him I got a psychic to confirm it, ask if Virgil's thrown furniture about his crib. I won't even mention you. I'll let him think this 'watching woman' is a separate problem."

She drained her glass, loosened the sash on her cotton robe. "There's more. Before Virgil came, Ritchie was talking to a white guy, trying to set up a meeting with a Charlie Hostler."

"Virgil's number two. Ritchie's moving right along, isn't he? The thing is, what do we do about it?" Zach rocked his empty wine glass back and forth. "We—you, that is—should at least observe the meeting when it takes place."

"I'm not a one-woman crime stopper, Zach. I only care about

you and your involvement here. Tell that Detective Warren what you know and let them handle it. I'll protect your body and your soul as well as I can."

"You care about me?"

"Uh-huh."

"You don't always act like it."

"I don't always want to admit it." Was he going to carry this confession into some analytical Q and A? It was late; it was bedtime.

He grinned. "Are you in therapy or something? Because I've never seen this side of you before."

She rose from the table. "If you want to see the best side of me, I suggest you follow me upstairs, right now."

CHAPTER 16

Zach slipped out of Keera's bed early in the morning, leaving her sleeping. For a girl who liked to live on the spirit side so much, Keera could get mighty physical once she returned to earth. These nights drained him; he hoped they invigorated her. Sure sounded like it. He left a sticky note on her laptop. I did so enjoy the best side of you. xxx.

He collected a coffee near the corner and joined the early traffic heading to the South Side. The Thai place not open for business but plenty of bustle around it. Crates of vegetables stacked against the front wall; two men carried sides of pork from a refrigerated truck to the kitchen, the slabs bigger than either of them.

Zach stepped inside the doors and all activity stopped. He scanned the workers, the guy with the cleaver back in the same place.

"Where's the manager?" he asked the cleaver guy. "It's a private matter." Didn't want to be mistaken for a health inspector.

The manager approached from the back of the main room. "What you want?" she asked, wiping her hands on a cloth. Her eyes grew wary as she remembered him. "He not here," she said quickly.

"I know," he replied, pulling out his notepad. Wrote his name and cell number on a page, tore it out and gave it to her. "This is for Mr. Ritchie. I need him to call me."

The woman accepted the note without breaking eye contact.

He cruised past the Post building, heading for the parking garage. No sign of Dash waiting to pick him up. Maybe Ritchie's boys were late risers. Maybe they were all busy fetching breakfast for the fat one. One of them wasn't. Zach's cell came alive as he reached the Post lobby.

"Whatchu want?" Dash asked.

"Well, good morning to you too, Sunshine," Zach said. "I just wanted to tell you about freaky shit happening to me."

"So? You wanna go on Dr. Phil and blub your eyes out?"

"I'm talking supernatural stuff. Somebody came to my place and moved all the furniture around like it was Lego blocks. Stacked it to the ceiling."

"Musta been a major style improvement if your clothes are anything to go by."

"Cute, Dash, but—"

"Is that my name?" Dash broke in. "I don't recall saying any such thing. You got me confused with somebody else?" Dash, getting twitchy, thinking he might be recorded.

"My bad. I don't know who I'm talking to right now. Anyway, I figured it wasn't your colleagues since you don't seem to be in the furniture-moving business."

"You right about that."

"So, I thought about it and thought about it, and eventually I remembered something about when people die violently their ghost comes back for revenge. You hear of anything like that?"

Dash took a while to answer, didn't have a jive-ass reply ready. "I never heard this kinda talk."

"I researched it. Found heaps of stories about this sort of activity. Poltergeist stuff. You must have heard of that."

"Shit, you think I'm ignorant?" He sounded hurt.

"Not at all. Not everybody has an interest in the supernatural, that's all."

Dash didn't reply.

Zach continued. "What I wanted to know was, is anything like this happening to you and your friends?"

"Why would it?"

"Well, you know we both have a connection with a violent death recently. Maybe that person's angry, wants to hurt us."

Dash forced a laugh. "Swear to God, man, you some crazy dumb fucker. You might have a connection with a dead man, I don't, none of us here do. You looking for clues in all the wrong places. If anybody's trashing your crib, it's because it lacks class and taste. Probably a fly guy turned over in his grave after he saw you carrying home Walmart shit and was highly offended. Serve you right."

Dash cut the call. Zach looked down at his cell and thumbed to recent calls. Dash's number sat there, a glowing beacon. He hadn't suppressed his caller ID, had wanted Zach to have his number. He couldn't figure out why and decided it was a mistake. Maybe Dash was more sloppy than he acted. Still, the call had done its job; a seed planted in their minds that it might not be a woman attacking them, it might be Virgil.

Zach rode the elevator to the Post floor. Most of the workstations still deserted at that hour of the morning; Edwina's outline visible behind her opaque glass walls. He dropped into his seat just as his cell rang. Warren.

"Detective," Zach said, "how nice to hear from you."

"How's the story on Ritchie getting along?" A warm-up line. He recognized the approach.

"I'm just at the information gathering stage, you know, background painting, that sort of thing."

"No interview, then, no proper one-on-one situation? Nothing you could share with me?" Stand by for the right hook.

"Not that I can think of."

Warren paused, gave him the punch line. "So how come you were seen getting into a car with one of Ritchie's boys?"

"I'm under surveillance?" This was news. Bad news.

Warren laughed. "You weren't so important that I could justify that in my budget." He got serious. "Now things have changed. You're consorting with criminals, and you could provide information leading to an arrest."

"You were watching me?" This changed everything.

"We got eyes out on the street, and your description turned up. A white guy hanging with one of Ritchie's guys."

"How do you know it was me?"

"Let's see now: tall, dark and ugly, obvious social misfit."

"Rules me out, then," Zach said, relaxing now. Warren had nothing but a suspicion. He moved to put Warren in a better frame of mind before the suspicion hardened into accepted fact.

"This Charlie Hostler guy you mentioned once."

"What about him?"

"Where can I find him?"

"Right now? Probably under a bed." Warren said. "Try the Lincoln Park area. Why are you asking?"

"You guys got a warrant out for him?"

"No. Answer my question now. This isn't a one-way street."

"His name came up in connection with Ritchie."

"In what way?" Warren interested now.

"Apparently there's a meeting coming up."

"You on the level?" Incredulous.

"Straight as."

Zach could hear him exhale. Waited a polite moment, then asked, "You got anything interesting for me?"

"Oh yeah, the reason I called. Trying to be nice after your awful snub. Emmett Hurtle, the perp in the Virgil murder? He might avoid a trial. He's been taken to a hospital. Gone crazy, can't sleep, won't sleep, keeps yelling that Virgil's trying to kill him every time he closes his eyes."

Dash walked in on Li'l Marie in her reading room at the back of her little store where she sold tarot cards, pendulums and crystals. One shelf held a row of books on the afterlife, written by those saying they'd been there and back. An easy way to write a book. Just make up any old shit, and people rush to buy it.

"Tell me more about the spook who locked my boss in," he said when he took a seat. A battered deck of tarot cards lay on the table between them, but never in any of Dash's visits had Li'l Marie used them. He understood they were a prop: Li'l

Marie took her visions direct.

"I gotta get set first," she said. "I can't just tune into the spirit world like that." She closed her eyes and appeared to be listening to somebody, nodding now and then. "Okay," she said after a while. "Here's what's going on. The spirit that's causing you concern is angry."

"You told me already."

"Stay polite, or I shut up."

She took a full minute to resume. Dash waited like he had a month of waiting time to spare. Didn't want her to feel she was getting to him.

"He knows your gang—"

"Not a gang, it's a business organization." Best to get that straight.

"Whatever. Your people are responsible for his death, he thinks. He's trying to make all of you pay for this, but he's not strong enough to achieve his aims."

"So we ignore him?"

"He's not yet able to harm you much. Yet. This person is determined, and he'll build energy over time. And then it'll be a serious problem for your ... organization."

Dash grinned. "Yo, you saying he's gonna mess with the locks all the time? I'm shaking already."

"It'll get worse. You won't be laughing then."

Dash recalled the brief glimpse of somebody standing next to Uncle at Rhiannon's. Preppy guy, pink polo shirt. "I seen a guy once; could be him. What does your guy look like?"

"I'm not getting any visuals, just the emotions."

"White guy, though, right?"

"Could be, hard to say."

Li'l Marie was supposed to be top class, but he was sure he'd caught her out now. She was fakin' it. Had nothing about what this menace thing looked like. He pushed her further.

"So, how do we stop him messing with us?"

"You can't. I can't. An outside force will come into play. This might be favorable for you, I can't tell."

Impatient, Dash shifted in his seat. "What's the point of seeing the future if you can't see the future that matters? I'm paying for good information here. Not 'maybe this, maybe that' shit."

Li'l Marie glared back at him. "I can only get what I get. If I don't get it all, it's because the future is not yet set."

"Like there's elements could alter things?"

"Exactly. I got something that might help you in the meantime." She walked over to a cupboard and took out a tiny vial of red liquid, put it on the table between them.

"What's in this dinky bottle, cheap perfume?" Dash said, picking it up, turning it around in his fingers.

"Four Thieves Vinegar. It wards off evil spirits."

"How it do that: make me smell bad?" Dash hooted laughter.

"It's made with wine vinegar and contains garlic, pepper and other herbal essences." She ignored his chuckles. "It's a long-time voodoo protection against psychic attack. You sprinkle it across your doorstep, and you'll sleep right."

"Good thing I don't have to drink it."

"You can sprinkle on your food, too. It's got a nice afterbite to it."

Dash slipped the bottle into his jacket, thought of something else to ask.

"I seen a woman, twice now, maybe a third time before, I'm not sure. She there the last time, when this spook got frisky. Who she?"

"You mean a woman in spirit?"

"What else would I be asking about? If she was solid, I'd ask her myself."

She glared at him again but closed her eyes and became silent. "She's not a dead one," she said, opening her eyes.

"What the fuck that mean? You can't be a ghost and not be a dead one."

"Sure you can," she said, laughing at him. "She's learned to leave her body at home, that's all."

"Why she following me around? She a spy or something like that?"

"Spying, that's the truth."

Somebody watching him, somebody without a body. What the fuck was this? "Who for? Who is she?"

"She's got her reasons. I hear no name to give you. She's not known to you at this time."

"She in with this other guy?" Seriously weird shit going on.

"Aware of him, not his friend."

A real person playing like a ghost, following him around. A thought hit him. "So, if this babe's for real, I can find her and ask her to stop?"

"Sure, if she'll listen."

"People usually listen to a Glock."

Li'l Marie regarded Dash with amusement. "If she can leave her body, Dash, she's more than a match for you. She'll know you're coming before you do."

Yeah, that a fact. Probably ride in the back of his car while he was driving over. "So, she got to leave her body somewhere, right? Her crib, for sure. It's her body that's the key. I find that, I control her. What can you tell me about her?"

"She has a link to the angry guy, that's all I know. I have his name, do you want it?"

"I know it. Virgil." Had to be, right? Bones done figured out the truth.

She beamed. "Oh Dash, you getting to be pretty psychic yourself."

"I can put two and two together."

"You gotta lot of talent." She closed her eyes again. "Men looking for you. Angry. It's about a gun."

Who she talking about?

"You took a shot at them."

Aah, those guys. "How close are they?"

"Not close but getting closer." She opened her eyes at him. "They will find you, and you have to be ready."

"I'm always ready," he said. "Born standing up and keeping a sharp lookout."

"Stay that way is all I can say. Anything else you need to know?"

"You said last time I'd be moving up in my organization. That's still good?"

She bowed her head. "You got a future ahead of you."

"I know it, but is it first-class?"

"Like I said, you're going to be making more decisions your-self, not waiting to be told. I get something else now: a packet of money. You holding money that's not yours."

Shit, she knew about Rhiannon's cash. "It's a temporary situ-ation," he said. He had forgotten about the cash; Rhiannon was supposed to call him and take the rest of it. Where was that bitch?

"Make it extremely temporary; it's going to cause a heap of problems." She sipped from a glass of water. "If that's all for today, I have another client soon, and that's fifty bucks I need from you. Plus fifteen for the potion."

"Shit, I was here like minutes," Dash protested as he reached for his money clip.

"I don't charge by the hour. Think on what you knew before you walked in here and what you know now. Fifty is cheap for what I do."

Dash dropped sixty-five on the table. She collected the money and held the bills in her hand.

"You wanna come over for dinner one night? You must be sick of all that eating out. Try some of Tish's fine home cooking?"

He knew Li'l Marie wouldn't give up on him and her kid easily. That girl? Shit, she couldn't even tell the difference between Donna Karan and K-Mart. Probably bought her underwear from the Dollar Store. "Nights is when I work the most," he re-plied, standing. Didn't bother sounding regretful.

"Sure, no problem. We'll find a way to meet up socially one day. I hope I was able to help your organization." She gave him a searching look.

"It was much appreciated," Dash said as he walked out. Like he

was gonna share any of this with Ritchie.

CHAPTER 17

Keera woke late and hit the shower. Rubbed her hair dry standing on a Turkish kilim alongside the bed. It didn't match the Navajo blanket covering her quilt, but neither were collected for style. She came home with the Navajo rug after a field trip to New Mexico. The kilim came back with her after a heady week in Istanbul with a fellow graduate. An affair that didn't survive the return to the USA. Her first inkling that she couldn't give men what they really wanted: undiluted attention.

Zach didn't clamor for attention. He wasn't needy that way; he knew who he was and what he was. That was part of the attraction. The rest of the bond was at the soul level. Too hard to explain, too hard to understand, even. She'd simply accepted it. Eventually.

Her cell trilled, Zach's name glowing on the screen.

"That Emmett guy," he said. "Virgil's harassing him, too."

"How do you know?"

Zach told her: Emmett moved to a hospital, a bit crazy, too scared to sleep, saying Virgil is coming after him.

Emmett was the easiest target. "Sleep," she said. "The best time for Virgil to make an impression."

"Why doesn't he come in my sleep, then?"

"Maybe he's got something figured out, how he can mess with you physically. We already saw the chocolate shake attack."

"You're turning it into a joke," Zach said, sounding aggrieved. "Glass is a lethal weapon, you know."

Keera laughed. "I imagined the headline: "Investigative Journalist Killed in Savage Chocolate Shake Attack.'"

"You'll never make a headline writer; it's too long."

"Okay, okay." She thought back to Emmett. "Doesn't Emmett's condition affect the case against him? Wouldn't he be considered unfit to stand trial?"

"That's what Warren said."

"Well, it makes no sense. It's in Virgil's interest to have a trial, isn't it? The truth comes out, and Ritchie gets implicated."

"You're so young," Zach said. "If Emmett stood trial, he'd stay mute. Or just explain crazy stuff in his head made him do it. Ritchie won't even get mentioned."

"So Virgil's just torturing Emmett. It fits his profile." She changed tack. "Have you seen any sign of Virgil today?"

"Nope. Not a single flying object came my way. Has he finished with me, do you think?"

"It helps to be optimistic, I know, but Virgil's got you on his list, and what's happened already is only a sample." She had put it right out there, but Zach had to assume he was in danger until Virgil disappeared. "Please be aware of this."

"I love the way you cheer me up, Keera," he said.

"I favor the truth with you whenever I can."

"I'm so blessed in that way." His voice softened. "Last night was fun, wasn't it?"

"It was," she said, a smile breaking out.

"I was wondering if I should stay over tonight and we, um, try it again?"

She cleared her throat. "About my nights, I do my best work then."

"I know. That's why I'm asking."

"I'm talking astrally, Zach. I'll call later."

She hung up, so he couldn't talk her into changing her mind. Not that a night of frolicking sex was a bad option, but she couldn't relax if tasks were left undone. Right now it was time to locate Virgil and see what influence she had on him.

She slipped into faded blue cargo pants and a white tee. Carried a cup of tea into the living room and sank into a sofa. "Bardo?" she asked hopefully, "can you take me to Virgil?'

That's not the best choice. Bardo soft in her ear as though he was sitting beside her.

"I have to tackle him sooner or later, don't I?"

Later is better.

"I don't want to avoid him, I want to take him on."

You can't avoid him. He's gathering strength and technique all the time, and he'll return.

"Is Zach safe?"

He's careless: doesn't understand his position.

The caution in his words worried her. "I've tried to warn him, but he's offhand about this. What can I do?"

He's a hard dog to train. Reaffirm the danger he's in, make him more aware.

"He resists me when I talk to him, I'm not sure he's going to listen next time."

Bardo didn't reply.

"Maybe I should see Virgil and convince him that Zach was an innocent pawn."

Maybe you should see this first.

She placed her cup on the coffee table and sank back into the cushions. Closed her eyes to concentrate on Zach and found herself watching Dash. He was pulling up outside the broken house where he'd come to deliver the money. The old man back on the porch, smoking.

"Yo," Dash said as he took the steps two at a time. "Rhiannon in?"

"She in," the old man said, "and not out of it—yet."

"Good to hear."

The old man tilted his head around to get a good look at Dash. "Why you coming here again, talking to another man's woman?"

"It's just business, is all," Dash said, peering through the mesh screen into the house.

"You reckon Emmett's gonna see it that way?"

"Reckon Emmett's gonna see it the way Ritchie says it is."

"You ain't him."

"You ain't the guardian of the gate either, my friend."

Dash pushed inside and came to a small girl watching television in the living room. About two, maybe three years old, she twisted to gaze at him impassively.

"Where your momma at?" Dash asked her. She pointed down the hallway, returned to the television. Ross and Rachel from Friends were bantering. What could she make of that, Keera wondered. How did it keep her interest?

Rhiannon was in the kitchen, smoking and tapping her fingers on a celebrity magazine. She wore a pink halter-top that hardly halted anything. She brightened when Dash walked in the room. Came up, wrapped her arms around him and buried her face in his neck.

He held her close at first but broke away to stare at her meaningfully.

"I ain't got no deposit box, yet," she said. "Not sure how to do that. You wanna come with me and help?" Her big eyes searched his.

"Yeah," he said, his tone husky. "We better do this thing."

"I'll get changed." Rhiannon looked at her bare feet and tiny shorts. "Get something presentable for the men in ties."

She moved out of the kitchen down the hall to the back of the house; his eyes tracked her swaying ass.

"Hey Dash," she called after a minute. "I need help."

Dash followed the hallway to her room. Rhiannon standing by her bed

"What do you think of this?" she asked him, holding a dress up in front of her. Nice cut.

Before he could reply, she dropped it. Wore nothing else. "What do you think of this one?" she asked, cocking her hip.

The vision darkened; Keera was back in her house. She rose from the sofa.

"Oh boy," she said. She walked back to the kitchen and

dropped her cup into the dishwasher. The picture of Dash carefully folding his clothes as he removed them fresh in her mind.

"Oh boy," she said again.

◆ ◆ ◆

"You get to watch people having sex?" Zach asked Keera when she called him. "You never told me."

"No, I don't," she said crisply. "What kind of person do you think I am? I left when I saw what was about to happen."

"I didn't mean it was a bad thing—"

"It's gross to watch. Shall we move onto what this means?" Let Zach start on what it was like to view sex scenes while out of her body, and he'd be absorbed for hours.

"Sure. Dash is starting a whole heap of trouble if he messes with Emmett's woman."

"Exactly. And guess who's going to tell Emmett what's going on?"

"His woman. Rhiannon. It'd be typical of a young girl to boast."

For God's sake; such a generalization. "She won't get the chance. I'm getting that Virgil will put the image in Emmett's head A.S.A.P."

"He'd do this to torture Emmett more?"

"Partly, but if Emmett thinks he's being made a fool of by one of Ritchie's men while he's locked up, he might change his mind about staying silent."

Zach stayed quiet for a while, figuring it out. "If Emmett starts chatting with the cops, and what Emmett says links Ritchie to Virgil's murder, then Ritchie will silence him. Emmett would know that."

"That depends on the state of his mind. Sounds like his nights are full of terror, and the days are filled with despair. Any hint of his woman cheating will have unpredictable results."

"Well," he said, "there's nothing we can do about this, is there?"

"I should see Virgil and talk with him." How to do this wasn't obvious, seeing as how even Bardo wouldn't take her to him.

"Slow your roll, girl. He's no shrinking violet."

"I'm not hanging around waiting for Virgil to do his worst. I'm going to find him."

"Now? Tonight?" The question hung heavy between them. She knew what Zach was really asking.

"Yes, as soon as I can, Zach. We can't wait. See you tomorrow."

"Yeah, tomorrow," he said, not able to keep the sourness out of his voice.

She put the cell back on the table and looked up.

Virgil stood in the doorway.

His body was as solid as the doorframe behind him. A hostile energy radiated out, enveloping her, tearing at her defenses. She imagined white light surrounding her, an automatic defense against psychic attack, but her efforts only amused him.

"You think you're protected?" he said. "I can slap you down like a mosquito." Her cell skidded off the table and thwacked into a wall.

"I told you to stay out of my business," he said, not moving, not taking his frozen eyes off her. "You must have a hearing problem, and I have a cure for selective deafness."

A cupboard door swung open and her plates sailed across the room, over her head, smashing into jagged shards on the slate floor. She willed herself not to flinch, praying that Bardo wouldn't allow her to come to harm.

"I guess your next meal's going to be takeout," he said. Another cupboard door opened to release her cups and mugs into the air. They circled her for several seconds while she tensed, waiting for them to rain down on her. When they fell, not a piece touched her. "You better get paper cups in, too," he said, but she saw uncertainty in him.

"You don't belong here," she said, surprised at her confidence. "Go from here, let go of this life."

"I belong where I want to belong. My life was terminated early, and I intend the same to those responsible."

"Leave me and Zach out of your plans. We're not involved."

"Your friend was a major element in the plan to kill me. He won't escape." A chair lifted slowly up, then whistled past her. It ricocheted off the cupboards behind. She took deep breaths, calming breaths.

"Zach was used. You must know that by now." She stood still, knowing that somehow there was a protection circle around her. "You're wasting energy on the wrong person. You don't blame a wrecking ball for demolishing your house."

"I have unlimited energy here," Virgil said. "Which is a good thing because I have large plans." Another chair flew at her but veered away, clattered noisily into the cupboards before bouncing on the floor.

"Your energy is strong but your aim is poor," she said and immediately wondered if she'd gone too far.

In response, the last two chairs rose up together, rocketed towards her but separated to pass either side before smashing down behind her. More of his uncertainty grew evident. He had meant to hurt her, but all his efforts had fizzled. His target still remained untouched amid the debris of the room.

Heartened by his misses, she poked him again. "You don't have the power you thought you had."

Virgil straightened, his face angry but controlled. "If I don't have what I need now, I'll get it. You'll be the first to taste it." He vanished with a pop loud enough to set her ears back.

She collected her cell from the floor, all three pieces: front, back and battery. When she reassembled them, it worked again. Another miracle. She called Zach.

"I've changed my mind. Come over."

"Should I bring wine?" His joy palpable.

"Bring everything you've got."

CHAPTER 18

Keera sensed Zach outside, opened the front door and wrapped her arms around him as he fumbled with his keys.

"Something happen tonight?" he asked, reciprocating with his own squeezy hug.

"Virgil came."

"You okay?"

She nodded. "He didn't have enough energy to harm me. I had protection, too."

"Bardo?"

"Probably. I haven't asked yet."

"What did Virgil do?"

"Take a look." She led him to the kitchen.

"Sweet Jesus," he said. The floor was all rubble: glass, china and chairs. To one side of the table a small space, not a yard square, lay bare. "What's that?" he asked, pointing at it.

"That's where I stood."

"Ah, the zone of protection." He inspected it. "Quite small."

"So am I," she said, smiling briefly. "It was all I needed."

"Well, I know what I need right now."

She looked at him, puzzled.

"A broom, then a drink."

It took less than an hour to clean up the debris. No chairs were broken, a tribute to buying old, solid workmanship. They drove to an all-night drugstore for mugs and glasses. She refused to buy more than the bare minimum she needed for the next couple of days. "It's always a mistake to accumulate too fast."

They picked up Vietnamese noodles and a bottle of Pinot Grigio on the way back and returned to the reassembled kitchen. They chewed and sipped and Keera said, "Virgil's going to come at you again soon. What are you doing about protecting yourself?"

"Nailing my furniture down."

"Be serious." Zach's safety would be a hard sell.

"What can I do? You're the psychic one, and you still got attacked."

"But not harmed. You need protection too."

"So, I'll stick with you; we'll both be protected."

"My students will be amused to find my partner following me around everywhere." She tried a silly suggestion. "You better talk to your guide."

"Keera—"

"I mean it. You need protection."

"I feel safe. Sort of."

"You won't if Virgil decides to destroy you. He can't kill you, but he can make you wish you were dead."

"Okay, okay, I'll wave smudge sticks about." He poured more wine for both of them.

"That's not a bad idea. Get a sage incense stick, have it going all night."

He swallowed half the glass. "That'll be most nights, right?"

"Look, I'm sorry you feel so toyed with, but it's been necessary for me to be alone. What would we know if I'd wasted those nights?"

Zach bridled. "Wasted? You call a night with me wasted?"

"I see you're in a snit about this. Believe me, it's not my ideal choice. It just has to be."

"Well, that's that, then," he said, rising. "I better be off so you can do your work."

"You're not going anywhere." She put her glass down and came around the table to him, slipped her arms around his waist. "You're staying with me."

She sensed his anger cooling, knowing that they were meant to be, and no occasional irritation, no flare-ups, no spot-fires that drove emotions to stupid places could break the bond between them.

Later, Keera woke with Zach asleep beside her. She asked Bardo silently if he was protecting her against Virgil?

I did what I could, but you did keep baiting him so. It made my job harder.

I thank you, but what about Zach? How can he guard against Virgil's attacks?

Your idea is a good one: he stays with you.

He comes with me to the university, too?

He's in little danger during the day. The mix of energies around him makes it difficult for Virgil to operate.

But the chocolate shake? That was effective.

Bardo laughed. It surprised Virgil, too. He didn't know he could manifest a desire so quickly. He learnt much from that.

Will Zach contact his guide?

It's not something he's comfortable with, as you know. His guide is ready, but Zach isn't. You're his only protector now.

* * *

Keera rose early and kissed Zach goodbye before he was fully awake.

"It's Saturday morning; mall time," she said. "Meet for lunch at the Post afterward, okay?"

He stayed in bed an hour longer. Figured it wouldn't hurt to call Dash, bitch about Virgil's antics, see if he let anything slip. Gave him till eleven to wake up.

"Where you get my number?" Dash said right away, his voice rising with anxiety.

"From you."

"Never."

"Scout's honor; you called and let my phone capture your number."

Silence while Dash worked through this unsettling information. Must have decided there was nothing he could do.

"The fuck you want?" he asked.

"I wanted to chat with your charming self, of course. This dead guy, he came around last night again."

"Didn't I give you style tips last time? You wanna ignore 'em; you take the lumps coming your way."

"He didn't come to me. He trashed my girl's kitchen. Plates, glasses, chairs tossed around the place like a hurricane. Reason I'm calling, I'm wondering if anything happened to you last night."

"Nothing happened. My Hennessey bottle broke when I dropped it in the trashcan, does that count?" Dash made with the hee-hees for a bit, thinking it was funny shit.

"Maybe he's coming for you tonight. After all, you're a lot more implicated in his death than I am. You've got more to be worried about."

"Don't do that implicated shit with me; you don't know whatchu talking about." Dash is staying cool and amused.

"I know enough to guess the rest. What about I meet with your man to figure out how to handle this threat from outer space?"

"He don't wanna be bothered with shit like that," Dash replied, a little too fast.

"He will if this stuff happens to him, and I don't want him to blame me for it."

"Is okay, I'll explain you too dumb to be that smart."

More hee-hees. The little shit was getting irritating now; time to push harder. Zach said, "Are you going to tell him I want to see him, or do I have to drive to the fucking Thai joint again?"

"He don't like that."

"It's not as if you're offering me a choice here, Dash."

"Don't assume who you talking to," Dash snapped. It was his dumb-ass way of telling Zach not to use names. Some security.

"Sorry, easy mistake to make when I hear stupidity."

He stayed silent; Zach could almost hear his lips tightening.

"You," Dash said," you be outside your place of employment in a half-hour."

He hung up.

Dash's black Chrysler barely stopped long enough to collect Zach, then drove to the next parking lot. He killed the motor and swung around to face Zach.

"Here's how things work in this town," he said. "I call you; you don't call me. You sure don't call me and bitch about your private life, and you never call me and use my name." His hands gripped and re-gripped the steering wheel.

"So how come I have your number if you don't want me calling you? I assume you wanted me to have it."

Dash considered this. "You want to talk; you text me a sign. Like a 'z'. Yeah, just a 'z'. Then I call you back at my convenience."

Zach deliberated Dash's new stupidity. Like Ritchie couldn't figure out who 'z' was if he checked the cell's texts. The kind of idiocy that would make Ritchie figure that he was planning something with Dash and might make both of them disappear. "What about a 'p'. Not so obvious."

"What's it stand for?" Dash asked, wary.

"Where I work, the Chicago Post, the whole fucking reason I even know you in the first place."

"Okay, 'p' is good. We go that way in the future." Dash nodded to himself as if he'd pulled off a hell of a smart move.

"So, you taking me to Ritchie or not?"

"Like I said, it's not worth bothering him about this. Whatchu wanna say?"

"I was going to say that if Virgil is attacking me and my girl, then he's surely attacked your mob, no matter what you say."

Dash stared out his window.

Zach continued. "Also, Virgil will be working on that Emmett guy, the man who did the killing."

Dash adjusted the rearview mirror like it was the most important thing in the world.

Zach tried a new line. "You heard Emmett has been hospitalized? Some freaky shit happening to him?"

Dash rolled a shoulder. "That crazy guy? Might've heard something. What's that got to do with us?"

"You know anything about dead people, Dash? They float around and watch over the live ones. They see everything that's going on. I reckon Virgil is watching Ritchie, and he's watching you. He could be telling Emmett stuff he ought to know."

"This of interest to me?" Dash looking out the window again.

"Just saying, is all. If you're not doing anything Emmett would hate, you have nothing to worry about."

The movement was almost imperceptible but Dash stiffened.

Bullseye.

Dash turned to Zach. "You think this Emmett guy is connected to us? You way off target, man. You looking to make up a story, make sure it's true. Ritchie hates bad reporters, know what I mean?"

He had recovered his poise, drummed his fingers on the wheel. "Got anything more to say? So far it's been a dull morning."

"Tell Ritchie what I said, okay? This Virgil business is a lot more complex than he thinks."

Dash started the car and drove Zach back to the Post. Zach opened his door; saw Keera approaching the entrance steps. She saw him and waved.

Shit, he'd forgotten she was coming over for lunch.

"That your woman?" Dash asked, ducking his head to get a better look at her.

"It is. I thought you guys checked that out."

"It wasn't my job." Keera paused on the steps, waiting. "She the one been getting shit from Virgil?"

"We both have," Zach said. "She gets more of it."

Dash said, "Why's that? She got connections to the afterlife or some shit like that?"

He didn't reply.

Big mistake.

Dash exhaled noisily, sank back against his seat. "Oh, baby."

By saying nothing, he had said the wrong thing. Dash taking his silence as confirmation of his guess.

His silence had made Keera a target.

Zach said to Dash. "She's not part of anything to do with us, you understand?"

"Everything is part of everything," Dash replied, putting the car into gear. "You getting out or what?"

He tried again. "Any harm comes to her, and I hold every one of you responsible. You understand?"

Dash grinned. "Yeah, man, my knees are knocking already. You want me to tell Ritchie? He hasn't had a good laugh for days."

Zach got out, held the door open. "I mean it. You know I do."

"Close the door, man, you letting in too much pollution."

Zach pushed the door shut and watched Dash glide down the street, indicate a right turn and accelerate around the corner. Like a messenger with the best news in ages.

He wheeled around to Keera. "I just did something really stupid," he said, reaching for her.

"I know."

CHAPTER 19

"**T**he best thing we had going for us was that they didn't know I could observe them," Keera said to Zach in the Post cafeteria. She forked salad into her mouth, not looking at him. "The next thing was that if they did spot me, they wouldn't know it was me." How could he forget that their biggest advantage was that nobody knew what she could do? Absolutely nobody.

"I know, I know." He sat opposite her, agonized eyes never leaving her face. "You can't make me feel any worse than I do. I was so stupid, totally forgot you were coming here. Last thing we needed was for Dash to get a good look at you."

She pushed her plate away; he hadn't touched his. "In some ways, it changes little."

"It changes something vital: it brings you to Dash's attention."

"I was always part of their plan. What can they do now? They can't stop me, and I'm sure I can hide from Dash if I have to."

"If he thinks you're spying on him, and he's doing stuff he doesn't want Ritchie to know about, then he'll act. He may shoot you."

"Wouldn't that weaken their grip on you? They couldn't use my safety as a weapon anymore."

He grew angry. "Jesus, Keera. How can you take it so calmly? I'm quivering in my gut at the thought of Dash shooting you, and you're talking like it's a fucking chess match."

"It is like a chess match." Zach was fearing the worse, but she sensed nothing to be afraid of. Yet. "We can assume our opponents have no scruples, and that makes it easier to work them out. They seek to gain advantage, and human life is only a factor in that the loss of it complicates matters with the police."

"Keera, this isn't a term-paper we're working on. We're trying to survive in a world we have no experience of. I have dealt with corruption. Those guys grab money when they think no one is looking. Put their activities in a spotlight and they cave in. I have no smarts when it comes to dealing with dealers. They make zillions, they control dozens of people, they kill some of them." He looked around the room as if gunmen were gathering. "We have to get you out of Chicago."

"Not a chance. If it's my time to die, it will happen anywhere I go. There is no hiding place from death."

"For God's sake, Keera. Get sensible."

"I'm staying, and we're going to put pressure back on them." He gave her the skeptical look. "Dash is clearly playing his own hand. He warned Ritchie that Emmett would crack up if Rhiannon messed with another man—and look who that turned out to be. What else did you find out today?"

"He wouldn't give me access to Ritchie. Fended me off. It matches what you're saying."

"I've picked up he wants to be a number one, not supplant Ritchie necessarily, but figure out an angle for himself. Have his own outfit."

Zach held up both hands. "So? He's dumb, thinks he's smart. Bad combination. You have to stop playing with him."

She tempered her view to accommodate his. "He's a dangerous one. He sees advantages where none exist. I know this, I'll be careful." His burger lay untouched. "Are you going to eat that?"

"Not hungry. I better take you home."

They rose from the table together. "It's okay," she said. "I'll grab a cab."

"You kidding? Dash could be waiting out there—"

"I'd relish the chance to speak to him."

"Keera, you're fucking crazy."

"Go back to your work, I can take care of myself." She shouldered her bag and strode to the elevator. He trailed her outside and waited in silence as she hailed a cab.

"I'll come over early to make sure you're okay," he said as she climbed in to avoid his kiss.

"I'll call you first," she said and swung the door shut. "Old Town," she said to the driver, and the cab moved into the traffic. Zach was hurting, she knew, but quick forgiveness downplayed the offense. Her private life was not to be shared; she had to make sure he didn't do this again.

She paid the cabbie off at her door and paused to find her keys in her bag. Ahead, a door swung open from a black Chrysler. Dash climbed out, came closer.

Like she'd expected.

"Yo, wispy woman," he said, stopping three yards away. One hand in his pants pocket.

She didn't wait, didn't give him the chance to set the tone. "Whatever you're selling, I don't want it."

"Ain't selling nothing. Just saying that I found you like I said I would."

"You're a stalker? Should I call the police?"

"Stalker? That's you more like. Hanging out in the dark like a witchy thing. I told you I'd find you."

He wasn't going to be deflected, he was certain he was right. She switched tactics. "Such a detective you are. It took you two weeks to find me after Ritchie knew my details?"

"Not what I'm talking about. You the woman been spying on me."

"Spying? What have you been doing that I would want to observe?"

"Talking psychic shit. You floating around, sitting in my ride."

"Ritchie ever suggest psychoanalysis to you? Because you sure need an opinion on your mental health."

Dash blinked as if she'd slapped him, searched for a reply. She pressed on, pushing while he was off balance.

"You want to prove it by hauling me up in front of him? Where I get the chance to tell him you got your hot hands all over that Rhiannon; and, well gee, I don't know how to put this, Mr. Ritchie, but your fine associate Dash hasn't handed over the money yet. It's still in his ride."

Keera held his gaze a couple of seconds, long enough to savor the unconcealed terror written all over his face, and she entered her house. She'd put him back on his heels, and showed him she wasn't easy to scare. That made her feel good for ten whole seconds before she grasped she'd upped the stakes too far.

She'd convinced Dash he was in danger.

Every second she lived.

"We're going to the San Souci restaurant in West Halstead," Tanner's voice came through to Dash's cell. "Come now, but don't even think about approaching the table."

Dash dropped the phone back in his pocket and returned to his car. How the fuck that Keera woman turn things around on him? Had her dead-set cornered, and she made it like he was in worse trouble than her. She didn't even care that he knew what she knew. Like it was nothing to her; like serious shit would come his way if he crossed her. No doubt about that; he wasn't taking her anywhere near Frankie.

He punched the restaurant details into his GPS and rolled the Chrysler away from the curb. How did stuff he knew become a danger? Ritchie believed in spooks, sort of. The bitch was right: Ritchie would believe her faster than him.

If he removed her, the boyfriend might run round crazy. He didn't scare easy, mightn't care if he be living or dead, would be after revenge. Like Emmett. Shit, another mess he got himself into. And Rhiannon, so fucking hot, how was he expected to leave her be? Dropping the dress, showing herself, timing it perfect.

Too much to figure out, he decided. Best see Li'l Marie and get hints on how to handle this. He swung the car past the San Souci and found street parking. Walked into the restaurant and stopped by the maître d's lectern. Swept a casual look over the clientele, Tanner seated with four others, caught his eye briefly before he looked away.

The maître d' hustled up. "We have no tables, sir, fully booked out."

Dash scanned the half-empty restaurant in a slow, deliberate way, telling the guy he knew he was lying. "It's okay, I'm not hungry," Dash said, making clear whose decision it was not to stay. He reached over and picked up a ballpoint pen from the lectern, wrote his cell number on the upside-down reservation sheet. Wrote "Hostler" under it and circled his work. "You give this number to Mr. Hostler over there and ask him to call me."

The maître d' returned a blank look. "Which diner would that be, sir?"

"The one at a table for five, you figure it out." He put the pen back and drew out a twenty-dollar bill, slipped under the booking sheet. "Thanks for your cooperation," he said and walked outside again.

His cell trilled a minute later. "Who's this?" Tanner asked. Voice hollow, like he was on speakerphone.

"Depends, where are you calling from?" Gotta make sure it was a genuine call.

"Where you just left the message, that's where."

Good enough.

"I'm making contact on behalf of a businessman who's interested in a profitable trading arrangement." Good. Sounded professional.

"How profitable?"

"We could double your turnover."

He heard muffled sounds like a hand was over the cell before Tanner came back. "We can meet tomorrow. Wait for a text."

"How will I know who I'm looking for?"

"You won't, but I'll know you."

"How?" Playing along now.

"We saw you come in, right? Wait for the text." Tanner shut down.

Dash dropped his cell into his pocket and started the car. Glanced in the rearview mirror but nobody there. Jerked his head around to the back in case the woman was there instead, but she wasn't. Damn bitch, giving me the creeps.

He drove back to the South Side and found Ritchie in his upstairs room, Tyrell inside the door.

"Got a call from Tanner," Dash said to Ritchie's quizzical eyebrow. "We meet up tomorrow."

Ritchie flashed his teeth in delight. "You doing well, my son. Have a seat, choose a cupcake."

It was afternoon snack time for Ritchie. Cupcakes in front of him, pot of coffee alongside them.

"Is okay," Dash said, "gotta watch my figure."

Ritchie's face tightened. "You mean I don't?"

Gotta watch my mouth, too, Dash thought. "I mean, I have a genetic disposition to rapid weight gain. I read about that stuff in a magazine once."

Ritchie glared at him. "I haven't noticed."

"It's happened to many of my relatives. Everybody okay until they thirty or so then whoosh, they blow out."

Ritchie held up his hand at Dash. "I don't want to hear it. Fuckin' depressing. What did Tanner say?"

"He couldn't talk, it was on speaker phone, said he would text me tomorrow to fix a place."

"Okay. Do it this way. Tell them we can get anything they want cheaper than they paid last time."

"How do we know what they paid?"

"They bought from us, that's how; what's the matter with

you?"

How'd he forget that? "I meant the time before."

"Who cares? We use the last figure as a starting point."

"That it?"

"Tell Tanner I gotta meet with Hostler face to face, just the one time to seal the deal. Make sure his underlings aren't chipping away pieces for themselves, telling us one thing and telling him another. Set up a direct line, know what I mean?"

"Sure, make friendly like, and then later we wipe him out and take over." Letting Ritchie know he had the big picture square in his mind.

"You dress sharp, Dash, but your brain's a mess." Ritchie sounding more exasperated than irritated. "Why the fuck would we kill a meal ticket? It'll take time, but one day he be into us for everything, and we not even a flyspeck on a police file. He gets all the aggravation; we get half the profit."

Made it sound easier than ordering cupcakes.

CHAPTER 20

Keera told Zach to come over late, a signal he could stay. Told him about meeting Dash, refused to answer his urgent questions, told him she was okay, told him to wait until he arrived. Her sharp exchange with Dash had done more harm than she'd anticipated. She'd let fly with unguarded opinions and exacerbated the whole situation. A couple of hours meditation might help. An agitated phone conversation wouldn't.

"So tell me, for God's sake," Zach asked at the door that evening. "What happened?"

"I gave him something to think about," she said, wrapping her arms around him, pleased how simple physical contact reminded her how much she needed him.

"You're good at that." The flippant response didn't hide his agitation. He was struggling to restrain himself, swallowing a million questions, clearly aware of how they had parted. Not wanting to provoke her by mistake.

"I told him what I thought of him."

"Bet that made him give up his naughty ways." Zach pulled a beer from the fridge, and they settled around her kitchen table. He unscrewed the top, waited for her reply.

"It didn't register with him at all. I sometimes wonder if these people have any moral qualms about what they do."

He took a long pull from the bottle before answering. "These people, as you call them, don't have a smooth-ish life path like you or me. They grab what they can. Their moral compass swings to a different north and south to ours." He took another pull. "Don't ever expect them to think like you or me. What else did you say to him?"

"He recognized me from when I was out of the body, but I didn't confirm it. I knew he couldn't tell anyone. Who'd believe him? I pointed out that if any information surfaced that only he and Ritchie could know, the first target of suspicion would be him, not me." A vision of Dash's obvious alarm came to her. "That shook him up. Then, I stupidly told him I knew about him and Rhiannon and that he still held the money."

Zach placed the bottle on the table. "Fucking hell, Keera, you've gone and put him on death row. He'll figure it'll only be a matter of time until you or I spill something to Ritchie. Then he's history. Trouble is, once he thinks this through, his first reaction will be to eliminate you, his second, to eliminate me." He took another pull on the bottle; nothing left now. "I can't believe I got you into this."

She reached across and took his hand. His energy fizzed and sparked, his nerve ends firing streams of tracers, not reaching calming conclusions. "You didn't. They were always going to use me to control you, we know that. Now they, or at least Dash, understand we aren't without power. We can cause as much harm as they can."

"Not so, Grasshopper. We're unlikely to kill, and killing is their preferred method of problem-solving."

"They won't be able to do any killing if we know their plans, will they?"

"You can't watch them night and day." A thought came to him. "Did you follow Dash afterward?"

She sighed. "No. I was frazzled from meeting him and from events earlier. Had to settle myself."

"Sorry," he said. "I can't say it enough, but I feel such a dick about that."

"I know, but I didn't do any better in the mistakes department either. That Dash has a knack for making us say stuff we shouldn't. Forget it, we can't change it. We have to move on, get on the front foot as they say."

He lifted the bottle, saw it was empty, put it down. "You're right. Let's go to bed; wake up refreshed with terrific ideas in the morning."

"Good idea." She stood, and he came around the table to hold her. She kissed him and nosed his cheek. "The thing is," she murmured, "I have to sleep alone to get refreshed. You get the couch." She took the stairs to her room, paused on the landing, heard the fridge door opening, thumping shut, bottles inside rattling.

Missed him already.

◆ ◆ ◆

The morning produced a fresh surprise. Keera gave him directions to where Rhiannon lived with the old guy who stayed on the porch all day.

"She'll be home," Keera said. "I get the feeling she'll be quite affable with you. Might reveal new information."

Zach didn't question any of this; any new material they gathered on Dash could be life-saving. He skipped breakfast and took off south.

Rhiannon's house was indeed where Keera had said. Kind of. It took a dozen runs down likely streets until he spotted the old man on the porch. No other humans outside. He parked the Mustang right outside, between two hunks of rusty Detroit.

"Rhiannon in?" he asked the old man. Weed in the air, but the man's hand out of sight at his side.

"Who's asking?" the man said.

"Name's Bones, from the Chicago Post. Just come by to see how she's keeping, with her man in jail and all."

"A reporter? Want my picture? I fought in 'Nam, you know. Could tell you shit make your hair go curly."

"I believe you. Must have been a bad place to be."

"Hell gonna be a vacation after that."

"Sounds like you have a good story; we can talk later. First, I'd like to see Rhiannon."

The old man jerked his head at the screen door. "She inside, call her name when you go in. When you done, come see me. I got a story you oughta tell your readers."

"Thanks, I will." He stepped inside. Wondered if Dash might drop in, hoped not. He called her name.

"Yeah?" A questioning tone from the living room.

Rhiannon was slumped on a couch, watching television with the sound off. A young child slept next to her, draped over the arm rest. Rhiannon's eyes a startling red and white where they weren't a glossy brown, her focus unsteady. Been sharing the weed with the old man, most likely. She wore microscopic shorts and a bare-midriff top. Zach fixed his eyes directly on hers.

She looked up with lazy curiosity. "Hey, a white fella. You no cop, you too pretty."

"I'm a reporter, Zach Bones. Like to talk about Emmett, if that's okay."

"A reporter." She considered this information, tilting her head this way and that. "You here to ask me questions?"

"Yes, about how you're getting along with Emmett inside."

"Emmett." She lifted an arm into the air as if waving goodbye to somebody.

"We're doing a series on women left behind when men are serving time. I was wondering how you're managing to get by with Emmett unable to work or support you and his kid."

Rhiannon giggled, making her face beautiful. "Gettin' by? Oh my, we gettin' by."

He tried again. "I see you have a young child, do you have enough income? Did Emmett leave you plenty?" Crass technique this was, getting right to the point, but anything subtle wouldn't work in her state.

She looked over to the child then back at him. "We got looked after fine. We look like we starvin'?" She was checking him over, lingered on his face, especially his mouth.

"How long do you think it is before Emmett gets out?" The question right off the topic but worth a try. Unexpected quotes came at, well, unexpected moments.

She made a face. "Could be old and cold before I see him again. He done more bad stuff."

"So I heard, terrible news. He could be gone for years now. You got a plan for that?"

"Got plans, paperboy." She smiled crookedly at him again. "They ain't for publication." She was well into the weed but not stupid. She would chew his words and play with them. He'd have to come back or meet her somewhere else.

"Don't see boys like you 'round here," she said, breaking into his thoughts.

"What kind do you see?" Go along with her a while, see what happens.

"They more fly, choose their clothes like they thought about it." She giggled again. "You not like that. But you're still cute as."

The dress code seemed a major part of life for the neighborhood. Everybody picking on his taste, too.

Rhiannon shifting on the couch, getting restless. Time to cut out. He said, "I see you're not in the mood right now, let's meet at a better time."

She rose to her feet and swayed in front of him, her breasts swinging one way then the other; no bra. "Oh, I'm in the mood."

"I'll give you my card," he said, scrabbling around in his pockets. "You call me when you want to chat." He handed it to her; she ignored it.

"Don't want no silly card, I lose stuff like that. Write your number on my boob."

He paused for a beat, grinned. "Which one?"

She yanked up her top. "You choose."

CHAPTER 21

When Zach emerged onto the porch, the old man was sagging lower in his seat. "You get any sense out of that girl?" he asked without looking up.

"Mmm. Wasn't the best time to come," Zach said, thinking of Rhiannon so amused at his discomfort.

The old man grunted as if he was laughing but it was hard to tell. "She's a tricky one to catch fully working. Try early evening sometime, before she go out somewheres."

"Thanks. Maybe we can do some preliminary work on that 'Nam story."

The old guy thought on that long enough for anyone to assume he was asleep. Zach started edging to his car before the man spoke again. "Not really a story. I got a weapon, got a tale to go with it."

"Sounds good. When do you want to do this?"

He had to think about that too. "How about today?"

"Okay. What's your name?"

"Call me Uncle, that'll do. I'm used to it."

Zach looked over the street. Still nobody walking, nobody driving. "It's quiet here, why is that?"

The old man grunted again. "You worried about your ride?"

"Sure, it's my only one."

"You got no cause. This is where Emmett lived, any ride out the front belong to him or a friend of his. Nobody gonna come around and check out its value." He raised himself out of the chair and took his time to steady himself, blew air out of his cheeks. "Show you something."

He shuffled inside, Zach following. They passed the living room with both the child and Rhiannon asleep, Uncle closing the door on them quietly. Kept going to another room out the back and sat on a single bed. The room was sparse and tidy, military style, and no place to sit except next to the old guy.

Uncle bent over and pulled a tin box out from under his bed. Opened it to display a bunch of papers. "This here my discharge papers and stuff."

"Interesting," Zach said and reached for them.

Uncle slapped his hand away. "My box, my fingers do the only walking in here."

He shuffled the papers to one side to reveal a brown paper bag, pulled it out. "This here's my favorite thing," he said and drew out an automatic. It looked as new and shiny as the day it was handed over to somebody. A thin oil slick covered it and Zach knew without asking that Uncle loved this gun.

"A Colt M1911, the best handgun ever made," Uncle said.

"This ever seen action?" Zach asked.

Uncle dropped back into his reverie again. Must have been a difficult question. "Never saw it used that way, that's the thing of it," he said when he was ready. "One time, VC is firing at us through jungle cover, we couldn't get a fix on where they were, didn't know if we were running toward good cover or into more trouble. We crappin' ourselves. The captain draws on a man too scared to go forward. He wants to make an example of how brave he is. By showing he's ready to shoot one of his own." He paused again.

The memories needed editing, Zach guessed.

"Seconds later the VC open up again; this time, it's like a million-fireworks night without the colors, and every bang is a bullet coming our way. We shooting back but what the fuck at? The fireworks stop. The Cong vanish, like always. We didn't know about the tunnels then. We see the captain dead; bullet passed through his head."

"The Viet Cong?"

Uncle looked up then. "Who knows? The army said they did, but I know which way he was facing at the time, and the bullet came the other way. I don't reckon they looked too hard either. Wouldn't have been a feel-good story for the public."

"A member of his platoon took him out? Why? I don't believe the US Army allows officers to shoot their own men, no matter what. His men had no reason to think he would use that gun." Uncle was manufacturing this tale.

"Somebody believed him, and that was enough."

"This the gun used?"

"Told you already, ain't never used in fear or anger. It was the captain's."

"It's yours now?"

"Guns belong to them that need 'em," Uncle said.

He drew out a cartridge box. "Somehow, all of this came to me." He rattled the cartridges in front of Zach's face. "Whenever I see people who are stepping outside their line of duty, I recall this box and what's in it, and I feel good."

He replaced the gun and cartridges in the tin box, pulled the papers over them and closed it. Pushed it back under the bed with his heel. "Thing is, Mr. Bones, when men get scared they don't think straight. They make stupid decisions, know what I mean?"

Uncle wasn't so stoned anymore. His eyes shone clear; his voice held steady. "It's late in the day, Mr. Bones. Rhiannon will receive callers soon, and it's best for you to be out of here."

He took him out to the porch. Zach's car was still waiting, still intact. "You come around here again, you better fix it with the right people, or you might spook somebody. Hear what I'm saying?"

"I hear you." Zach gripped his hand. Uncle didn't seem too keen to grip back. "I'll come back another time to get the rest."

"You got all you gonna get," Uncle said and walked back inside.

Zach drove to the Thai place to find Ritchie and bitch to him that Dash was bugging Keera by sneaking up on her. See if Ritchie would keep Dash in check. It wouldn't hurt to have the kid cop pressure from both sides. It wouldn't hurt either for him to know he could get to Ritchie without him.

That Rhiannon, Jesus. So hot, and so out there with it. No wonder Dash couldn't resist her. He'd had to jam hands in pockets and walk away before he did something stupid as well. Thought about Dash and Rhiannon, and her telling Dash who had dropped by. Lingered on that delightful image.

Dash would be thunderstruck to hear that Zach was moving into his territory. He'd look for him soon after. How much would Rhiannon tell him? She might forget to mention the sassy move she made on him. He hoped not; that would make Dash even twitchier.

He found a parking place right near the Thai. Like the locals knew who might be inside and left a respectful space. Found the same woman gliding up, her expression darkening as she approached.

"People don't want you here," she said.

"I don't want me here, either," he said. "I need to see Ritchie, tell him not to send Dash."

She blinked as if memorizing his request, a lot simpler than a four-course meal with sides and afters. "You go outside, you not customer."

Zach took himself out and leaned against his car, frowned at a new ding on the Mustang's front fender.

A black man came out of the restaurant, stopped close. Had the build of a family refrigerator, voice soft as a priest. Melvin. The guy who had thrown him across the room the first time they had met. Time to act respectful.

"This is the wrong place for you, my friend. You out of your neighborhood." His demeanor was calm, not expecting conflict, not expecting to lose if there were.

"I'm not here for the balmy weather," Zach said. "I came because it was important. I need to say my piece, and then I'll return to a place where people can breathe without paying a street tax."

"We don't need any comedians around here; we're hardworking folk. Go home."

"I have to see Ritchie, it's important."

"Tell me what you want to say."

"This is the problem: I already have middlemen on my case, and I know they're creating a little deal for themselves. That's why I don't want to talk to another one. I want the top guy."

Melvin smiled at Zach as if he were simple. "Top guys aren't available to people like you. You got a message, give it to me or get back in your sweet li'l antique and chug-chug out of here."

Whether Ritchie was inside the Thai joint or not, Zach wasn't going to get in. Melvin had been told to head him off. All he could do was say his piece and wait for Ritchie to send somebody to collect him for a lengthy chat.

"Tell him that Dash is shadowing my girl and making threats. He's gone crazy. He has to stop."

"That all?"

"Don't wanna give you lots to recall."

Melvin's hand shot out, grasped the back of Zach's neck. Squeezed and squeezed again. Soft tissue crumpling, bones protesting and nerve endings shrieking. His knees buckled at the pain; tears blurred his vision before the big hand let go.

"I'll see what I can do with your message," Melvin said. "But sounds like beggin' to me." He walked back inside.

◆ ◆ ◆

"You came alone?" Tanner asked Dash.

"Think I need an armored division to talk to you?" Dash said. "We just business people. Discussing areas of mutual profit."

Tanner had an associate with him in the diner booth. Dash had walked in, looked at the menu board and waited for Tanner to wave him over, pretended he hadn't met him before.

Dash sat down and Tanner's man leaned across the table and

said, "Unbutton your shirt."

"I don't swing that way," Dash said back, giving him the dead-eye.

The man tapped Dash's chest. "I need to see you aren't wearing electronics."

He waited a bit then unbuttoned his shirt and pulled it away from his chest. "No wires, see? Just a manly front panel."

"Says you," the man said. He held Dash's arm and felt along the jacket material methodically. Did the same for the other arm. Dropped his hands below the tabletop. "Put your foot in my hand," he said. Ran his hand along Dash's pants leg to the thigh, then the other. "Put your head on the table."

"What?"

"Lay your head down like you're taking a quick nap while I run my hand over your back."

The bug inspector prodded his back like it was a wheat-filled sack. "It's done," he said.

Dash rebuttoned his shirt. "You think I look like a cop?"

"I don't think," the man said. "I act."

"What's the proposition?" Tanner asked.

"We supply all you want for a better price than you pay now."

"That's a mighty big offer. How do you know what we need?"

"You tell us and then we know, right?"

Tanner shot a glance at his companion, Dash couldn't read it. Might figure it out later. "We give you top quality South American, not that brown you've been messing with."

"How do you know what we've been doing?"

"We watch, we learn."

"You credit us with the fifty percent like discussed?"

"That's carved in stone already."

"You do realize it's not smart for us to have just one supplier, don't you?"

"You do realize it's not smart to pay a higher price," Dash said, mimicking Tanner's lofty tones.

Tanner ignored the barb. "We don't need you, to be truthful, but it wouldn't hurt to see this further."

Tanner getting clever now, making like it's all happening against his will. "You want to do this soon?" Dash said. "You got my number."

"We can do a sample, see if your talk is good."

"Okay, call me. Rent a car, park the money in it and leave it for us to load. Then take it back. Don't forget to return the car on time. The extra rental messes up the bottom line." Dash allowed himself a small smile.

"We know how to do this," Tanner said, rising. "Maybe not the way you say."

"One more thing," Dash said. "Our principals have to meet, if we go further than one time."

Tanner paused. "That might be difficult."

"It's a condition of play. It's a trust thing, you see?"

Tanner shuffled out of the booth. "I'll put your suggestion to the right person, but I'm not hopeful."

"It ain't a suggestion. It's part of the second part."

The bug inspector also slid out of the booth. Tanner stood there thinking. "What happens is what happens," he said finally.

"They teach you that at business school?" Dash asked. "Good thing I didn't waste my money there."

He watched them leave. That went well. Got to first base, showed them they weren't dealing with no amateur. He would become the main contact guy for this operation, for sure. Future looked fine as a brand-new day.

Except for that Bones and his wispy woman. The fucking woman checking him out anytime she wanted, and her guy saying shit would happen if he did anything about it. No doubt about it, the two of them would have to go. Grab the woman, and get Bones to hand over his written notes and stuff. Then boom-boom baby. Explain some shit to Ritchie, like he stopped them going to the cops.

He slid out of the booth, the waitress between him and the door and wearing that look. He glanced back at the table and saw the check in the saucer, no money on top. They'd left him holding the check, cheap bastards. He dropped some bills and walked out.

CHAPTER 22

D ash stopped by the old man on the porch when he arrived. "This your favorite place in the world?"

"It's a good place to see things," Uncle replied.

"You should be careful what you see, I reckon."

"Maybe, but I'm seeing you coming here more than you should." The old man wasn't stoned. Had an attitude this afternoon.

"I told you before. This is business with Rhiannon. I'll be a short while, that's all. It ain't what you're thinking."

"If you're thinking I'm thinking that, then you've got a conscience to deal with."

Dash laughed. "It ain't bothering me none." He pulled the screen open and stepped inside. Found Rhiannon asleep on the couch, her baby awake, just lying and watching him.

He tapped Rhiannon on the cheek. "Time to rise, baby. We got work to do."

She opened her eyes, blinked a few times. "Hey, Dash," she mumbled as she sat up. "How you been doing?"

"Working my ass off to stay alive, as usual. Listen, you ready to take the rest of the money now? I don't like to hold it for so long."

"Money. Is all about money today." Rhiannon yawned.

"Whatchu mean?"

"Had me a reporter here before. So cute. Asked if I was getting by. Did I have enough money with Emmett not able to provide and all."

Fuck she talking about? "Who was this guy?"

"Don't recall his name. Left a card." She giggled.

"So funny he left a card?" Dash asked while he looked over the coffee table, found a card, picked it up.

"Sure is. Asked him to write his number on my boob and he freaked."

"You did that?" Dash said, looking up. "What the fuck for?"

"Said he was cute, didn't I? Don't see white goodies around here much."

"White?" Dash read the card and read it again. Zachary fucking Bones.

"What did you tell him?" He kept his voice calm, not wanting to spook her.

"Told him nothin'. Told him I was fine. Let him know I'd be finer if he wanted to try me out."

"He make a move?" Her talk stirred him.

"Nooo, he kinda rushed out the door. Said he'd be back at a better time." She stood, her top sideways, plenty boob showing. Looking at him, like she knew he was hot for her, like she was waiting for him to close in. Couldn't, had to do the money thing. Then get to Ritchie and tell him that Bones was meddling. Fuck that guy, wrecking his life.

"Listen, baby, we gotta do the money. Now. You want it here, or did you fix up a bank?"

"No bank. Thought about it. Want a locker at the train station or maybe the airport."

"Okay, I'll get it out of the car and you deal with it," Dash said. The fuck that Bones asking about money for?

"Uh-uh." She moved right up to him, ran her hands around his ass and pulled him closer. "Take me to the train station, Dash. I don't feel safe alone." She kissed his chin. "Later, we'll have a time in one of those fancy hotels nearby."

"I don't have time for a time. If you want me to take you to the station, get your things and let's go. I have urgent stuff."

She pressed her body against his, giggled and kissed his neck. "I reckon your urgent stuff is urgent for me."

He pushed her away. "Like I said, I gotta hurry. I'm in the car waitin' five minutes only. Then I'm gone, and you get to the station by yourself."

She straightened. "I don't need to bring things, got money. We gonna shop then we gonna—"

"We're going to the station then I'm leaving you to shop. Got it? Call me after a couple of hours; I'll see if I can spare the time."

"So sure of yourself," she said. "The money I got, I don't need to beg for a good time."

Getting all rebel now. He knew the money would get to her sooner or later. "Listen, I'm not blowing you off, got major stuff to do, okay? Meet me in the car."

He walked outside and clattered down the steps, lifting a hand to Uncle. Sat in the car, figuring out what that woman had told Bones.

Rhiannon came out in a yellow dress, spoke to Uncle before sliding in next to him. "Uncle will babysit. We don't have to be home until tomorrow."

Dash didn't reply, slotted the gear stick into drive, and they rolled away. He wondered how many times he'd have to shoot Bones before he felt better. Figured the whole clip.

At the station, Dash showed Rhiannon to a locker, swiped his card to pay for it. "Eleven bucks a day is expensive storage for an envelope, baby," he said.

"It's just for now. And it's not all in there, is it? I'm keeping some on me; I gotta refresh my wardrobe." She was happy as a kid skipping to a birthday party.

"Call me when you done, but be at least four hours." He dropped his hand to her fine ass as he pecked her cheek goodbye. Thought about Emmett. He wouldn't see any cash, that's for sure. All gone in six months, quicker than that if she found the wrong bro to shack up with. Like he'd told Ritchie, too much cash make some get silly.

His cell buzzed in the car. Ritchie.

"You still thinking of coming back to report or what?"

"Yeah, Frankie, on the way. Got held up a bit. Got extra news."

"Make it sound like good news; it's been a day lacking in highlights so far." Ritchie terminated the call. Sounded calm, like he did before he pulled off a stunt. Should have sounded keen to hear the news, not cool. Something had happened since this morning.

Had Bones been there already? Not likely that Ritchie would see anybody just because someone asked to. Ritchie survived because he didn't show himself around. Didn't flash his style.

Outside the Thai restaurant Dash deleted all his call logs and text messages. Satisfied, he walked inside. Tyrell, at the back room door, gave him a look. He knew what it meant: shit coming your way.

Ritchie had a beer in his hand, another jug nearby and a bowl of Thai salted snacks in front of him. Melvin stood guard duty.

Ritchie motioned to a chair opposite and said, "Speak. Tell me everything."

"They going for it. Try a sample run first, see how good the price, how good the quality."

"When?"

"Didn't say. Will call when they ready."

"Who was at the meet?"

"Tanner, another preppy checked me for bugs. That all."

"You check them?"

Dash smiled like it was a silly question. "They say no, what can I do? We asked for the meet, not them."

Ritchie drained his glass and refilled it from the jug. "See anyone else today?"

This had to be about Bones. Give him what he doesn't know, get him thinking, not asking. "That Bones guy," Dash said. "He came to Rhiannon's crib. Asked about money."

Ritchie lowered his glass. "What money?"

"He asked if she was being looked after, seeing as how her old man is away and all."

"What did she say?"

"She said she was fine. Whaddya think?"

"You were there?" Ritchie not letting go of the original

thought.

"Not then, caught him later, told him to stay out of the hood." Fucking ace move. Getting the times around that way, so it sounded right. Bones not about to be asked the truth of it, either.

"What you doing visiting Rhiannon?" Ritchie still hadn't picked up the glass.

"She wouldn't take the money the first night I came over. Said it was too much to keep in the house. There's the truth. Asked me to hold it while she sorted a bank out." He paused, didn't want the words rushing out like he was nervous. "Saw her today and she wanted to deposit the cash in a locker. At fuckin' Union Station. I took her there, she told me about Bones."

"You think about telling me this stuff before I hear it from elsewhere?" Ritchie still without his glass—not a good sign.

"This was a li'l logistics problem, Frankie. Stuff you don't need to be bothered with."

"I need to bother with everything. Attention to detail is what made me." He leaned forward. "Rhiannon gonna back up your story?"

Dash drew his notebook out. "I took precautions."

"I bet you did," Ritchie said with a dirty laugh. Melvin laughed with him. Things were lightening up.

He showed Ritchie the page Rhiannon had signed. "I made her sign for the money she left with me, see?"

Ritchie took the notebook and read. Flicked through the other pages, slammed the book down on the table. "You done anything else as stupid as this, you frozen piece of parrot piss? You wanna write down any more evidence of your doings for others to read sometime?"

"I had to have something—"

"You had to do what I said to do. No improvisation, got it?" Ritchie lifted his glass and poured half the contents down his throat. Dash didn't take it as a good sign, either.

"Sorry, Frankie. It won't happen no more. What you say is what you're gonna get from me."

"Don't I know it," Ritchie said. "You back to being a driver while you figure out how to be smarter."

Dash nodded acceptance of the demotion. Not as bad as disappearing altogether. Waited for Ritchie to send him out.

Didn't happen.

"When you seen the Keera woman last?" Ritchie asked.

Shit. "She was with Bones when I found him." That should hold up. He now knew it was Bones somehow bitching to Ritchie about this morning.

"What did you say to her?" Ritchie pressed without raising his voice.

"Nothing much."

"Exact words, Dash."

Ritchie staring at him like he was trying to catch him out on something. Time to get all indignant. "How can I remember? It was late this morning; she was meeting him outside his work, where I was telling him to behave. Told him to keep away, told her the same thing as an extra. He got all macho shit going and tried to look good in front of his bitch. That's all." Sounded good, sounded right.

It must've sounded right to Ritchie, too. He sank the rest of the beer. "Okay, Dash. Go and wash the car; bring it back. You staying close to me tonight."

Dash stood, found his legs shaky.

"Gimme your cell," Ritchie said.

Dash handed it over, left the room, passing Tyrell, who said, "You still alive or you a ghost?"

Dash drove the Escalade to the Drip'N'Zip Carwash a couple of blocks away. The bros there worked a fine job with the rags, drying off the duco and making sure no water marks left behind. When you watched them. If he brought the car back gleaming like a black diamond, it could work in his favor. Might make Ritchie contented enough to stop buggin' out about the reporter and his girl.

In front of him, in the wash bay, sat a ten-year-old Lincoln. A stretch of duct tape covered a piece of the front passenger door. Two bros standing close by, turning around to look at him.

Dash climbed out of the car before he figured who they were: half of the young fools who messed with him that night. They approached him, one of them showing a limp.

"Look who's come to pay his bills," the bigger one said, stopping a couple of yards away. The Limper said nothing.

Dash recognized him: the driver. The one who'd called everyone back. Probably looking to get a better outcome this time. "Don't believe I've had the pleasure," he replied. Dropped a hand inside his pocket in case they'd forgotten who'd walked the taller last time they met.

"You had all the pleasure that night," the driver said. "Time you righted a wrong."

"Don't recall doing no wrongs. Just warning off a bunch of puppies who shoulda been cozied up in their cribs that time of night."

The driver jerked his thumb back at the Lincoln. A car wash guy was power hosing it down. "There's an itty-bitty hole in my door. Shouldn't be there, that car don't deserve damaging."

Dash tilted his head as if to examine the car. "That yours? That what you saying? It so raggedy-ass, look like your mama's car. She let you borrow it that night to fetch her some feminine products from the drugstore? Bet she was downright vexed when you returned late. Come to think of it, I ain't seen you round awhile. You get grounded?"

The driver showed teeth, a mocking smile. "You got no Chrysler today. Come up in the world, all the way to a Caddy. Your sugar daddy letting you have a taste of style, in exchange for a little butt play?"

The car wash guy brush-soaped the Lincoln, not looking over at them.

"Well, this conversation's fascinating," Dash said. "We oughta meet up for coffee and cake sometime and keep it going. Discuss how bad starts lead to bad outcomes. But right now I got me a ride that needs some loving care."

The driver shifted his feet, took a wider stance, blocking any movement forward. "Here's the nut of it, bro. I need twenty big ones to forget about the car door."

"For that old thing? It ain't worth half a gee. You should drive it to City Hall, tell 'em to stick it in a park somewheres. Call it a monument to stupidity."

"The money ain't the whole of it, either," the driver said. "There's a question of personal satisfaction."

"Aah. I gotcha. You saying you were humiliated. I can understand that. You stick your beaky snout into my business, you always gonna be humiliated."

The Limper sneaked a glance at the driver. Pulled out a cell and spoke softly to it. Bringing up the rear guard. Five minutes from now he'd be surrounded by a bunch of bros looking to cut him good. And his own cell in Ritchie's hands. Fuck.

The Limper pushed his cell into his back pocket and withdrew a closed blade. Played it around his fingers like he was getting ready for a magic trick.

The driver said, "I see there's no talking to you and expecting things to come out right."

"Let's make that the first topic of conversation when we get a chance to hang. Right now, you've messed up my intended bay with your mama's muddy ride. I hafta find another place." They hadn't figured out how to stop him leaving. He pulled out his Glock and held it by his leg.

"You gonna use that in a public place?" The driver waved a hand around.

"Seeing as how your lopsided friend has a knife, I figure I got legal right to defend myself."

They had no answer for that. But he didn't want to give them time to think, either. He climbed back into the Escalade, never taking his eyes off them, but neither one moved. He rolled down the window. "Been such a pleasure, again." He reversed out into the street and drove away.

When you're outnumbered, that's a good time to quit. Should ask Ritchie if that was in The Art of Fuckin' War.

Oughta be.

CHAPTER 23

"**W**hat's wrong with your neck?" Keera asked when Zach arrived at her home.

"It's lucky to be still in place, but how do you know?" He looked haggard, searched the fridge, found a Heineken and popped the top.

"Your aura. It's black around there. Not your normal ruddy-health color."

"Right, I forgot. You got a health eye as well." He sucked most of the bottle dry in his first attempt, inspected the balance, then finished it. "Thought I'd chat to Ritchie about Dash coming at us. Epic fail."

She came over and laid a hand on his neck. "Still aching?"

"No, just immobile. This fucker crushed it with a spare hand."

"I can heal it if you stop drinking."

"No need, I have found that drinking heals most things," he said, but he placed the bottle down and took a chair.

She moved behind him. "Close your eyes and sit for a few minutes." He obeyed, and she held her palms over his head, waiting for his natural energy flow to re-establish itself.

"He was big but fast. Jesus."

"I know you're still shaky, but you have to stay quiet for best results."

She dropped her hands to hover over his shoulders; his inner fires pulsed erratically. She held that position, noting the increasing heat emanating from him, the strengthening of his life force. Held it for another five minutes before she stepped away. "How do you feel?"

"I feel like another beer."

"Sounds like you're cured."

He scooped a bottle from the fridge. "I am, a bit. My neck moves better; I can tilt it easy now."

"And you've found a good use for that already." She took a chair opposite him. "What was the point of seeing Ritchie?"

"I thought it would be good to press Dash from the other side. I wanted to be sure he knew there would be consequences if he harmed us. He was waiting for me today. Wasn't happy with you, he said. I told him my notes identified him as an inform-ant, and my notebook would be delivered to the cops if some-thing happened to either of us."

"I bet he loved that idea."

"He was rather perturbed," Zach said, turning his neck one way then another. "He's frustrated that he can't control us."

"Who hurt you?" A finger of revenge scrabbled around her heart. She didn't try to suppress it.

"This wide guy, Melvin. Talked soft but carried a fucking big stick—his hands. Ritchie must have sent him out. He told me to go away but took my message. I got lippy in the process, and he retaliated."

"You, lippy? Surprised to hear it."

"It's a failing, I admit." He finished his second bottle and eyed her speculatively. She didn't need special powers to read these signals.

"I better go out and see what our friends are doing tonight," she said.

His shoulders drooped, just a fraction. "Do I get the couch again?"

She came around behind him and wrapped her arms around his neck, rested her cheek against his. "I'll come to you when it's over, and we'll lie in each other's arms until dawn."

"You been reading those romance books again?" he said, but she felt his heart glow.

Later, when no sounds came from downstairs, she lifted out of her body. Thought of Ritchie, and found him in the bar where he'd ordered Dash to take money to Rhiannon. No Dash in the booth this time, just Ritchie and the lieutenant who had also suffered from Virgil's toying earlier.

"Tyrell, Dash is becoming a real worry," Ritchie said. "Think he's telling me everything he does?"

Tyrell said. "He the kind who thinks a lot, gets stuff muddled up. Forgets his priorities."

"He wiped his cell phone. How fuckin' suspicious is that?"

"Standard operating procedure, Frankie. He don't want the cops having a look over his private moments."

"Or me."

"He's just careful."

"Yeah, like that fuckin' notebook. So careful that was."

"Okay, it was stupid. But he must've been scared you'd think he'd taken the money. He tried to show everything was on the level."

"All I know is, he could've been leaving a trail all the way back to me. Like Hansel and Greta."

"Gretel."

"Whatever. The man's a liability. Thought he could be a top assistant, know my mind before I knew it myself. Jump around, get things done. Leave me to work on the big picture."

"He'd like to be that man."

Ritchie drummed his fingers on the table between them. "He ain't sharp enough. Why you so for him?"

"No reason. You might be judging him too quick, is all."

"Think he's against me?"

Tyrell stiffened at this. A child could see he was figuring out if it was a trick question.

"Nah, Frankie. He's just eager to please, that's all."

"He wanna take over from me?" Ritchie's directness alarmed Tyrell further.

"Not possible, Frankie." His words tumbled out. "None of us would go with him. We with you, and he knows it, or he's dumber than we think."

Ritchie gave him a hard look. "You hundred percent on that?"

"Two hundred percent."

"Where he now?"

"Outside with the car, like you told him."

Keera glided outside to be sure and found Dash leaning against the car and talking to a large man she knew instantly was the one who'd hurt Zach. She moved up and behind Dash.

"You saying that Bones never saw Frankie?" Dash was talking to Melvin.

"You got it, Dash. He gave me a message to give Frankie. He say you gone crazy, hanging around his girl, scaring her and shit."

"Never fuckin' was. She came up when I was letting him know where he could go and where he couldn't. The dude is lying."

The man laughed softly. "Sure he is. You just keep saying that."

Dash bounced off the car, indignant. "You don't believe me?"

Melvin held up his hands in peace. They were huge like Zach had said, bear paws. "Your story, Dash, you stick to it, is all I'm sayin'."

Dash asked, "What plans Frankie got for Bones, anyway?"

"Frankie's plans are born in his head, and they come out when they're fully ready. He doesn't try ideas out on me. He sure wouldn't try them out on you."

Dash heating up again. "You suggestin' he don't value my opinion?"

"He might, when he needs to."

"When that gonna be?"

"When he needs a new shirt." Melvin burst out laughing, inches from Dash, who could only glower.

Keera saw the anger pour out of Dash, watched him fight to retain it, to put a cold expression on his face.

"You sure is funny, Melvin," he said. "I better get a doc on standby in case I bust my sides from laughin'."

The retort made Melvin laugh harder. He stumbled away,

bending over, resting his hand on the car for support. A big man, confident enough to turn his back on somebody he was insulting. The big man who had crushed Zach's neck.

She wanted to trip him, shove him, hurt him in some way but couldn't. Dash turned and stared at her, mouth open.

"You," he said, squeaking.

If he could see her, then his channels were open. "Brace yourself, Dash," she said and flew into him, Dash not resisting, not knowing how to.

She forced him forward, kept her balance. Melvin still with his back to her, bent over, laughing. She lifted Dash's foot, planted it on Melvin's butt and shoved. He staggered forward, lost his footing and sprawled on the road. He sprung to his feet, an angry bull.

She withdrew out of Dash's body and moved back to observe.

"Never touched you," Dash said quickly.

"I didn't trip over my own feet, you fuckin' clothes rack," Melvin said, took two steps and drove a fist into Dash's temple. Dash hit the ground softly. A jacket sliding off its hanger.

The bar doors opened, and Tyrell stood outside. Dash, moaning on the ground, clutching his head.

"Yo, Melvin," Tyrell said. "Frankie's leaving now, and he prefers to have a driver with a head on his shoulders, okay?"

Melvin dusted his knees off. Dash stood up but fell over again.

"Guess you driving, Melvin," Tyrell said. "Dash needs a li'l R&R." He bent down to help Dash up.

Ritchie burst through the bar doors and into the back seat, Tyrell barely able to get the car doors open in time. Melvin took the driver's seat. Dash, upright but without conviction, scrabbled at the passenger-door handle. He climbed inside with the dazed movements of the aged. When Tyrell joined Ritchie in the back, the car sped away.

Keera didn't follow. She had meant to hurt Melvin but had only dusted his pride a little. Dash had copped a pounding instead. She almost felt sorry for him.

Almost.

Zach woke to Keera's soft body sliding under the blanket next to his, her arms pulling him closer. "You couldn't wait until we got to the bedroom?" he asked. "It's not as if I've got another appointment this time of night."

"You keep talking, we're going to lose the mood," she said and wriggled herself closer to him. Closed her mouth on his, and silenced the next thing he was going to say.

Later they moved upstairs, and she told him what she'd done.

"You what?" Her startling information jerking him out of his post-sexual languor. "What the fuck you do that for?"

"I was angry with Melvin. I didn't stop to think it through. But Zach, did I do any harm?"

"You've shown Dash another way how you can make his life much worse. I'd call that a provocative act."

"Well, they both deserved what they got."

Keera defensive now, the ramifications of her actions hitting home. She hadn't, not to his knowledge, channeled into a person's body since the time they first met. It wasn't normal for her, nor, as she once explained, easy to accomplish by somebody in the physical plane. She must have built up such a rage that her energy soared to unexpected levels, and she succeeded. He wished he'd been there. The imagery made him smile.

"You kicked a man over, and that made you sexually excited? You rushed back to help yourself to my body?" He laughed softly.

She punched him lightly on the arm. "When I spend time in the company of misfits I realize what a treasure you are."

"Who wouldn't?" he said and received another punch. Decided not to go further with the banter. She might freeze up at some accidental slight. Changed the subject. "I have to say that channeling into Dash, and getting him thumped is a delicious irony."

"We need more than irony. We need to be free of that crazy mob. I can't see how to do it."

"You could channel into Dash, walk him into the nearest precinct and make him turn in Ritchie."

"He'll resist me like crazy after tonight. It won't work."

Zach thought on this. "Do you think Virgil could channel into Dash? Get Dash to shoot Ritchie?"

"I was lucky. Dash wasn't expecting me, didn't know what to do, and I only needed a few seconds. He won't be so easy to take over next time since the first experience wasn't a good one. Any fresh intrusion by Virgil or me will panic him, make him fight off any invader."

She snuggled closer. "You aren't thinking that killing people is a way out of this, are you?"

He kissed her face, said, "We're dealing with violent types. What if it's the only way?"

CHAPTER 24

As soon as Zach arrived at the Post, Edwina beckoned to him from her glass-walled office. "You're safely back from the urban war zone. How did it go with the girl?"

He took a visitor's chair. "Not so good. She was too stoned to be real coherent but managed to indicate she was doing fine. I'm going back."

Edwina tapped a pencil on her desktop. "When?"

"When she calls me."

"Uh-uh. I need material sooner than a stoned kid's phone call. Drop by today and try again. Get me a quotable line or two. I don't need a feature, just something that shows the story developing."

A vision of Rhiannon lifting her top came back.

"And you're waiting for what?" Edwina asked.

"I got a problem with Rhiannon. The girl. She's, um, pretty out there with the sexual attitude. Practically offered herself to me."

"I'm sending you out to chat to a hot, nubile thing, and you're scared?" Edwina roared her delight. "You a choirboy, or what? Okay, let's see ... take an intern with you. Debbie Krasnowski looks so proper; bet she could do with a walk on the wild side."

Debbie Krasnowski wasn't only proper; she was downright prim. About eighteen, nineteen, blonde hair pulled back in a brisk ponytail, sensible skirt and top, good body but draped with disinterest.

Zach filled her in on the way. "We're interviewing a young mother on the South Side regarding her financial position since her partner, and I use the term loosely, was incarcerated."

Debbie gazed out the window. "Do you want me to take notes? I do shorthand. Or should I record the interview?"

"Bring out a recorder, or a pen and paper, and the subject's likely to shut up. Best to talk to them like a friend. They say more. You memorize the answers like I do, we write and compare notes later. Mostly you shut up and observe. You might see things I don't."

"I can do that."

"But it's not your main role."

"What is it, then?" she asked, turning to him.

"Last time I was with Rhiannon, she got a bit frisky and flashed her boobs at me. I'm hoping this time she won't, not if you're there."

He glanced over to catch her reaction. Steady gray eyes back at him. Not shocked, just sorting things out in her mind. She faced the front. "Like a chaperone, you mean?"

Uncle's porch was empty when they arrived, but he came to the screen door as they approached it.

"You brought backup this time," Uncle said. "Got a girl to talk to a girl, huh?"

"Last time I didn't get so far," Zach said. "Must be my clumsy ways with women. I thought young Debbie here would help Rhiannon with her story." He tilted his head at Debbie beside him.

Uncle looked her over for a whole ten seconds. "Shouldn't she be finishing her homework, then working on a quilt or something?"

"She's learning the job; she's good. Rhiannon home?"

Uncle swung the screen door open. "She home all right, been in front of a mirror since her shopping expedition yesterday."

They entered the hallway, and Rhiannon called out, "Dash, that you?" She came out of a room, handsome in a silk dress straight out of a swanky cocktail party. It was blue, with a little shimmer in the color, and it had shoulder straps, thank God.

"Say, it's the cute reporter and his li'l sister," she said, pouting with exaggeration. Uncle laughed as he went into the kitchen.

"That's a gorgeous dress," Debbie said. "Where did you get it?"

"Debbie is also a reporter," he said, annoyed at having to explain her again. "You expecting Dash? I know him."

"At Herman's," Rhiannon said. "Got a whole bunch of stuff there. Nice people." She said to Zach, "Dash? Was supposed to meet me after shopping and take me out. Never showed, never called. You see him, tell him not to come over no more. I'd tell him myself, but he don't pick up the phone."

"I'll pass the message on," Zach said.

"Can I see the other dresses you bought?" Debbie said.

That surprised him: Debbie so assertive. He followed the girls to Rhiannon's room, but she stopped him with a hand on his chest. "We having girl talk now, you wait outside." She slid her

206

hand down and drew it away when it reached his waist. "You want a proper conversation, well, a girl likes to be appreciated, you know what I mean. Taken somewhere nice, where I can wear my gorgeous dress."

She smiled and closed the door.

He joined Uncle in the kitchen, accepted a coffee, black, and waited for the girly meet-up to finish.

"I didn't expect those two to get on," he said to Uncle.

"Rhiannon don't have many female friends. It's because their men want Rhiannon instead."

"No surprise there," Zach said. "She's a beautiful woman."

"Yeah," Uncle said. "And she knows it."

"Must have caused Emmett a lot of worry."

"Emmett adored her. Never let her out of his sight. Everybody too scared of him to even talk to Rhiannon."

"Doesn't seem to bother Dash now."

Uncle raised his eyebrows. "You really know Dash? I thought you were smoking her when you said that."

"We don't hang, that's for sure, but we talk now and then. Rhiannon's name came up. I was surprised to hear it, especially as we were doing a story on the families of—"

"Cut the crapola, Mr. Bones. The story you working on ain't the one you talking about."

Zach swallowed coffee. "That's the funny thing about stories. You start working on one, and another, better one pops up and takes over. I got all sorts of leads to follow. Rhiannon is one of them, but she's a safe distance from any trouble. She's not coming to any harm from me."

"I hope not. I showed you the Weapon of Justice for a reason; I hope it's not called upon."

That killed the conversation for a while. "Does the Weapon of Justice protect Dash as well?" Zach asked.

Uncle grinned. "The Weapon is itching so bad to talk to Dash, it tries to climb out of the box by itself every time that boy come over."

Debbie came into the kitchen. "We can go now," she said.

"I haven't talked to Rhiannon yet," he said, rising.

"She doesn't want to talk anymore today. We don't need to bother her." When he still hesitated, she said, "A girl's dressed up and nowhere to go, with no man to take her. She needs time to herself."

Zach offered his hand to Uncle. "Maybe we'll meet again," he said. "Who knows?"

Uncle's grip was firmer this time. "Bring a six-pack next time, or I might mistake you for a poor relative."

He took the car onto the freeway before saying to Debbie, "You better have something real good for me to come away empty-handed."

"Rhiannon went to Herman's. You heard of it?"

"You think I shop in boutiques?"

"Not a boutique. An expensive fashion store. Couture things. She bought six dresses, none of them under a thousand dollars."

"Jesus Christ."

"I have to say she's got wonderful taste."

How would you know, he wondered.

"Plus a Fendi clutch bag and two pairs of Manolo Blahnik shoes," Debbie said. "That's another three thousand right there. You still want to ask her what her financial position is? I'd say it was sound."

She stayed silent for the rest of the ride back, until Zach eased the Mustang into its parking slot.

"That dress she was wearing," she said to the windscreen. "It was fucking divine."

Dash woke with his head pulsing itself to pieces. Checked the mirror. Purple bruising from cheekbone to hairline, tiny cuts above his ear, blood congealed there. He swallowed an aspirin, drank coffee and figured he needed advice. Grabbed a cab to Li'l Marie's storefront.

"Whoa, Dash, you need a hospital, not a psychic," Li'l Marie said when he walked in.

"I need to see in front of myself, is what I need. You talking about my face? It can wait." He settled himself in her client's chair.

"You getting psychic yourself now. How'd you know I didn't have a client booked right now?"

"Something happening to me for sure. I saw that woman again last night."

"She wave hello?"

"The bitch got inside me somehow, used my foot to kick my associate. This bro busted me across the head for it."

Li'l Marie looked shocked. "This woman is developed, getting into you like that."

"Is why I'm here. Stop her doing it again. She could damage me in a bad way she do that shit to me again. How the fuck she do it, anyway? I had that potion shit you gave me in my pocket."

"There's your trouble, Dash. You gotta sprinkle it around, on yourself if you have to."

"I ain't gonna have it on my clothes. Smells worse than Creole takeout."

"I have another way." Li'l Marie hesitated like he wasn't ready for this. "I can give you a psychic self-defense technique."

"A gun that shoots spooks?"

"No such thing, Dash."

"What you got then?" Maybe she had something simple, a word, "Shazam" or shit like that.

"You heard of Chakras?" She didn't wait for an answer. "They major energy centers in your body. You have to visualize them, one by one—they're all different colors, you know—and then surround yourself with a protective white light."

This woman didn't understand his situation. "You think I got time to sit around thinking of this shit while this bitch gets at me again?"

"You do this every morning and night, and you'll be safe." Li'l Marie firm on this.

"You sure this voodoo is gonna work?" Just thinking of good stuff stopped bad stuff happening, is what she was saying. How about that. And people believing this shit.

"It's not voodoo; it'll work if you want it to work. It'll do against this woman, anyway. Any entity that turns up with more energy, well, I'm not laying down any guarantees."

"No point in trying it then."

She leaned forward. "The thing is, Dash, you're getting psychic, bit by bit. That's a problem for you."

"How so?"

"The more psychic you get, the more open you are to them stronger than you."

"You saying I attract spooks?"

"Yes, you do, but this woman not a spook, is she? Didn't we get that last time?"

He thought of the stuck-up bitch, talking to him like he was a fool. "What if I warn her off me?"

"Didn't you already try that? I'm picking up that she dissed you. Made you angry."

"Gonna talk to her again." Stop her for good this time.

Li'l Marie said, "Not a good idea. Only more trouble for you if you go that way. She's more powerful than you."

"She just a dinky girl, it won't be a problem."

"I say it again, don't go to her."

He rose out of the chair. "Not getting quality advice today, Li'l Marie. Gotta get going."

"Still a fifty."

"Put it on my account," he said and walked out. His face must look bad; Li'l Marie didn't even try to fix him up with her daughter.

Dash caught a cab to the Thai restaurant, walked in. The owner bustled up.

"They not here today," she said. "Not expected." She waited uneasily.

"It's okay," he said. "I forgot."

Did he get told the hangout for the day last night? Had Melvin knocked the information clean out of his head? Couldn't even remember being left at his crib.

"Gotta use your phone, okay?"

She nodded.

Called Tyrell. "Yo, dog. Where we at today?" he asked. "My head don't recall a thing."

"You lucky it balanced on your neck," Tyrell said. "The fuck you doing, messing with Melvin? You wanna die young, just ask me. I find a painless solution. We at the bar, Frankie's waiting." He cut off.

Frankie still on his case, fuck. What else was there to bitch about? Give him a big telling-off for kicking Melvin? Maybe. He'd have to explain how he got real angry, just for a split second, and did a stupid thing. Wouldn't happen again, that'd be sure. Next time, Melvin's fist would go right through and come out the other side.

"You got a direct line to a cab?" he asked the woman, his head throbbing again.

"I get for you," she said and lifted a yellow phone at the end of the counter.

When Dash arrived at the bar, Ritchie had no food, no drink in front of him. Just the cell. Melvin off to the side, watching.

Ritchie surveyed his face. "You look like shit, and you deserve it. We don't tangle with each other, got it?"

"Got it," Dash said. "I lost control, just for a second. Can't explain it." Turned to Melvin. "Sorry, man. Disrespectful of me to act like that."

Melvin didn't respond. Gave him the stare.

"It was an unusual event," Ritchie said. "You not noted for being a wild child." He checked his watch. "Where you been all morning?"

"Went to see that voodoo woman, got something for you." Hoped it got Ritchie happy. He handed the vial to Ritchie. The shit didn't work, no point keeping it.

"What's this, bat's blood?" Ritchie inspected the vial with suspicion.

"Called Four Thieves Vinegar, stops bad spooks attacking you. Those voodoo types use it all the time."

"I drink it or rub it on?" Ritchie being jokey.

"She said sprinkle across the doorway, but you could put some on your food if you want."

Ritchie unscrewed the top and sniffed the contents. "Vinegar all right, some pepper and herbs." He screwed the top back on. "This shit works, we could sell it by the gallon. Get the Thais to make it up every night." He picked up Dash's cell. "You wiped all your data from here."

The cell. Frankie couldn't get him on that, not with all the calls gone. "Didn't want to leave evidence there," he said. "Easy to forget who you call, so I wipe it often."

"How do you remember the numbers?"

"Keep them in my notebook. You still got it."

Ritchie blinked once, twice. "You fuckin' what?"

"In code, see. Not just a list of names and numbers, I write the numbers backward."

"The names backward, too?"

Dash smiled, but it hurt. "Too obvious. Just an initial."

"You think nobody could figure that out?" Ritchie's voice rising.

"Not the right one. It's in code, too."

"So you have a code book where you match up the right name to the fake initial?"

"Takes too much time. I use a page at the back of the notebook. I got the alphabet, and alongside it the real initial."

"Fuck me," Ritchie said. "What makes you think the cops wouldn't flick through your notebook and find the code-breaking page, you dumb shit?"

"That's the page I eat when they come," Dash said. "Evidence gone for good that way."

Ritchie sank back in the booth. Looked over at Tyrell leaning on the bar. Tyrell real interested in his shoes. Ritchie tugged Dash's notebook out of his back pocket.

He thumbed through the pages until he found what he wanted. Turned the book around to show Dash. "This the important page?"

Dash nodded.

Ritchie tore the page out, crumpled it up and held it out to Dash. "Eat it."

Dash took it and nibbled away at the edges. Each chew made his head hurt more.

"We ain't got all day, Dash," Ritchie said. "Faster."

Ritchie read every page, one by one. Tearing out more of them until the notebook was reduced to a slim volume of blank pages. He folded the torn ones in his hand and thrust them into his side pocket.

"I'll deal with these myself," he said. "You done eating?"

Dash swallowed the last piece, briefly gagging on it. Didn't ask for water, had to look strong.

"Dash," Ritchie said, "You don't look like my driver, right now. You look like an alley cat that lost a fight with a dumpster. Take a week off, come back when your face looks human."

Dash sidled out of the booth, didn't look at Melvin or Tyrell. Stopped outside, the Caddy parked there, his Chrysler behind it. Walked to his car thinking if anybody, just anybody else bugged him today, he would pull the Glock and drill a thousand holes in the fucker.

CHAPTER 25

Keera sat through a two-hour meeting at the Anthropology Department; nodded when asked to cover for an absentee; raised a questioning eyebrow when a field-trip budget surplus of seven thousand dollars was brought to notice; agreed to help draft a request for more staff for the faculty. In between she thought of Dash.

Visions kept crowding in, one of them showing Dash walking up to Zach and drawing his gun. Dash had to be hurting after Melvin's assault, and he had to be thinking of her. He understood what she had done; revenge would be his first reaction. In the moments before she used him to kick Melvin, she had also picked up that he blamed her and Zach for his troubles. He couldn't see he was the one to blame: the only one to blame.

Dash was sure to come to her again. Before then, she had to locate him and prepare. The first thing she did when the meeting was over was to call Zach.

"Saw Rhiannon today," he said, sounded delighted. "She's spent near ten thousand bucks on clothes yesterday. We're doing a piece on it. Where did this money come from, that sort of thing."

It sounded like Zach was chasing a story and forgetting about consequences. "Doesn't that put her in jeopardy? Won't Ritchie silence her in case she says too much?"

"I'm thinking of seeing him first, explaining he'll only strengthen the link to her if she's harmed."

She remembered his neck throbbing darkly the day before. "Didn't you already try chatting to him, and found your access skills were lacking?"

He grunted, acknowledging her point. "I'm not going around there this time. I got Dash's number. I'll call and ask him to put Ritchie on."

"Let me look over the scene first. Dash's behavior yesterday would have caused ructions."

"Ructions. Nice description. Sweet. Vintage sound to it. Who knows how these people think? It might be normal for them to go head-to-head like rutting moose."

"Whatever. I'm going to take a look; then we figure out a new plan."

"We haven't had a plan yet," he said. "We've been reacting."

"Fine, we'll figure out a new contingency. See you tonight. Don't force any issues before then." Zach might have an excellent scent for a story, but he had a terrible nose for self-preservation.

Two hours later she was home and lifting out of her body. Ritchie was in an expansive corner apartment overlooking Lake Michigan and standing, staring out a window, flanked by Tyrell and Melvin.

Nothing indicated Ritchie lived here; the place wore the sterile ambiance of a hotel room. Probably one of his crash pads. What was it like to have an occupation where it was crucial that hardly anybody knew where you were each night?

"Figure Bones is loose in the head, you know?" Ritchie said

to Tyrell. "I point out exactly where he stands, and he pokes around like he didn't hear me. Talking to Rhiannon, Dash said. What's the go with that?"

"Dash said she went shopping," Tyrell said. "We should find out what she bought."

"Good idea. Ring Dash and find out."

"Uh … we can't, you got his cell."

Ritchie pulled the cell out of his pocket. "Fuck it, we can't work with smoke signals. Take it back to him tonight." He tossed the cell on the sofa. "Tell him to see Rhiannon, tell her to shut the fuck up or get out of town. Tell him to find out if she's going crazy with the money."

"Not a problem. Talking about crazy, Frankie, what's the word on Emmett? He still in the psycho ward?"

"Far as I know. Makes it easier for us. Call his lawyer, see what gives."

Tyrell moved away from Ritchie to use his cell. Keera stayed in a corner, behind her a wall with generic flower prints that should obscure her outline if anybody here had the ability to see her.

Ritchie said to Melvin. "What the fuck you hit Dash so hard for? You leavin' me a man short. What if the cell rings and it's Tanner for Dash. Might not talk to me, might hang up."

Melvin massaged one hand with the other, kept staring out the window. "Don't take dissin'. Had to show consequences."

"Might have thought it through before you thumped him. Shit."

Tyrell listened to somebody on his cell, saying "Uh-huh". Closed the cell and said to Ritchie, "He says Emmett's not improving, practically in a coma from the shit they giving him.

Cops pissed off, trying to find out if Emmett's faking it but the medical staff saying he's for real."

"No trial anytime soon, then?"

"That's his opinion."

The cell on the sofa beeped and they all looked at it. Ritchie nodded at Tyrell who picked it up, switched on the loudspeaker. "Yeah?"

Keera knew who was calling: Tanner. It came to her as loud as a proclamation. They must have had the first meeting and she'd missed it.

"This isn't the person I expected," Tanner said.

"He not around," Tyrell said. "You call in coupla hours, he be back then."

"I'll do that," Tanner said and hung up.

"Tanner," Tyrell said to Ritchie. "They ready to boogie."

"Sounded like they wanted Dash."

"Sure, wouldn't you? Tanner's gotta cover his ass and other precious organs. It's a tricky operation for him."

Ritchie moved across the carpet to the kitchen area, pulled a beer from the fridge and a jumbo bag of chips from an overhead cupboard. Broke open the bag and crunched on a single chip. "Better get Dash back here now. I'll make sure he sees Rhiannon tonight. That Bones, we oughta take his girl and hold her, make sure he stays quiet. He won't see her again until she's seventy-five years old."

"That's a new way of thinking for us," Tyrell said. "We need more people to hold someone."

"Can't be hard to organize. Shit, the Tijuana economy runs on kidnapping and weed. If a bunch of Mexicans can do it ..." Ritchie's voice trailed away as if the details weren't worth developing further.

They were going to grab her? Just like that? And hold her like a sack of wheat? Keera burned, her energy fizzed and sparked at the outrage of it. Behind her, one of the framed prints rattled and banged against the wall.

Ritchie and the others turning in her direction. The picture jumped off the hook; the glass front shattered on the ground. She slipped away to float behind them. Still angry.

"Musta been a loose hook," Ritchie said.

"Dunno, Frankie," Tyrell said, looking around but not seeing her. "The picture was jumping like crazy. Hook's still there."

"You sayin' that spook just came back?"

"Could be." Tyrell inspected the broken shards on the ground. "Getting frisky, breaking shit."

Ritchie swept the room with unseeing eyes. "I thought all spooks stay where they die, or maybe where they were hangin' just before they died. You know, a favorite place."

"Never heard that." Tyrell scanning the room himself.

Melvin said, "Get a priest, some religious guy, have him sprinkle holy water around."

Keera stared at the shards, small pieces that might move. Hadn't tried this before, didn't know how it worked. Stared at them fiercely but they simply lay there. Bardo, she asked, I need help.

This is not the place to be active.

I want to disrupt them as much as I can.

It's not your role today. I recommend you watch and learn.

I want to make them nervous. Please, show me how to move those shards.

I don't do circus tricks.

Bardo didn't say goodbye, but she knew he wouldn't respond anymore.

Ritchie said, "Dash said something about seeing a spook the last time this happened."

"He could sort this out," Tyrell said. "He keeps seeing his voodoo woman, getting advice. She can tell him what's going on, and he can tell us."

Ritchie kept staring at the broken glass as if expecting it to fly around the room. "Know what? I wouldn't be surprised if he already had conversations with his woman, and he knows a lot of shit we don't."

"Could be."

"Get him now."

Keera was being pulled away, and as she came past Ritchie she slashed her hand across his head. Knowing it was futile but wanting to just the same. Ritchie didn't react, felt nothing. She got that he was thinking of her.

Back home she sat up and rolled off the bed. Her legs wobbly, she half stumbled downstairs, grabbed her cell and dialed Zach.

"Good thing I went along," she said when he answered. "They're sending Dash to warn Rhiannon about talking to you. You know what they're going to find out?"

"What? That she hasn't said much anyway?"

"That she spent heaps on clothes. Clothes way too flashy for her neighborhood. If she is a liability, Dash is to get her out of town."

A pause at his end. "Better than the alternative I suppose. And I don't think she'll mind too much. Rhiannon likes exciting moments, I'm sure. New York or Los Angeles would be attractive."

"They figure Emmett isn't coming back, so that gives them freedom to move on Rhiannon." She stopped, then said, "There's something else you should know."

"You're so dramatic. What is it?"

"Dash is to tell you that they'll take me if you see Rhiannon again."

A pause. "What do you mean 'take'?"

"They'll kidnap me and hold me for as long as they need, to control you."

"No!"

She gave him the rest of the news. "But Ritchie doesn't intend to keep me at all. I saw his thoughts. He means to kill me."

It sounded like she was talking about someone else.

Dash watched Tyrell walk in the Thai joint, and hoped for some scene setting would set his mind at rest. But Tyrell didn't have a lot to say.

"Frankie wants more chat," he said.

"What now?" Dash asked, already rising to his feet. Ritchie still mad about something?

"Mmm," Tyrell said. "Best let him say."

Alarmed, Dash put a hand on his arm. "Tell me. Don't leave me hangin'."

Tyrell handed Dash's cell back to him. "That spook come by again, up in the apartment. Broke a picture. Frankie wants your opinion, is all."

"Shit, the spook again. What do I know about spooks?"

Tyrell didn't answer, just led them to his car and took him to Ritchie.

"See that mess over there?" Ritchie jerked his chin at a pile of glass on the floor. "That spook followed us from the chop joint and got frisky. Whatcha know about that?"

Dash inspected the shards, took his time, looked back to Ritchie. "What would I know about this?"

"You see your voodoo woman regular, right? She tell you stuff you forgot to pass on?"

"I gave you the Four Thieves Vinegar." Not the best answer, he knew it.

Ritchie glanced at Melvin and back at Dash. "I'm talking about information. Tell me everything she said if you don't want the good side of your face to match the bad one."

Melvin stirred on the couch. Dash hurried an answer. "She said it was a … white spook, but I thought nothing of it so I didn't mention it."

"Don't pay you to filter information, just to deliver it. What kind of white spook?"

"An angry one."

Ritchie laughed. "Angry? I hope you didn't pay money for that. I could've told you for free. Shit, you could have figured it out yourself, after seeing the mess it leaves behind."

He couldn't tell Ritchie it was Virgil now; that would make him mad. He'd let Melvin work on him for a bit as punishment.

"You want me to get some ID on this spook?" He'd tell him it was Virgil afterward. It be the safe way to go.

"Yeah, you do that, but there's something else first. The girl. Rhiannon."

Dash waited, his heart still.

"She went shopping, right?"

Dash exhaled. "I dropped her off. She was gonna buy dresses and shit."

"Go and see what she bought. If she be buyin' stuff she can't afford normally, she broadcasting her new situation. If that's the way, you get her on a plane to somewhere else. Today. Got it? Never, ever comes back."

"It'll happen just like you want it." Dash turned to leave before Ritchie came up with more tricky shit.

"I haven't finished."

Dash halted.

"Find Bones, tell him if he keeps being pesky we're gonna take his babe. Hold her until we tired of it, then throw her off a high bridge."

"Be a pleasure," Dash said. About fuckin' time Bones got told what was what. "Anything else?"

"Sure is. A new situation has come up."

Dash couldn't think what. Couldn't be serious if it was last on the list.

"Got word some bros looking for you," Ritchie said. "A couple of our street guys said these guys were gangsta-ed up. Asking about a skinny dude in a black suit and a Chrysler. Remind you of anyone?"

"Let 'em find me," Dash said. "I got ways of negotiating."

"Uh-huh. You don't do that so well. They find you, say sorry, a big mistake and how can you make it right. Let 'em know you're looking at a financial settlement."

"That's crazy. They'll ask for the highest number they can think of."

"Sure. Then come back to me and I'll work something out. At least you're alive while we're talking."

Alive and heading for the nearest poor house if Frankie meant what he'd said about no health plan. He'd offer anything he felt like since it wasn't him paying out.

"What you don't do," Ritchie said, fixing the hard stare on him, "is pull your piece."

"Shit, they be carrying something themselves, for sure."

"They'll be expecting you to, seeing as how you were so quick before, and that'll give them a reason to decorate your body with a bunch of holes. Don't fall for it."

"Gonna have to back my judgment on this when the time comes." Dash returned the hard look. "It's not you facing down this situation; it's my ass sticking out there."

Ritchie spread his hands in a gesture of surrender. "Okay. Do it your way and see how your ass gets by."

Dash turned to go again but Ritchie stopped him.

"Funny thing is, these guys are asking my people about you," he said. "Means they know you connected to me, but nobody's talked to me. What you think 'bout that?"

"They being polite, not wanting to bother you until they're sure of who they looking for."

"Uh-uh. They not interested in me, they want you. I feel a

financial settlement ain't a priority."

Ritchie didn't seem real concerned. Dash wondered if he should ask Li'l Marie for advice on this.

CHAPTER 26

Ritchie means to kill me, Keera had said. After kidnapping her. That made it near impossible to concentrate of his big scoop of the day, but somehow he completed the piece. Zach checked it once more and sent it to the copy editors. He shoved his chair back from his desk and stood up.

"You have fresh news?" Howard, startled, looked up from the next desk.

"I certainly have," he said and nearly broke into a run heading for the doors. He guided the Mustang through the afternoon traffic, holding one thought in his head. That he had to create a situation where Keera's life would be assured. That meant extra pressure had to come Ritchie's way. On his patch.

Uncle was back in his favorite chair but stood up in alarm as Zach took the front steps in two leaps.

"Dash here, or been here?" Zach asked him, stopped in front of him.

Uncle shook his head. "That boy still not appeared. Rhiannon's never gonna forgive him for not taking her someplace fancy in her new clothes. I hope."

"Then he's still coming. Coming with bad news."

"That boy himself is bad news. What could be worse?"

"He knows I've been here, twice. Thinks I'm onto something I shouldn't be."

Uncle laughed, a scratchy, growling thing. "Well, that ain't hard to figure out."

"The problem is he's going to take Rhiannon away. For good."

Uncle stopping grinning. "How do you know all this?"

"I have sources. Can't reveal them as you might know."

"Yeah, Supreme Court decision somethin'-versus-somethin'-or-other." He looked through the front door screen. "I heard Rhiannon take a call ten minutes ago, saying yeah, she was home. Guess that's him on the way."

Zach wondered how much he could share with Uncle, decided a little more wouldn't hurt. "Is Rhiannon safer away from here? I ask because where Dash takes her might not be in her best interests."

Uncle took a long while to work through what he had said. Then opened the screen door and yelled into the darkness. "Pack your bag right now, baby, you gotta leave in seconds."

Rhiannon tumbled through the door, hair done nice, lipstick in her hand, half-applied to her lips. "Pack? What?" She saw Zach. "Oh."

"Dash has orders to kill you for talking to me," Zach said. "You have to get out of here, now." Not totally true but could become true at any time.

Rhiannon turned around, and they heard sounds inside, feet walking fast, soft words to the baby.

"Dash doesn't seem too worried about Emmett these days," Zach said. "Guess the word is he won't be back anytime soon."

Soft sadness crossed Uncle's face. "Emmett's my nephew, and I care for the boy. But he was always easily led by others. Never had enough watts in his light bulb to help him see things clearly."

"His father had no influence?"

"Father no smarter than the son he produced. Not with us anymore."

Rhiannon was out with them again. A small bag in one hand, the child holding the other.

"You sure Dash has it in for me?" she asked as they drove away. "I did nothing to him."

"Not him, his boss. You spent too much on those clothes. You're advertising that you came into money. Emmett's money."

"He would've spent it on me; everybody knows that." Defiant tone.

"I don't doubt it. You're surely worth keeping happy."

She flashed a smile. "You sweet-talking me? Saving me from evil, then taking advantage of a poor girl? You the kind I should be careful of?"

He felt himself coloring. "I'm not sweet-talking. I'll take you to the airport." They were running up the ramp to the freeway when he though to ask, "You got money?"

"Shit, I got money, but I left it behind," she said. "Go back to Union Station."

He waited outside in a drop-off-only zone, eyed the child in the back seat. She stared back at him with huge brown eyes and a dazed face. Fucking doped-up. Fed marijuana all day long to shut her up. Probably lost ten percent of her brain cells already.

Rhiannon came back clutching a brown envelope. Sat inside and kissed it. "Airport, driver," she said, her face shining with excitement.

"Where are you going?"

"LA. My sister's. She's always sayin' come on over, don't freeze your ass no more."

"Here's a tip. Don't come back. You're not safe."

She nodded then exclaimed. "My dresses. Can't leave them there."

"I'll have then sent to you. Uncle know your address? If he doesn't, call him and tell him. In the meantime, don't answer your phone if Dash calls you. Get yourself another one."

"Sure thing." She fell silent until they drew up at the domestic terminal. She struggled out of the seat and pulled the child upright next to her. "Goodbye, my white knight," she said and pulled his head to hers, kissed him on the lips before he could move. "Drop in sometime when you're in town. I'll bake you some pie. Keep it nice and warm 'til you ready."

He watched her walk into the terminal flanked by her bag and her child. Hoped he would never see her again.

Uncle was back on the porch when he returned. "Dash came," he said. "Told him Rhiannon gone out, coming back in a couple of hours. Made him more cranky than he was to start with."

Zach leaned against a post. "You tell him that? Why not tell him she's gone away? Not coming back, ever?"

Uncle inspected his fingernails. "I figured you and Dash better meet up and sort things out. He comes back, he don't know you're here if you move your car."

"You think I should ambush him?"

"Sensible military tactics, just trying to help."

"You get more helpful every time we meet."

"And you still don't bring any beer."

"You got other ways of relaxing, I'm sure."

Uncle looked up at him. "Some situations require a clear head. I think we got one coming up. Dash had a purple face, yellow patches of bruising. He's been disciplined for something, and he wasn't happy. I seen dudes that way before: anger simmering close to boiling. They'd likely to put a full clip in the next bush that rustles. If Rhiannon's not here, he could take out his feelings on you. Put your car away."

"Fuck it. I'm not scared of the guy. I'm going to talk to him and tell him to lay off me and my girl."

"Or what?"

"He knows or what."

Uncle rose to his feet, agile and economical with his movements, put his hand on Zach's shoulder. "You can't point out logical outcomes to an angry man," he said. "We better wait inside."

He led Zach to the kitchen and set a coffeepot on the stove. "You'll find cups about. Gotta make a short stop," Uncle said and left the kitchen.

Zach organized two mugs, found the sugar, heard the toilet flush and Uncle returned.

"You the sissy kind that has to have sugar?" Uncle asked as he sat down, taking the chair facing the door.

"Can't help myself," Zach replied. "Got energy needs you don't know of."

"Sugar gets you hopped up just when you need to have a calm

temperament."

They heard a car door slam outside. Just the one.

"Sound like Dash is alone," Uncle said, putting down his coffee and pushing his chair back from the table. Dropped his hands to his lap.

The screen door slammed, and quick footsteps brought Dash to the kitchen door. He looked worse than Uncle had described. His head, purple and yellow on one side, had several cuts where Melvin's knuckles had broken skin. His eyes darted around the room, his hands shook and he rested his left hand on the doorframe to steady it.

"You," he said to Zach. "You have no business here, and I say get out before you get carried out."

"And I say, you stay the fuck away from Keera or Melvin will have a reason to go after you again."

Dash straightened. "That bitch is gonna get no chance to do that shit to me again."

"How you going to stop her?"

"We'll arrange it so she comes to stay with us for the duration."

The guy talked like he grabbed lines from movies without understanding them. "I repeat, how are you going to stop her doing shit to you again?"

Dash had to think about that, and it wasn't easy. The internal calculations were practically written on his face while he figured out that holding a body captive didn't include the capture of the spirit. That Keera could come and channel him anytime she wanted to.

Dash came to a conclusion; the solution gleamed in his eyes.

"This is how it's gonna be," he said. "The next time she comes near me, I come for you and switch your lights off. You tell her that."

"Does that mean the next time she comes near you has to be the last moment of your life?"

In his side vision, he saw Uncle glance at him as if he'd gone mad. Provoking Dash like that wasn't the smart option, but he was angry enough himself.

Dash ignored him, probably needed the time to think of a smartass response. He looked over to Uncle. "Rhiannon come back?"

Uncle turned to Zach, who said, "She's gone. Forever. You'll have to find some other guy's treasure to steal."

Dash's right hand kept lifting and falling like it wanted to hold a gun and blast away at soft targets.

"You fucked up bad, Dash," Zach pressed on. "You took her shopping, and that's on the front page tomorrow. The whole town will know she's cashed up, and it won't take any effort for them to guess why. Will Ritchie give you a promotion for this?"

Beside him, Uncle moved restively. Wasn't agreeing with what he was saying.

"Or did he slap you around for a while?" He couldn't stop. "Looks like your face ran into a brick wall somewhere. You should hang a bag over it before you scare dogs and children."

Dash found words. "Rhiannon's gone, not coming back?"

"You got it."

Dash relaxed a fraction. "That bitch better off somewhere else."

Uncle lifted a hand off his lap with his Colt in it. "Did I hear you refer to Rhiannon in a disrespectful manner?" He rested his gun hand on the table, his other hand steadying it, the muzzle aimed at Dash's stomach.

Dash stiffened. Left his hands hanging by his side. "Didn't mean to, Uncle," he said carefully. "It's just the way I talk."

"You don't talk that way here, understand? You come into a man's house you need to be mindful of his ways and preferences."

"Sure, not a problem. Won't happen again."

Dash had enough survival skills to know when to retreat. Zach grinned at his backtracking, knowing it would make him madder and half hoping Dash did something so stupid Uncle would shoot him.

Dash made to leave. "I guess I'll be going now. Seeing as how Rhiannon's not here and seeing how she's never gonna be here again, I guess I won't be back."

"You don't know how much pleasure your words bring me," Uncle said. He stood up and jerked the gun toward the front door. "Your car's out there, I believe."

Zach beside him, Uncle walked Dash to the porch and watched him drive off. They walked back to the kitchen where Uncle pulled a couple of long-necked beers from the fridge, handed one to Zach. They sat opposite each other at the table, touched bottles, drank, and Uncle said, "It's time you told me a story. The one about you, Dash and Rhiannon. I'd like it if it had a sweet ending."

"What I'm doing," Zach said, "is trying to find out if Dash's boss Frankie Ritchie had Emmett kill Jason Virgil. This Jason Virgil was a major drug dealer."

"How far have you got?" Uncle asked.

"Dash, Ritchie's man, has given Rhiannon money that was earned by Emmett for the kill."

Uncle thought on this. "There's no stopping that Emmett from reaching new heights of stupidity. That boy already going to be doing years for robbery, and now he likes it there so much he aces somebody for money he's never going to see."

"I guess he wanted to see Rhiannon looked after."

"She's got money, I guess, spent some on clothes and shit."

"You know how much she spent?"

"Didn't look at no price tags."

"North of ten thousand bucks."

Uncle stared at him, frozen. "Those itty bitty things, slinky things hanging off her shoulders?"

"She bought top-end brands. Debbie, the girl I brought along, she knows fashion, figured out the cost."

"Shit, that kid got no more brains than Emmett."

"That's the problem. She wears that stuff around here, and there's going to be talk."

"That why Dash came tonight?"

"I heard he was coming to see if she was a problem. If so, she was to disappear."

Uncle leaned back in his chair. "How come you know all this stuff you couldn't possibly know?"

"I get stuff the same way cops get stuff—I pay for it."

"Bullshit. No bro would talk to you."

"Was I wrong about Dash tonight?" Uncle wouldn't be able to refute that point.

"You might have got lucky. Dash come here a lot these days."

"You see how pleased he was when you told him Rhiannon was gone for good? That sound like a guy coming around to play?"

"There's that," Uncle admitted. He sat straighter. "You think I'll have a peaceful time of it now? No more unwelcome visits?"

"No more visits. Rhiannon's gone; you can sleep tight each night."

Outside, his cell trilled as he started up the Mustang to drive back to Keera's. It was Warren.

"Tomorrow's papers just hit my screen, and I read your piece," he said without preamble. "You suggesting that Emmett Hurtle's girl got a payout from somebody and spent most of it in a day?"

"Something like that."

"You saying that it's linked to Virgil's' death?"

"Not saying, exactly, but thinking it."

"What makes you think that?" Warren was calm, questioning without attitude.

"She told me Dash took her shopping."

"Dash? That the Ritchie lieutenant you been hanging with?"

"Not hanging with, Detective—been seen with, momentarily."

"Dash confirm this?"

"Haven't spoken to him, probably won't bother. He's not the loquacious sort. You can check his association with the young Rhiannon yourself."

"How so?"

"She told me she left the money in a locker at Union Station. Dash took her. The two of them must be on closed-circuit television footage there."

A muffled rustling came over the line as Warren moved the phone, probably to write stuff down.

"What else can you tell me?" Warren letting excitement creep into his voice.

"That's it for now. Did you get anything on the supposed meeting with Ritchie's mob and Virgil's outfit?"

A long sigh from Warren. "Haven't the manpower to observe all those citizens we'd like to."

"What about in Virgil's old territory? Betcha that's a priority."

"Hmmm."

Warren was clamming up. Might have some surveillance out there anyway. Zach said, "Well, Detective, it's been a long day for me, writing interesting stories and all. Is there anything else I could help you with?"

"I got something for you: Emmett Hurtle's dead."

The news sat him up. "What? How? When?"

"Officially, heart failure. Died while under heavy sedation. About an hour ago."

"Unofficially?"

"I have only one version at this time." Warren getting sarcastic. "There will be a press conference tomorrow morning at nine. You are cordially invited as of now. Hope this makes up for the earlier disappointment. Goodnight."

CHAPTER 27

Zach's key scratched at the door around midnight. Keera shook off her sleep, and they met in the hallway, holding and absorbing each other.

"You were in trouble," she said in reproach. "I sensed it, but you didn't call me."

He led her to the living room and a couch. "I got Rhiannon on a plane out of here. Dash came for her later, then annoyed Uncle, who pulled a gun on him."

"God." She checked his aura for stress fractures, but he had none.

"It was okay, Dash backed down and left." Zach paused. "Warren called. Emmett's dead."

An image of Virgil flashed into her head and evaporated. "Did Warren say how he died?"

"Heart failure, he said."

"Dropped dead, just like that? A young guy?"

"He died while under sedation. Sounds strange to me. We'll find out more tomorrow at the press conference."

"Isn't that the place where lies are born? You said that once."

He grinned. "That's true. The trick is to figure out the truth the lies are based on."

She rose to her feet and pulled him up. "You need calming fluids before you get too cynical."

"You're such a mind reader. Beer would be perfect."

"I was thinking herbal tea," she said but laughed to show she didn't mean it. He didn't need a health lecture right now.

In the kitchen, Zach opened a beer and took a long draw before speaking. "My piece on Rhiannon and her dresses is out on the website. Warren's read it already."

She sat alongside the table and stretched her legs out on the next chair. "Does that mean the police will interview Rhiannon?"

"They'll try. It'll be a while before they find her." He finished the bottle. "In the meantime, Ritchie will be very tetchy with me. My Rhiannon piece will spoil his breakfast now that I've publicly linked Virgil, Emmett, Rhiannon, and a heap of money."

He placed the empty bottle on the table and rotated it a couple of times like it helped him marshal his thoughts.

"Rhiannon told me Dash took her to Union Station, to park her money in a locker. The cops will find security camera footage of them together. That'll be my follow-up piece. Virgil, Emmett, Rhiannon, money and now Dash: a known associate of Ritchie's, as the cops will describe him."

She swung her legs off the chair. "It'll more than make Ritchie tetchy, won't it?"

"I assume I'll be sent for again."

"Don't go."

"I assume they'll have ways of convincing me."

"Don't go. I mean it."

"Do you foresee terrible trouble?" He played it lightly, but she felt his internal unease.

"Refuse to go with them. They won't shoot you in the street," she said, knowing it was an inadequate answer.

"People get shot in the street every day in Chicago."

"Not you, not white guys. There'd be too much publicity."

"I feel better already."

Irritation welled in her. "If you want good news, find a fortune teller and pay her to tell you what you want to hear. I see what I see."

"Sorry. Sarcasm comes naturally to me. I didn't mean it."

She said nothing, leaving him uncertain of her mood.

"Ritchie will be expecting a string of stories after this," he said. "He'll have to stop them. He'll send for me, that's certain." He caught her eye. "They'll come for you, too. Like you said."

She stood. "That's their intention, but I'm not without resources, am I?"

◆ ◆ ◆

The press conference was short. The Lieutenant, a dour-looking cop with a tossed salad for a face, introduced a Detective Carbone, who stood next to him and never took his eyes off Zach. No Warren. The Lieutenant read a brief statement pretty much repeating what Warren had said the night before. Took questions.

A female reporter Zach didn't know lobbed up the first one. "Was the death related to the sedatives Hurtle had been administered?"

"At this stage we have only conducted preliminary investigations," the Lieutenant answered. "The autopsy should be more conclusive."

"Does this conclude the investigation into Jason Virgil's death?" Zach heard himself asking. A few yards away, Jeremy Brackett swore aloud. Must have thought it was his turn to ask.

"Unless suspicious elements are uncovered in the autopsy," the Lieutenant said. "This death concludes the investigation into the Virgil case."

Zach followed up fast before the press officer pointed to somebody else. "It doesn't strike you as strange that the person the police were anxious to interview refused to talk, became unable to talk due to sedatives, and then expired of a heart failure? A young man in his twenties?"

"It's been a frustration for us, but we had to defer to medical advice." The Lieutenant sounded grateful for that.

The press officer pointed to somebody else, but Zach wasn't giving up.

"Does the fact that Emmett Hurtle's partner spent over ten thousand dollars on clothes a few days ago suggest that money was paid to Hurtle for his murder of Virgil?"

"That's a wild statement there," the Lieutenant said. "We don't have facts; we have only a news story."

"When are you going to check it out?"

The Lieutenant shot a look at the press officer, then said, "We are going to keep our investigations confidential, is what we are going to do. When we have something to announce, we'll let you all know."

The press guy pointed to Brackett.

"Have you any idea what motivated Emmet Hurtle to kill Virgil?" Brackett asked.

"Inmates of correctional facilities often harbor resentments and grievances that to us would seem trivial," the Lieutenant said. "It's not unusual for tensions to explode in a violent manner."

Other reporters asked questions about Emmett's known history, budgetary constraints and the disproportionate level of young black men in jails before the press guy said, "That's it, folks."

The Lieutenant and Carbone turned and left the room in step.

Brackett strode up to Zach. "This is my story, you fuck. I'll ask the questions. That dresses shit you wrote; you should have told me about it."

Zach put his arm around Brackett's neck like he was a best friend. Brackett wasn't fooled; he flinched. Zach said, "Your story just died. My story just came to life." He crunched the guy's neck for a couple of seconds and let go. Felt like a bully. "Go cover a dog show," he said. "You're good at sniffing butts." He walked out hating Brackett and hating himself for how he made him act.

He found Warren in the main corridor, waiting for him. "This Rhiannon," the detective said. "She left home yesterday and hasn't come back."

"I don't know her that well, Detective," Zach said. "I only spoke to her twice, but I got the impression she was the playful type, seeking adventures here and there. Keeping regular home hours probably wasn't part of her makeup."

"Hurtle's records show she was his partner, and they had a child. I saw no child there either, only a relative."

Shit. He'd forgotten about Uncle. Forgotten to warn him police would be knocking on his door.

"You searched the place?" Did they find Uncle's gun? Was it registered?

"The uncle of this Rhiannon wouldn't let us in without paperwork. But he said the girl and her baby were gone. Can you confirm a child lived there?"

"She had a two or three-year-old girl when I visited. The kid made like a zombie in front of the TV. You should get the child welfare guys to look at her." He wondered what Uncle was thinking now. Maybe he was thinking that the Weapon of Justice should be used on a pesky reporter.

"Sure thing, I'll add that to my to-do list."

"All I'm saying is that the kid looked totally doped-up both times I saw her."

"I know what you're saying, Bones. I am aware of your reputation as a social reformer, and I will act on this information."

Zach ignored the sarcasm. "Did you find Dash on the surveillance tapes?"

"As I mentioned before, we don't operate as fast as we'd like. Maybe you could run a piece on enlarging the police budget?"

"I'll add that to my to-do list."

Warren flashed a row of perfect teeth, acknowledging the riposte. "If we find that Dash is caught on camera with Rhiannon, can you help us find him?"

"Tell you what, Detective," Zach said. "I'll consult my notes; maybe I wrote down where I saw him. I'll be in touch."

Zach pushed through the glass doors of the entrance and stopped at the first row of concrete pillars flanking the street. Pulled out his cell and called Keera. That morning she had insisted on taking her normal route to the university despite his fears. "They won't do anything today, it's too soon," she'd said. "Ritchie will have to talk to Dash first. Stop fretting."

"I'm not fretting," he had replied. "I just want to see you alive again."

She smiled and kissed him goodbye. Left him wondering what she knew that she hadn't shared. Worried she was ignoring the dangers.

Now his heart relaxed when she answered. "You in class?" he asked.

"In ten minutes."

"Okay, do me a favor so I don't die of worry. Don't go home alone tonight. We, especially you, shouldn't be there alone anymore. Meet me at Rocco's when you're done and we go home together."

"Okay. Gotta go. Bye."

She had agreed so fast he was worried again.

Zach lifted a hand to an approaching cab, and it stopped. No roof box light on. The cabbie sported a gold crucifix and a pentacle or maybe a Star of David hanging on chains from his neck.

"Can you take me to the Post?" he asked the driver, indicating the unlit box with a glance

"Oh that, the light's broke. I'm for hire."

The cab merged briskly into the traffic, and the driver had questions. "You don't look like a cop," he said. "You just been released after some kinda interrogation?"

"A press conference," Zach answered from the back seat. This guy was going to talk for the whole ride.

"A reporter. What was it about? A new atrocity where man is inhumane to man?"

"A jailhouse murder."

"Like with a shank, or something like that?"

"They didn't give a lot of details." He didn't want to discuss it either. Changed the subject. "Death comes to all of us," he said. "I see you trying to cover your final moments with two religions. Why's that? You can't make up your mind to be Christian or Jewish?"

The cabbie pulled up at a stoplight. "I drive this for a living, you know; that gives a man plenty of time to think."

"And that's left you undecided?"

"They both got rules how to live your life, you know what I mean? But what happens after that? When you're dead."

The lights changed and the cabbie hammered down on the gas.

"So, you're still searching for answers?"

"Been reading books about the afterlife and there's some pretty interesting shit going on there."

Not exactly the way Keera would put it, but Zach knew what he meant. "What did you find out?"

"Well," the cabbie said as he made a left, checking all his mirrors like he had neck strain. "I thought once you crossed over you got to be a good guy. Saw all your faults clearly, felt sorry for your transgressions and shit."

"And?"

"Not true. You can stay the way you were, hang out the same

places like before. Stay a good guy or a piece of shit."

"That's what you'd do?" He pictured the dead cabbie riding hundreds of cabs and sprouting his ideas until the end of time.

"I'd spend every minute with my family. Two kids, beautiful wife." He pulled up outside the Post. "You got a family like that?"

Zach climbed out, passed a couple of bills through the window. "I'm too young to start a family," he said.

The cabbie said, "You're never too young to start living right."

"Thanks for the tip," Zach said. "I'll write it down, stick it under a fridge magnet."

Keera lied to Zach and went straight home after the first class. Made excuses, rescheduled the rest of the week. The reason was simple. To argue with Zach, an argument which could explode into a major conflict, would leave her senses jangling and useless for psychic work. She had to see Ritchie again, had to know what was approaching. Nobody was going to snatch her off a street. Not if she stayed alert.

She took her tea to the living room and settled on a couch. "Bardo," she asked, "what's the best way to get Ritchie out of our lives?" Maybe Bardo had a quick answer. But he didn't respond at all.

"Is that too much to ask?" She persisted, but she knew Bardo would twist the question back on her. "I feel we're in danger." Perception of danger is not the same as danger itself.

Of course. Another homily. Bardo, back to his elliptical worst. Not a good sign.

"You mean we're safe for now?"

"Safe" is a relative concept. So is "now."

"Please, I ask only this: no philosophy today, just simple answers."

Simple answers are for simple people. You deserve better.

"Thanks. Can you take me to Ritchie, now?"

Of course.

She stretched out on the couch. Closed her eyes, absorbed the rushing, the blackness, the glimmering in the distance, and found herself back in the apartment of last night.

"Emmett was a good man," Ritchie said while the three of them watched the news. "Worked as a team player, never figured a private angle for himself."

The broken picture leaned against the wall where it had fallen. Some glass shards remained, suggesting Ritchie hadn't called in a cleaner.

"Think this will kill any more investigating?" Tyrell asked.

Ritchie pointed the remote at the TV and cut the sound. "It would have if that fucker Bones hadn't run his story on Rhiannon. They won't let that go. Not without going over and asking tricky questions that she's too dumb to avoid answering." He inspected the buttered toast in front of him on the kitchen counter, pushed it away. "Hear from Dash yet? I wanna know if he's taken that girl out of town or not."

"Hasn't called, hasn't answered either," Tyrell said. "You want me to get him out of bed? He might be still feeling poorly."

"Fuckin' hope so," Melvin muttered from the couch.

"Bring him here, Tyrell," Ritchie said. "Bring back coffee and muffins. I'll be hungry by then. Can't believe I'm not hungry now."

"Didn't he say he was going back to his voodoo woman?" Tyrell said. "That's where he is, then. Probably had to turn off the cell so it didn't interfere with all that psychic shit."

Ritchie reflected on this. "Yeah, you're right. Was gonna find out the name of this spook keeps following us." He tapped the remote on the counter. "Let's leave him be for a while. See if he turns up with something useful."

Ritchie said to Melvin. "What did Bones say to you at the Thai that day? Something about a middleman?"

"Said he already had middlemen on his case, which is why he wanted to talk to you direct. And Dash was shadowing his girl."

His girl. Zach said that? Keera grew warm at the thought of it.

Ritchie reached into the fridge and pulled a carton of milk, took a long drink of it. Put it back. Wiped his hand across his mouth. "Think he was telling the truth about Dash?" he asked Melvin.

"Why not? He was angry about Dash getting to his girl."

"Dash said he only talked to her when Bones was there."

"Think he was smoking you. Dash musta done more than that for Bones to come around."

Ritchie looked over to Tyrell. "Think Dash was hot for the girl?"

"Uh-uh," Tyrell shook his head. "He don't no have the taste for that type, white, uptown. Dash knows his limitations."

"So, why would he dog the girl?" Ritchie said. "Makes no sense."

"Dash gets some crazy lines of thinking sometimes. I can't always understand what's pushing him."

"Think he's cutting himself some action?" Ritchie's tone was soft, but Tyrell tensed. Keera picked up that he had translated the question as an accusation: that he wasn't telling Ritchie everything.

"He only wants to appear clever in front of you. If he's figured out some independent plan, it's because he figures it will benefit us. He's not the solo kind."

Ritchie tossed the remote onto the counter in disgust. "I hate that. I hate independent thinking. You can't have a bunch of drivers for one chariot." He picked up a newspaper. "This Bones, he didn't listen so good, did he? We better have another talk."

"You want me to fetch him?" Melvin asked.

"No, Dash can do it later. You too scary looking. Look like you mangle people cos' you're bored. Bones sees you waiting for him, he'll run. Maybe all the way to the cops if he's scared enough."

His cell buzzed and Ritchie picked it up. "Yeah?"

Keera heard Dash's voice, and it brought an image of him in his car. Ritchie scowled as he listened then he barked into the cell, "You get your skinny self down to Rhiannon's and grab any dresses she left behind. Got it? Get 'em, lose 'em, don't bring them near me."

Ritchie killed the cell, opened the fridge, closed it again. Exasperation creased his face. "Fuckin' Dash. He went to Rhiannon's yesterday, got told she was gone for good, and he left. Not thinking to check the place over."

"Where he been all morning?" Tyrell asked.

"The voodoo woman, like you said. You know who our spook

is? Virgil."

Tyrell laughed. "No way. No fuckin' way. He lost his outfit, and he throws a picture to the floor? Like a cranky kid?"

"That's the word." All three grinned at each other, surprising her.

Ritchie said, getting into the moment, "Next time we see shit moving around we say 'Wazzup Jason baby. Wanna move the couch? Be our guest. Put it over there, see how it looks.'"

Tyrell eyed the couch, said, "How does he move stuff? I mean, he's got no body, no hands?"

"Never studied that particular field," Ritchie said. "But is all about energy, is all I know."

"Got that vinegar bottle, right?" Tyrell asked. "If Virgil comes back we sprinkle that shit all over the place."

"Can't think where I left it," Ritchie said tapping his pockets. 'I'll get Dash to bring over a whole bunch of them just in case."

Like that would help. She almost felt sorry for their poor bedraggled hopes.

Bardo took her home. She sat up and sipped her cold tea. "How long before they come for Zach?"

Complications will delay them.

"A day or two?"

Perhaps.

"No need to stay so noncommittal. You can be more specific." There were times Bardo had to understand her urgency.

I can't be more specific because much depends on what you do now.

She ran fingers through her hair. "How do we escape this ... this madness?"

You can't escape. You have to face it and defeat it.

"I'd like to, but I don't have the power to do more than observe. Even Virgil has more power than I do. I could barely move a hair."

Throwing dishes isn't you.

"What's Virgil doing now?"

Watching. Planning.

A new thought came. "Emmett Hurtle's death ... was that Virgil's doing?"

He concentrated on the young man for several days. Focused his energy on one thing: to drive him mad through dreams. He succeeded better than he expected because young Emmett had a weak heart, and he died during a psychic attack.

"God," she said. "I've never heard of anybody dying of a dream before."

It's rare, but it happens.

He was gone then. She left the living room for the kitchen and boiled more water. Brewed fresh chamomile tea and sat at the table. Checked her watch and decided to call Zach at the end of the day. That way he wouldn't know she'd left early and come home by herself.

CHAPTER 28

"**G**ood piece on the dresses, Zach," Edwina said, holding the folded paper. Around them, the newsroom was only half full as reporters drifted in from press conferences and interview assignments and copy editors back from lunch grimaced at their screens.

"Thanks," he said.

"Fine piece of investigative reporting. You're a credit to a disappearing breed."

"I thought so, too."

"One thing you forgot."

Zach waited. "Does it mean I have to go back?"

Edwina said, "Pictures. We have no pictures of the dresses. With those, we can run this story a little bit longer. You should've seen that."

"I should have, you're right. But the situation was too delicate to whip out a camera. Even a phone camera."

"But now that the story has hit page three status you're going to trot back and ask for photos, aren't you?"

It was hardly a question, but he tried for wriggle room.

"Detective Warren talked to me today. He says the girl has skipped. She might have taken her dresses with her, don't you think?"

Edwina dropped the paper to her side. "I don't surmise. I ask, I find out. Get me the photos."

"Where's Jerry? It's his job, isn't it?" Every paper had a Jerry: the staff photographer who helped reporters beef up feeble news with an unflattering snap of the subject.

"Jerry's out for the day."

He tried again. "Here's me, a plain ol' reporter, no eye for imagery, unable to frame a picture, useless when focusing, leaves a cluttered background with every shot. Elsewhere in this city are real photographers, award-winning guys and gals. Why don't you send one of them?"

"Because, Zach, they will ask dollars plus unrealistic expenses. You, on the other hand, are already employed here. Times are tough, as you know. Take yourself off to where you were and come back with photos. We don't need fashion shoots; just the garments draped over a chair." Edwina turned to go then turned back. "The girl's gone? Skipped town, you say? Call her and get her to take snaps with her cell. With those photos, this could be front page."

Zach pulled his keyboard closer and tapped out all the details he could recall of his meetings with Ritchie, Dash and Melvin. Dates, places and outcomes. It looked damning on the screen but without corroboration, it was useless in a court, but it was the only weapon he had.

He posted the document to Dropbox in a folder he shared with Howard. A place where they placed news snippets useful to each other. "Um," he said to Howard. "I've left a doc on Dropbox. Take it to the cops if I don't come back by tomorrow noon."

Howard stopped gazing at his screen and gave his full attention to Zach. "You joined the SEALs and going off on a delicate expedition?"

"Worse. I have to face the guy who's collecting the wrong attention for my piece on the dresses."

"He's angry enough to kill?"

"If he's nice, he'll kill me before he dismembers me."

"You shafted him?"

Zach shifted, uncomfortable. "Not so much shafted. Got careless, forgot that the spotlight would fall on him also."

"This forgetfulness has consequences. Is that what you're saying?"

"Exactly."

"So what's up? This guy wants to wear these dresses or something, but the cops will take them as evidence?"

"Howard, he's not a cross-dresser. He's going to get attention from the cops, yes. He will also get attention from Ritchie, which is way worse for him. Also, his nephew died in a jail hospital last night. He won't be pleased to see me." That was an understatement. It'd be a miracle if the Weapon of Justice stayed in its box.

"And your mission is?"

"Edwina has sent me back to take photos of the dresses."

"That's her mission. What's yours?"

"The same."

"Uh-uh." Howard looked ready for some finger-wagging. "You have to make peace with this guy. Apologize, explain, grovel like you've never groveled before and beg forgiveness. Or you'll dump your job in disgust sometime soon."

"I will?"

"Yes. Because you're honorable." He didn't even smirk when he came out with this.

"Howard, I don't need this moralizing. The day ahead looks pretty shitty already."

"I'm suggesting a course of action that will settle your mind."

"You got a course of action that will stop bullets?"

Howard turned back to his screen. "I just point to the right mountain. I don't cut the trail."

◆ ◆ ◆

Uncle sat on the porch like before, a newspaper across his lap, his face as cheerful as a tombstone. Empty cans of Pabst Blue Ribbon at his feet.

"They tell you about Emmett?" Zach asked from his spot beside the bottom porch step. Figured he should stay there. Unless Uncle smiled.

"They came, they told me." Uncle examined Zach with cold eyes. "What late-breaking horror you bring now? You want another hot story? Another way of making me an easy target?"

"Aah, about that story. I told you yesterday it was coming out and you didn't remark on it. I figured you had it worked out, knew the consequences." He said this too quickly, way too quickly.

"Fuck you say," Uncle spat out. Not on the weed today, beer fueling his anger. "You know the trouble that stupid shit you wrote is going to cause me?"

"I assume the cops wanted the dresses."

"They came, offered their condolences, asked for the dresses, left without them. Had no warrant but they'll be back with one. That's not the worst of it."

"Dash came back?"

"Fuck, I forgot about him. No, not him. Everybody around here now knows that I have over ten grand in garments lying around the house. Valuable items, know what I mean. All-too-easy to steal items. All day they gonna drive past real slow and look this place over. Come dark they'll be creeping up like hyenas, figuring out how to keep an old man quiet while they take those fucking dresses. No more Emmett to worry about taking revenge one day. You know how much sleep I'm gonna get while those things are in the house? Zero. I'm gonna sit in my chair all night, listening to jungle sounds. You happy now?"

"I didn't think it through. I'm sorry." Zach moved onto the front step but Uncle stiffened.

"Don't think about taking another step or I will shoot you for being a robber." He lifted the paper on his lap to show the Colt.

Zach stepped down again, tried for the truth. "I should've thought of warning you. Slipped right out of my mind, what with Dash and all."

"Fuck you did. You thought you'd never be back to see the damage you caused."

So much for truth. He tried for forgiveness. "How can I make it up to you?"

"What can you do?" Uncle snorted. "You sold some extra papers, made a few bucks for the corporation, why you care about the result for ordinary people? Your readers got some excitement for breakfast. I got a shitload of sleepless worry."

"I lost sight of details," Zach said. "I was after Ritchie. I was blind. I'm sorry."

"You'll be sorry until the next story. Then you'll spike somebody new."

"I helped Rhiannon, didn't I?" He felt like he was pleading for his life here. He wanted respect from this old guy.

"You had to. Even a snake like you could see she'd get hurt." Uncle leaned over and picked up a Pabst. Drank from it without taking his eyes off Zach. Put the can down. "What you here for anyway?"

"I didn't have your number, so I came to see how it was going for you."

Uncle cracked a laugh. "Don't gimme more of you shit. Be gone."

No way could he photograph the dresses now; all he had was a slight story about Uncle warning off reporters.

"Your problem is the dresses. You get rid of them, you're home free. You got nothing to steal, nothing to show the cops."

"Ah, I get it. It's about the dresses," Uncle said. "You need 'em to prove your story. You're such a weasel, trying to butter me up, but it's something else you want." He reloaded from the can again. "Like I care," he added as an afterthought. "You ain't gettin' nothing."

"I don't need them, I had a witness see them, and there'll be camera footage of Rhiannon spending her money somewhere."

"So, why you here?"

"I came to apologize to you."

"Bullshit."

"And photograph the dresses."

"At last, something you say has the ring of truth."

Maybe the truth worked with Uncle. Zach tried for more. "Let me take the dresses away and you can resume your peaceful life."

Uncle lifted the Pabst off the ground and raised it to Zach. "I hafta admit it, you're a stone-cold mother. You take the dresses, the proof of what you wrote, and I still get to fight off the night-comers who don't know the dresses are gone."

"They'll know in the morning. My next piece will feature them."

"Will you run it next to the story about an old Vietnam vet left for dead after a firefight with armed predators?"

The beer was bringing out Uncle's dramatic side. "You can go somewhere safe," Zach said. "You can stay at my place for a few weeks if you want."

"You want me to be your roommate?" Uncle shook his head at the wonder of it.

"It's yours. I'm not using for a while."

Uncle leaned forward, his forearms on his knees. "You don't get it. If I leave this place unoccupied, it'll be cleaned out. With no Emmett, there's no holding back the worst elements of this 'hood. They'll come and come again, strip the place until there's nothing left but a shell and a lingering smell of evil."

Zach grinned back at him. "Uncle, you ever think of a career in Hollywood, writing outlines? You're a natural."

"Never gonna live on the same coast as Rhiannon. She's a baby, but she brought a heap of shit into my life."

A car turned into the street, and Zach glanced at it. A black Chrysler, Dash at the wheel. "Looks like a new heap of shit just arrived."

Uncle shifted in his seat and slid his hand under the newspaper.

"We saw him off last time," Zach said as he watched Dash emerge. "We can do it again."

"What do you mean 'we'?" Uncle said. "Didn't see you doing much sending-off last time. I recall it was me who convinced Mr. Armani to leave."

Dash hurried across the road and stopped near Zach. Spoke to Uncle. "Here's what's going down. You got a small boutique inside, and I need to remove your stock. There was an error in delivery."

"Is that so?" Uncle pulled out the Colt and rested it on top of the paper.

Dash looked at it and back at Uncle. "I gotta say I leave without them garments, brothers will come here and burn your house down, with you and the garments in it." He paused to let the words sink in. "Before bedtime."

Uncle held Dash's gaze for several seconds, then nodded. "Go and take them."

Dash waved a hand at the front door. "First, you and the paper boy go inside. Leave your piece on the seat."

"You think that's ever gonna happen?"

"Wanna live in a smokin' ruin?"

Uncle leaned forward. "Wanna be one of the bodies found in the ashes?"

Dash smiled widely. "See how we've reached a misunderstanding here? It shouldn't be like this between friends."

"The day I call you a friend, I'll eat my gun."

Uncle, Zach saw, just itching for Dash to reach for his own weapon.

Dash raised his hands. "It's simple, right? I want the garments; you want me to have 'em. Can we conclude this transaction in a professional manner?"

Uncle rose and extended an arm, indicating Dash should enter the house first. His right hand held the Weapon of Justice. A slight tremor told Zach how close it was to being fired.

Dash opened the screen door and Uncle followed him inside. Zach right behind them. The best part of the story unfolding in front of him.

"The kitchen is on the right," Uncle said to Dash. "Get yourself in there and sit down. Put your hands on the table."

Dash did as he was told. Uncle sat opposite, the gun still in his hand, the butt resting on the table, the muzzle aimed just above Dash's sternum.

"Mr. Bones, would you fetch the garments for us?" Uncle asked.

Zach moved along the narrow corridor to Rhiannon's room. The dresses were still there. Some in boxes, they had been tried on and thrust back; others hung on plastic hangers from her closet door. The favorites, he guessed. They must have made her feel like a princess every time she put them on.

The shoes were sitting like trophies on top of their boxes. The room a shrine to loveliness. He understood then, dimly, the power these things had over women. He pulled out his cell, stabbed at the camera icon. Grabbed a couple of shots and prayed Dash didn't catch a glimpse of the flash bouncing off the walls.

He repacked the dresses and shoes and carried them back to the kitchen. Uncle and Dash still sat opposite each other. They had run out of conversation. He dropped the boxes on a chair, sat in the last one left.

"You are one stupid fuck," Dash said to him. "You think you can write shit without Frankie's permission?"

"I'm more nervous of my editor than him. She wanted the story, she got it."

"And you came back to give Uncle a free copy of the paper?"

"That's what I'm known for, spreading kindness everywhere."

Dash took this in. "Frankie's gonna want talk with you. Like to escort you myself, but my orders don't include you. Not right now."

"That's a shame. I've enjoyed our rides together in the past, was looking forward to more."

Dash grinned. "You sure got a mouth. Can't wait to see what Melvin does to it."

"Looks like Melvin's been practicing on you. Would that be right?"

Dash dropped the grin. Said to Uncle, "Those boxes, they all there is?"

Uncle looked at Zach.

"They all there is," Zach said.

"A pleasure doin' business with you." Dash rose and stood by the box pile. "You people sit here while I load the car. Quietly. When you hear me drive off, you may resume your shitty lives."

Spoke like he was holding a gun, not Uncle.

Outside, car doors slammed, fast feet pounded the porch steps. The screen door banged open, Dash ducked his head into the hallway, his hand scrabbling at his waist.

"Thass him." A new voice. "Do it."

Two shots exploded in quick succession and Dash jerked back like a dancing marionette. He lay, twisting in pain on the ground, a shape bent over him. Another deafening explosion and Dash was still.

The killer straightened and saw Zach and Uncle. Both of Uncle's hands under the table. Another dude appeared behind the killer. The two of them scoped the kitchen.

Uncle spoke first. "You done the city a public service. We saw nothing. Go in peace."

The killer stared at Zach. "You good for the white thing?" he asked Uncle.

"He's my friend and he's tight."

The killer lifted his gun, pointed it at Zach's head. "We could make sure."

"You'd be starting something," Uncle said. "Killing a white boy in this 'hood will bring lightning up your ass quicker than you can explain to your brothers why you did such a stupid thing. Best you go while you can. We'll be the cleaning ladies."

The killer considered this, nodded and lowered his gun. Walked out. His companion followed, a limp slowing him down.

CHAPTER 29

D ash's body lay in front of them. A dead man, in the same location as Zach. Warren was going to love this.

"Know the best story of all?" Uncle said. "The one you don't need to tell."

"That going to apply here?"

"We can make it apply."

Uncle dabbed carefully at his cellphone. "Veejay? Get over here; I got a task and a reward."

Veejay must have read a lot into that message because he was tapping on the front screen door ten minutes later.

Uncle pulled latex gloves out of a box under the sink. "Stay here," he said to Zach. "Be like a mouse."

He took Dash's car keys to the front door. The screen door squealed open, and Zach could hear him talking.

"Put these cute things on and drive that sweet Chrysler away from here."

He couldn't hear the response; maybe there wasn't any.

Uncle continued. "Got yourself a nice ride for about half an hour, then get it gone. You didn't find it here."

The screen door banged shut, and Uncle came back. Bent over Dash's body, rummaged in his jacket pockets. Found a wallet and a money clip, a notebook, too. Joined Zach at the table and counted the cash.

"You know who those guys were?" Zach asked.

"Disciples wannabes is all I saw. Dash musta riled them up good. They weren't in no mood for talking, you notice?"

"This is some complication, isn't it? Cops come here and find no dresses, but a body?"

Uncle grinned. "You heard of the Ways and Means Committee?"

"Sure, Government is my beat."

"You just been promoted. Me and you; we're got the ways and the means of fixing this."

Ah, two determined people would remove all evidence of Dash's presence in Uncle's house. "I guess that nobody will report the gunshot," he said.

"You guess right. People don't want cops to come cruising along here anyway. They ask funny questions and hate all the answers." Uncle folded the money back into the money clip. "Five big ones and change," he muttered, stowed the cash in his jeans pocket. The wallet he flicked through. "Nothing to keep, plenty to get rid of." The Glock 26, he pushed to one side of the table. "Pop gun."

"What's in the notebook?" Zach asked.

Uncle flipped the pages. "All blank. Some torn out. You expecting the names and phone numbers of his contacts?"

"It would've been helpful."

"What you got in the trunk of your old Mustang?" He placed

the notebook next to Dash's wallet.

"A tool box and shit. You thinking of using it as a funeral car?"

"Something like that."

"I'll never get rid of any blood, you know. The second I'm linked to Dash, and the cops know I've spoken to him, they'll check my car over with the biggest magnifying glass in the world."

"I've had to handle bodies before."

This was getting worse. "Why don't we call the cops and tell them about a home invasion that went bad? The good thing, it's all true. Unassailably true."

"Got an Army groundsheet. Tough, waterproof."

"We're got the right narrative, they'll believe it."

"We truss up Dash tighter than a leg of smoked ham."

"You're not listening."

Uncle swung round to him. "You're thinking of a white solution. We go your way, you might get to lead a normal life. Me, I get to be hunted by Ritchie. Forever. Rhiannon, too. They won't leave her alone." He stood. "Got work to do."

He strode down the hall. Came back with a ground sheet, dark green, and still in its packing plastic. Opened it and spread it out on the floor. Inspected Dash's body, rolled it over then peered down the hall.

"We got ourselves a clean job. Three shots, one exit wound. Two slugs in the body, we can leave. They didn't come from my weapon. The other slug went right through that skinny hustler, probably stuck in the bedroom door. Get a pointy thing out of the drawer and start digging it out. Don't leave any pieces behind."

He rolled Dash onto the sheet and folded it over him like it was a giant deli treat he was wrapping. Went off, came back with duct tape. Left Dash looking less like a body, more like an unclaimed FedEx parcel.

Zach stepped over Dash. The dumb kid had been so obviously desperate to figure out the world and his place in it. Somewhere, somehow, he'd crossed the wrong people. More dumb fucks like himself, but who were faster to get riled and quicker on the draw. Jesus, what a short and stupid life.

All Dash had demanded was respect, and he'd thought sharp dressing and a gun were enough to gain it. The trouble was, you have to be ready to use a gun if you carry one, and the people he annoyed must have assumed he'd pull on them again. So, they shot first. There are rules in any 'hood, and Dash had forgotten the main one around here: be harder than the next guy.

Zach found lumpy metal embedded in Rhiannon's door, scraped at it; the slug dropped into his hand. Uncle took it, bounced it up and down on his gloved palm a few times. Slipped it into his pocket. Looked at the small pool of blood on the wood floor.

"We gotta clean that off," he said. "Ever done anything like that before?"

"I have, actually," Zach said and instantly knew it was the wrong thing to admit.

Uncle grinned. "Scrubbing brush, detergent and a bucket under the sink. Get to it."

It took twenty minutes before Uncle passed the clean-up, every one of those minutes creeping Zach closer to his jailing.

While he worked a new thought gained traction.

"How come you got them to leave me alive?" he asked while

he scrubbed. "It wasn't your beef; you're not my bodyguard either. But I do thank you."

"Been thinking. Watched Dash's crew mess up Emmett, watched them buy Rhiannon with gaudy flash, and most of all watched Dash come around here like he owned the place, owned Rhiannon, and I was a sideliner."

"That explains why you hated him. Doesn't say anything about me."

"There's the way they make their money; that was a factor." Uncle ignored his point. "The way they run the area, remove all chance of a good life from the young men and women. Dealing in that shit, it makes boys think that car stealin's a respectable way of life."

"Most people thinking your way would try and create a program of sorts," Zach said. "Something to help the youth break out of this pattern. You, you accept guns and violent death as reasonable outcomes. It saved our necks today, but it's not an answer." He stood and surveyed his work. "Clean as I can make it."

"We'll bring the brush and bucket with us," Uncle said. "Too hard to clean that thing. Let's go and find a dumpster." He patted the Colt stuck in his waistband. "It's not the answer, but it's part of the answer."

He glanced back at the boxes. "You still want those dresses?"

They waited until dark, sipping slow beers until they ran out. Zach laid the dresses over the backseat; lowered the shoeboxes to the floor, sat the handbag on them.

Uncle placed the body without reverence in the trunk and directed Zach to a strip mall three miles away. The pizza joint was open and held the evening's waiting customers; a Chinese takeout held a few less. The liquor store, Zach saw through the windows, contained one browsing customer and a bored guy behind the counter. They circled around to the rear where the dumpsters sat. One was for recyclables only, another wasn't.

"Round here," Uncle said, "they ought to have one for street trash." He heaved the sack that was Dash into the dumpster marked as general garbage. Bent over the rim and moved stuff about to cover the body more.

Uncle directed Zach farther south, and when they passed a pile of junk on the sidewalk he added his bucket and brush to it. As they drove away, he slid down the window and flung the third slug at the gutter.

"Drop me off at my corner," he told Zach. "When you get home, lose all the clothes you wore today, scrub your body twenty times. After that, never come near me again." When Zach stopped he put his hand out, took Zach's and gripped it like he meant it this time. Got out, leaned back in for a final word.

"I never did get those beers," he said, and he was gone.

Zach turned for Old Town and remembered that Keera hadn't called him to meet up. He jabbed at his cell, praying she would answer, was relieved when she did.

"You okay?" he asked. "Still at the university?"

"I'm home," she said. "Everything's fine. I've got something for you."

"What kind of something?" he asked, surprised that she'd gone straight home.

"I watched Ritchie today. They're coming for you. They're going to send Dash."

He drifted off his lane and corrected. "It figures. When did you find this out?"

"About lunchtime."

"I got something for you, too."

She didn't reply. Made him continue.

"This afternoon," he said, "I saw Dash die."

He heard her sharp intake of air. "Zach?" she said. "You heading here?" Saying it like it was the best thing to do.

"Not right away. I got a dress shop in the back seat, and I have to get it photographed before the cops come and take it. You stay there, don't go out. Don't answer any doorbells, either."

He loaded the dresses onto a hand cart and took them up to the *Post's* newsroom expecting to be met by a string of office wit. He wasn't wrong. Some of the boxes had opened slightly showing silk and gossamer dress fabric. The remarks flowed freely.

"Whoa, Zach, we didn't know you were that way," a sportswriter said as he passed by.

"I'll date you, Zach, if you wear an off-the-shoulder number," a copy editor said.

"Anything more revealing in there?" a laughing voice demanded.

Zach ignored them and pushed into Edwina's office. She looked up from the proofs she was perusing.

"I asked only for pictures," she said. "We don't have wardrobe space for those."

He dropped the boxes on the floor, pulled out a dress and draped it over the visitor's chair. "I had no time to grab good shots, but I was allowed to remove them. Rhiannon's uncle didn't want them around to attract thieves."

Edwina moved around her desk and fingered the fabric. "I'd work for less if I could wear this every day."

What was it with women and dresses? Edwina never looked like she was short spending on outfits and she still wanted better?

"Thing is," Zach said, "the cops will find out pretty quick we have them, and they'll zoom over and grab them. We need a photographer fast."

Edwina picked up her phone. "Is Jerry back?" She nodded at the answer. "Send him to me."

"We'll shoot them now but it's too late for tonight's edition," she said to Zach. "Give me the story by the morning, we'll have it on the Web at least. How you found out, how the dresses became a target for thieves, how you retrieved them and where this Rhiannon might be now."

"Sure. I'll maintain a high moral tone throughout."

Jerry knocked on the doorframe and walked in. Saw the dresses. "Sweet." He looked at Zach, kept a straight face. "Which one you wanna wear first?"

Why Keera hadn't picked up that Zach would witness a killing puzzled her. She could never grasp why sometimes she received clear images of inconsequential events to come, and at other times, events that were quite vital to her well-being exploded without warning.

Bardo had explained, as patiently as only he could, that she couldn't see as far into the future as him, which was why some events that appeared trivial to her were, in fact, important in her development. She would only understand that many years after the event.

She supposed that the reason other events that hit her without warning were also to do with her development. Whatever this development meant. She understood the general nature of spiritual development: to reach a greater understanding of the universe and her place in it. But there was always the feeling that she was being groomed for some reason, some special reason. And Bardo wasn't revealing it.

Except that Zach was part of it.

Bardo had practically browbeaten her to consider Zach as a soul partner. Her first impression was that he was too cynical, too ready to take life lightly, and enjoyed larking about like a schoolboy. Not her type. Eventually, she became aware they had a deeper connection than a simple social attraction. Maybe forged during past lives for all she knew; she hadn't yet dared explore that aspect. It's not always pleasant to relive past life experiences.

Keera quickly discovered that one of her roles in this partnership was to protect Zach from his impulsive, and dangerous actions. But she hadn't been able to stop him walking into a killing scene. This was acutely worrying.

"How do you feel?" Keera asked Zach when he arrived later that night.

"I'm getting used to guns pointed at me," he said. "Seems normal now. Ever stops happening, sure gonna miss it."

She took him to the kitchen, handed him a beer, sat opposite and said, "Tell me everything."

"That Dash," she said at the end. "I know he was a low life, dealing, part of a mob that makes money out of misery, but still ..." She stroked the table in front of her. "The police, will they link you to the killing?"

"Can't see how. It was a random event, no motive they'll ever figure out."

She searched his face. "But Ritchie? That's different, isn't it? He sent Dash for the dresses, was going to send him to collect you. When Dash's body is discovered, and the dresses are published in the Post, what else can he think but that you were responsible?"

"He'll know I didn't do it. It's not my style; that's the first thing."

"The second thing will be that he won't care either; he'll punish you anyway."

"You got that much from being there?"

Zach didn't seem very interested in her answer. His energy was low, negativity and uncertainty eating him. He needed good news.

"I got a lot we can use," she said, reaching for his hand. He grasped hers, absently, as if thinking of something else. "We need insurance. Like telling Ritchie we know two places where he hangs out. Like telling the police that you're going off to interview Ritchie, so they'll believe me when I call and say you're missing."

"I'm going to be missing?" Alarm raked him, and she regretted using the term.

"No," she said quickly. "I meant if you are taken. I saw nothing in the near future, but don't go with them if they come for you."

"That's fine advice, but it doesn't lead to a resolution. Sooner or later, Ritchie and I have to talk a deal. He leaves us alone and we leave him alone."

She took her hand back. "Bury that thought. He'll never let us go."

"He say that?"

She tightened her lips. "Some things are self-evident." She stood. "You're exhausted, you need rest, you need to lie beside me all night long."

He flashed a grin, but there was little life in it. Maybe he'd be stronger in the morning. The worst was yet to come—that much was certain.

CHAPTER 30

Someone trilled Zach's phone before he reached the Post in the morning. Zach hit the hands-free unit on the visor.

"Whazzup?"

Warren. "We pulled Dash out of a dumpster this morning," he said. "What can you tell me about that?"

"Not his preferred place of rest." They had found Dash quicker than Uncle had imagined. He wondered if Dash's car was still cruising around instead of halfway to Florida by now.

"He didn't have a choice," Warren said. "We found wearing a large hole in his chest, plus a couple of others for insurance."

"Are you thinking it's part of a gang war?"

"I need more than one body to think that. When did you see him last?"

"Three days ago."

"And?"

"And what?"

"Bones, if I have to drag information out of you syllable by syllable, I'll bring you in and do it in the comfort of the interviewing room." Getting heated. "Tell me everything you have

274

on Dash and don't fuck around."

"He came to see me. Caught me outside the *Post.* Warned me off trying to talk to Ritchie." Pretty much the truth there.

"Did you see him again?"

"I tried to get to Ritchie again, but ran into this big enforcer who handled my neck like it was a string balloon. I didn't go back."

"Bet that was Melvin Meat Hands." Sounded like he hoped so.

"You always take pleasure in another man's pain?"

"I have a professional interest in calming techniques." His tone changed. "How did you know where to find Ritchie? He's a slippery guy to pin down. Has no fixed patterns in his movements."

"I have my sources. You know, the ones I can't discuss."

"Dash one of them?"

"Dash was a messenger, which is why I'm thinking he might have been killed delivering a message."

"To who?"

"To whom. That I don't know, but as I said before, there was an attempted linkup with Virgil's group. I have no idea if it came off, and as you said, you don't either. Maybe there was bad blood between the two sides."

"I still find it hard to believe they even knew of each other."

"The link is clear. Jason Virgil killed by Emmett Hurtle. Afterward, large money is received by his girl Rhiannon who is seen with Dash, a confidant of Ritchie. Have you got that security footage from Union Station?"

"That takes time, dozens of cameras and dozens of hours to

check over. The wheels of justice turn slow around here."

That's because Uncle isn't in command. "Well, here's a thought … maybe Dash took some of the money and was punished."

"Not Ritchie's style to make a public statement like that. If Dash had stepped out of line, he would've just disappeared." Warren switched back to his earlier line of questioning like the cop he was. "Did he tell you about the meet with Eric Tanner?"

Zach hesitated but figured this information couldn't be contradicted. "Yes, he did. He was a walking encyclopedia if you knew how to play him."

"You saying he gave you a lot."

"Not as much as I wanted."

"He give you those images you brought to me?"

"Nice try, Warren, but I'm wide awake."

"So am I. I've been figuring out how you got to be interested in Ritchie in the first place, and those images keep coming back as the answer. I figure Ritchie sent them to you, and you found you weren't the hotshot reporter you thought; you were somebody's patsy instead."

Warren had nailed the right picture to the wall. All it took was thinking time, and even the obscured became obvious.

"Stay with that theory if you want," Zach said. "If it makes you feel warm inside."

"It does, the truth always does. A question. We got another body on our hands earlier. A one-time corner guy for Ritchie called Elon Washington. Found in a car junk yard. Neck snapped, no other injuries. You know this person?"

"No. I don't interview those kids; they wouldn't talk to me anytime."

"Who said he was a kid?" Warren sharp with the question.

"Give me a break, detective. I've never seen anyone over twenty-five working a corner, and neither have you." Zach saw his parking station ahead. "I'm about to go into a car park. You got any more questions right now?"

"Yeah. Where are the garments? This morning, the uncle said you took them."

"I didn't take them. He gave them to me because I asked nicely. We needed to photograph them. A good story needs good pictures. You can have them now."

"You ever think you might be removing evidence from a crime scene? Ever hear of the chain of custody?" Warren's voice was rising.

"Crime scene? It's not a crime to buy dresses. The price tags are still attached to most of them. You'll be able to link Hurtle's girl to the purchases."

"Can you not instruct me in police work? It irritates me so much, I don't feel like being polite to you anymore."

Zach took the down-ramp to the garage and stopped at the boom. "Sorry. I'm about lose the signal. You have a last question?"

"More than one, and I'm thinking that after Homicide spends a day on Dash's murder I'll have enough to bring you in for a longer chat than this."

"Just remember the First Amendment when you do."

"There's no such animal around here." Warren cut the connection.

He was losing it. Wouldn't normally say anything like that, not to a reporter, even if it was a one-on-one conversation and totally deniable.

Zach parked his car, remembered Keera sitting beside him that morning while he drove her to class. "You have to promise," he'd said to her as she made to get out, "you won't go home. You catch a cab to the *Post* and meet up with me." She nodded, but he made her say it aloud as if a promise was more binding that way.

They had spent the night locked together like it was their last time. If Keera knew something, she wasn't sharing, and in the morning she stayed quiet. Wouldn't discuss plans, not that any came to his mind.

Edwina was alone in her office when Zach stuck his head in the door. "I have a follow-up on the dresses. It involves the guy they pulled out of a dumpster this morning."

She leaned back in her chair. "You're a fast worker. Were you on this thing all night?"

More than you know. "Rhiannon told me that a Dash had gone shopping with her. That guy was found dead today."

"You didn't mention him in the story at all."

"I had to check it out. She was a bit, um, hazy at the time. Now there's a body, we got something to work on."

"The police know this?"

"They called already. I told them what I knew. Which means they'll let this fresh news slip to our rivals real soon."

"Okay, get on it." Edwina picked up the phone in a gesture of dismissal. Some people were so grateful for front page stories.

Back at his desk, Zach wrote of Rhiannon linked with an associate of Frankie Ritchie and then her subsequent disappearance. The body of the same associate being found in a dumpster the next day, the police not yet releasing his name. He wrote captions for the dresses' photographs. Noted that Jerry had made an effort, creating a white soft-focus background, bounce flash in use, and a model with a pixelated face. Debbie Krasnowski. Zach knew where all her income would go in the future.

He sent his piece to the copy editor's in-box, leaned back and stretched his arms. Nothing left to do but wait for the explosion called Frankie Ritchie.

He wasn't good at waiting; he lasted ten minutes. Scrabbled in his pockets for the card the Thai woman had given him. Called the number, recognized her voice when she answered. "Thai Style," she said.

"It's me again, Zach Bones, the guy with a stiff neck. Tell Ritchie to call me, okay? He's front-page news tomorrow if he doesn't."

"No Ritchie here," she said. "You have wrong number."

"He better be close, or you'll be on the front page instead. Found in a dumpster." He hung up. If that didn't get a response, he would drive over and wait at the restaurant until Ritchie showed.

There was no call back from Ritchie. No word from Keera either.

"You're twitchy today," Howard said.

"Trying to force an issue here," Zach replied, "but I don't know how it'll play out."

"You forcing it by wriggling around in your seat?"

"Waiting on a call, Howard, waiting on a call." Thought about that some more and knew he would have to confront Ritchie, not wait around like a supplicant. "You're right, it's not me. I'm going to back to the dragon's cave. I'll get results faster that way."

"Whoa, I didn't mean to suggest you put yourself in danger. Leave me a name and address at least."

"They put a bag over my head once, so I wouldn't know where I was. They might do that again." He rummaged in his jacket pocket, pulled out Warren's card. "Call this guy if I don't call you by the end of the day, tell him I went to interview Ritchie about his man Dash. He'll be interested." Handed over the Thai Style card. "Ritchie hangs here often. That's where I'm going now."

"May I remind you that this would be a good time to mind your manners when in the company of wolves?" Howard getting protective. "Be especially mindful of your speech. You know what you're like."

"Thanks for the tip."

He caught the elevator down, his mind working through his possible opening questions to Ritchie. Decided to grab a coffee made by craftsmen, not by gravity. Stepped off the curb to cross the street. A Cadillac Escalade stopped in front of him, and Melvin climbed out of the rear door.

He beckoned to Zach.

"Thought I'd get coffee first," Zach said. "Your boss offers insufficient hospitality every time I see him."

"Get your sorry ass in there, or I tear it off and make you wear it as a hat."

"Okay, but call Ritchie up and tell him to put on the coffeepot." He climbed inside, and Melvin took his position next to him. Tyrell up front driving. They entered the next parking garage.

"Ritchie moved closer to the Post, then?" Zach asked. "Wants to check the early editions as they come off the press?"

Melvin grunted a response, levered him away with an elbow, then slammed a fist into his kidney. The pain overwhelmed all his other senses. Zach sucked in air like it was an analgesic but it didn't help. The car stopped as Tyrell took a ticket, then descended the ramps until they came to a level with few parked cars and stopped.

Melvin dragged Zach out and propped him up on sagging legs. Removed his cell and wallet. Patted him down for a weapon. No one in any of the cars, nobody walking to or away from one. The trunk opened, and Melvin steered him to it. It already held an occupant.

Keera.

She blinked as she focused on him but said nothing. Didn't have to. The situation explained itself in milliseconds.

Melvin pushed him inside, against Keera, who gasped as she was forced back against the bodywork. Melvin folded Zach's legs, his hand movements as precise as a robot's. Arranged his arms across his chest.

"You two rest easy until we need you," Melvin said and slammed the lid; the compression of air deafened Zach for a moment.

"You okay?" he asked Keera. "How long you been in here?"

"I can't tell." She sounded calmer than he expected. "They grabbed me as I walked to the El. Took me to a parking garage, put me in here, no conversation. We waited a long time somewhere before the car moved again. Then you turned up."

Zach took it easy as instructed: breathed in and out, waited for the pain to subside, knowing he would pass blood for a few days. He tried to track time but couldn't concentrate. The

Caddy made too many turns to count after it emerged into the street. Guessed he was heading to the South Side. Where else?

"Do we have a plan?" she asked him.

"Staying alive is plan A."

"Plan B?"

"Dying quickly."

She shifted behind him, her thighs pressed against him. One of her arms was free, curled around him protectively. It was stupid he knew, but that made him feel braver.

"I thought you said we or, at least I, wouldn't be taken by them," he said.

"I must have muddled my impressions. Once I get too involved in desired outcomes I tend to interpret what I'm getting in a favorable light. I let my conscious wishes override my psychic input." She sighed heavily as if this was something she'd been running through her mind since she was shoved into the trunk.

"What do you think now?" he asked. "You getting any images?"

"Sure. I see two bodies."

CHAPTER 31

After a half hour or more, the Escalade slowed and descended. Zach guessed they'd entered a car park. When Melvin opened the trunk and pulled him out, his legs folded.

"You stay on the ground," Melvin said, "and my foot will find your other kidney."

That announcement worked better than adrenaline. His feet found steady ground, his knees locked in place, he hauled himself upright and leaned against the trunk.

Melvin grinned. "We have reached understanding."

Keera untangled her limbs and emerged. She stood up with only a slight sway, a tribute to her daily yoga routine.

Tyrell walked toward elevator doors, Melvin strolling behind, an arm around each captive's shoulders. The elevator rose eighteen floors, no stops, and they emerged into a carpeted corridor with shoulder-high Chinese vases guarding it at regular intervals. They held gravel and artificial flowers. No cigarette butts. Classy.

Tyrell knocked on an end door in a rhythmic pattern. Ritchie opened it and scowled at Zach. Said nothing until they were all inside.

"You fuckin' cockroach, Bones. Sorry I ever thought of you." Ritchie took up a position leaning back against a kitchen counter; Melvin pushed Zach and Keera onto a couch. Tossed Zach's cell, wallet and notebook on the counter in front of Ritchie. A large-screen television flickered on the opposite wall.

"Where's the girl's ID?" Ritchie asked as he reached for Zach's cell and turned it off. Glared at Tyrell.

"We left her bag in her car," Tyrell said.

Ritchie gave him a look, and he left the apartment.

"More fuckin' notebooks," Ritchie said, opening Zach's. "Get a man into trouble." He pointed at Zach. "When you see Dash last?"

"That's what the cops wanted to know."

"Answer my questions straight, or Melvin will remove your head."

"That'll cut the questioning short, won't it?" Figured the more confident he sounded, the more likely they would listen.

"The cops know you know Dash? How's that?"

He said know Dash. Hadn't got the news. "They saw us together once, by accident they said. Kept pestering me about it. They've got a heavy interest in you, in case you don't realize."

"You putting the dresses shit in the paper guaranteed that, Bones. That'll cost ya."

"I'm a reporter; I'm supposed to write stuff."

"Should've stuck to flower shows." Ritchie glanced over at Keera and back to Zach. "What you want to see me about?"

"The cops have vision of Dash with Rhiannon at Union Station. They have the link they need to tie you to Emmett Hurtle. You're fucked. Not today, not this week, but soon."

Ritchie gave with the bored look. "Dash is one with the ladies. It don't mean shit. That babe's a tasty morsel, I hear. How come you're so anxious to gimme this news? You worried about my safety?"

"There's more."

"Yeah?"

"Dash is selling you out."

Ritchie kept a straight face, but he blinked. "The boy's loyal."

"He contacted me several times. That your idea?"

"For what?"

"He never said. But he turns up so often, I've come to think I'm part of his plans."

"What plans?"

"Whatever he's setting up with Tanner."

The name exploded like a stun grenade. The following silence told him everything—they believed him.

Ritchie ripped his gaze away from Zach and leafed through his notebook, found the fresh entries. Pulled notebook-sized sheets out of his pocket, spread them out on the counter. "What's your cell number."

'The number next to a 'P'."

Ritchie scoured through the pages and stopped. "It's here. You had a code name?"

"Dash likes codes. Makes him feel clever, I guess. The 'P' stands for the *Post.* His first choice was a 'Z'."

Ritchie smacked his hand down on the loose pages. "The fuck. Stupid doesn't begin to describe his thinking."

The door opened, Tyrell came in, dropped Keera's bag and briefcase on the counter. Glanced at the television, said, "What's goin' on?"

They turned to the screen; Tyrell increased the volume. A blonde newsreader talked about a body found back of a take-out joint. Images of police tape around a yellow dumpster filled the screen. "Police say the young African-American man was wearing an Armani suit. He had been shot twice in the chest and once in the head. There was no identification on the body, which had been wrapped up in a ground sheet."

"Is that Dash?" Ritchie said. "No fuckin' way."

"Who else?" Tyrell said. "What other bro wears Armani? More usual to drop their pants down to they ass crack."

"Shit. Not Dash. I loved the kid. He was just starting out, could've gone a long way."

Ritchie's view of Dash had swung around now that he was dead. "Who did this?" Ritchie watched police cars parked around the crime scene, lights flashing, watched the ambulance drive away.

"Who was he going to meet? Rhiannon, then come back here?" Tyrell counted off on his fingers. "There was the call from Tanner. I told Dash. He might have called him back, or might've taken another call."

"Where they say he was found?"

"Over at Bronzeville. Not far from Rhiannon's."

"She got no beef." Ritchie stared at the television, adding up, multiplying, calculating to a conclusion. "Those fucks, they clipped Dash to tell us something."

"Weren't they gonna to do business with us?"

"Could've been a fake move, setting us up for an easy hit."

"Think they saw the news item on Rhiannon's dresses and figured something out?"

Ritchie turned away from the television, now showing a weather chart. "Nah, the timing's wrong. Dash musta got hit last night somewhere, before the story came out. Shit, I feel bad. I send the kid out to pick up the clothes and somebody whacks him."

Tyrell dropped the volume on the television, pointed the remote at Zach. "Bones. He's been sniffing around Rhiannon, tried to talk to you. Maybe he went off to talk to Virgil's men. Told them about the dresses to get a reaction."

"It's how they work all right. Give a little to get a little." Ritchie eyed Zach. "What do you say, Bones? You cause this?"

"Not my doing," he said. "I write about people getting shot; I don't shoot them myself."

"Not what I'm talking about. You see Virgil's team? Talk to them about me?"

Zach spread his hands. "I wouldn't even know how to find them. And, seeing as how that photograph got me involved in Virgil's death, I'm guessing they wouldn't appreciate me coming around to say hi."

"You see Dash yesterday?" Ritchie not buying his story yet.

"I didn't get the pleasure."

"You wrote about those fuckin' dresses. Where they now?"

"Take a guess. I'd say they're locked up in the evidence room." Almost true. If not now, it'd be true in an hour or two.

"What about Rhiannon? You see her yesterday?"

"Unfortunately no. She's a lot easier on the eye than Dash."

Ritchie was less interested in the answers that he should have been. Like he'd made his mind up already.

Tyrell said, "What about the Disciples? Weren't they looking for Dash?"

Made Ritchie think for a second. "It's not likely they'd clip one of my guys. Some physical shit, yeah, but a gun? They doing fine out of us, they wouldn't do Dash. They'd talk to me."

Tyrell was eager for action. "What do we do then? Hit Tanner? He must've had a hand in this."

Ritchie ran a hand over his hair. "Like I said before, I don't want a war. We better be sure what happened. Let's see if Dash got to Rhiannon's last night. That old guy she lives with, the weed puller, he might know shit. Melvin can hassle him until he's believable."

Tyrell waited, and Ritchie spoke again. "If Tanner was part of it, he would've called us to say it wasn't him, shit like that."

"Makes sense. You think it's not his people?"

"Don't know for sure yet. We'll get Tanner in, listen to his story, shake it up and see what pops out. It just doesn't figure they'd move on Dash at this time. We weren't laying heavy shit on them, terms had been agreed."

"The groundsheet," Tyrell said. "Makes it a calculated hit, not some holdup going bad."

"Yeah, that's what's throwing me. You get over there later, bring back useful news."

"You're missing the obvious," Zach said. Behind the couch, Melvin tapped sharp knuckles on his head. A reminder not to speak unless spoken to.

"Whatchu mean?" Ritchie asked.

"The cops will figure you've got the best motive for wiping

Dash out. He was endangering your operation. Letting Rhiannon throw the money around, showing everybody she'd come into a heap of it."

He eased his body into different positions to stop the ache in his lower back, but nothing worked. Felt Keera's hand rest there. Thoughtful of her, trying to soothe the pain. The biggest problem, which she couldn't do anything about: Ritchie and his thugs were talking too freely. Not caring what he and Keera heard. He didn't like where that thought took him.

Ritchie reached into the fridge for a beer. "Oh, I might have done him if what you say is true, but I woulda had a conversation first. And a shorter one with you." He twisted the top off a Heineken and stopped drinking when the bottle was empty. "We come back to my question: when did you see Dash last?"

"A couple of days ago."

"He come to you?"

"He did. Came to warn me off talking to Rhiannon."

"How would he know you gonna do that?"

"I called him, asked if it was true that Rhiannon had a lot of money all of a sudden."

"You had his number?"

"Sure. He gave it to me, the second time we met … you know, when I was blindfolded."

Ritchie worked through the new information until he came to a new question. "How'd you know about any money?"

"I didn't. I guessed there might've been a payoff. When Dash showed up, he confirmed it."

Ritchie grunted something and pulled a bag of Doritos out of a cupboard. "What's your angle on this? I don't see you trying something on me here."

"I want out of your life, is what I want. You leave Keera and me be, forever."

"In exchange?"

"I stay quiet."

Ritchie grunted again. "You're going to stay quiet no matter what. You've caused too much trouble already. Your girlfriend can fuckin' join you."

"Join me where?"

"Wherever the fuck Virgil's hanging out."

Keera watched with suppressed anger as Ritchie picked up her bag and briefcase, tipped the bag upside down on the counter and scanned the pile. He checked her cell was off and pushed the rest of the contents around with one finger: her pocket-book, coins, a notepad, pack of tissues, lipstick, store receipts. Her life spilled out like scattered garbage.

He opened the briefcase and pulled out a couple of files. "You the intellectual one of the team?" he asked her. "Don't answer that. Gotta be. Your boyfriend couldn't cut it in a carwash."

He checked a folder inside. "What's this about? 'Explain how the food-gathering techniques of the Incas were dictated by climate, terrain and their technology?' You asking your students how they ate? Shit, I can tell ya. They grabbed fruit off a tree and pushed it in their faces."

"The Incas were more organized than that," she said. "They built canals and irrigated crops. You want to know more, you can come to my lectures."

Ritchie snapped the folder shut, shoved it back into the brief-case.

"Don't need to, lady. Got all the food-gathering techniques I need." He pulled a chip out of the packet. "So, we remove you from our lives and get back to making a living."

"We have insurance," Zach said. "My files go to the police if I don't come back."

"Insurance, eh?" Ritchie waved the chip around dismissively. "I'll take my chances. You know shit, and your chief witness is dead."

"What about Virgil?"

"Virgil?" Ritchie at the fridge. "He been bothering you?"

"I heard he was bothering you. I heard Emmett too frightened to sleep, claimed Virgil was tormenting him. Looks like he tormented him to death."

"You seen Virgil?"

"I've seen what he can do. Made a junkyard of my place. Heard he messed around with you guys, too." He didn't mention the chocolate shake. Keera knew it sounded demeaning any way he told it.

"Ain't no ghost worry me," Ritchie said. "He can lock and unlock doors all he wants, drop pretty pictures on the floor, even. He a nuisance like a moth's a nuisance."

Ritchie had no idea what a truly angry Virgil could do.

"Been dangled out of a high window, had a cocked gun jammed in my nuts, that was fear." Ritchie making his position clear. "This is nothing. Gonna fetch me one of those voodoo women to put the frighteners on him. He'll go. Us humans can continue our busy lives again."

"Humans," Keera said. "I don't rate you that high."

"We could swap opinions all day," Ritchie said, "but I got a situation to take care of." He turned to Melvin and Tyrell. "Take these cuties to the Iron Man."

Melvin pulled Zach upright and marched him to the door. As Tyrell turned to Keera, the couch moved, then shook. She came off it fast.

A sudden chill. A presence.

Virgil.

He wasn't waiting and watching, either. The couch shimmied and shivered, leather and steel dancing to his commands.

"What the fuck?" Ritchie tilted his head, trying to see behind it. Nothing there.

The couch slid across the room until it bumped the full-length window at knee height. The glass flexed but didn't crack.

"That Virgil here now?" Ritchie asking anybody.

Nobody answered, all eyes fixed on the couch. It slid back across the room, rucking the rug hard against the door. No fast way out for anybody.

"Yo, Virgil," Ritchie called, looking around. "You wanna make decorative changes, go right ahead. Let's see what taste you got."

Melvin moved to kick the couch away from the door. It reared up and crashed down on his foot. The steel leg splintered Melvin's bones.

He screamed and staggered back, releasing Zach and falling to the floor. The couch leaped forward to finish off its wounded prey. It plunged the leg into Melvin's skull, cracking it open far enough to spill brain matter. Melvin twitched once, twice, before the nervous system collapsed and the muscles sagged in death.

Keera pulled Zach to her as the room regained its warmth. Virgil was gone. For now. He'd gained much more power; he was done with throwing cups and saucers.

She said to Ritchie, "You still think you can scare Virgil off?"

He didn't answer. Nothing in his life could have prepared him for this. He clutched the counter, his dazed face shifting from Melvin and the blood and brains seeping out of his head, to Tyrell standing frozen.

"Tyrell," he said after a while. "We got a change of plans."

CHAPTER 32

A change of plans didn't amount to much, Zach realized. Only that Melvin's body was swapped for theirs. It seemed that anybody wanting to set up an illegal drug distribution network ought to invest in a funeral parlor to increase their profits.

Tyrell closed his cell.

"Van's coming, twenty minutes, meeting us in the loading area," he said to Ritchie.

Ritchie put his beer down. "Here's what's going down, newspaper man. You and Tyrell roll up Melvin in that nice rug. Take it to the basement, stick it in the van. You do what Tyrell says. Your girlfriend, she stays here. Tyrell tells me your report card isn't too hot, you were uncooperative or some such shit, I get to slap your bitch around until she can't stand up. Got it?"

"You touch her," Zach said, "and my behavior will get much more than uncooperative." Letting him know it was two against two now. A whole new problem. Maybe.

"Whatever. Her condition depends on your attitude. That's all you need to know." Ritchie's equilibrium restored: he was giving out orders, taking charge.

He helped Tyrell drag Melvin's body into the end of the rug

and roll it up. Keera back on the couch, sitting as if waiting for room service. Cooler than any cucumber. Did this mean she knew the day would finish on a happy note? Or was trying to keep his spirits up until the last second Ritchie snuffed out their final spark?

"Ready, one, two, three," Tyrell said, and they hoisted Melvin and his rug onto their shoulders. Tyrell with the heavy end, the head and the massive shoulders.

Ritchie opened the door, took a quick peek along the hall. "It's good."

Tyrell and Zach carried the carpet to the elevator and stopped, the carpet sagging in the middle. Tyrell hoisted his end higher on his shoulder after he pressed the down button. Something moved inside the carpet.

Toward Zach's end.

Better not be a piece of brain, I'll throw up.

It was solid; he could feel its heft through the weave.

The elevator doors slid open, and Tyrell led them inside. They shuffled around to fit in Melvin and the carpet.

While Tyrell reached for the buttons, Zach freed a hand and groped for the sliding object. His fingers closed on metal: Melvin's gun. If ever there was a message from above, this was it. Whatever Keera said, he was going to use this. There was no other way. The next life might be fine for her; she'd seen plenty of it. For him, this life was fine. Without Ritchie.

The elevator stopped a couple of floors down.

"The fuck?" Tyrell unhappy.

The parting doors revealed a lone woman waiting. Past middle age and weighing up the options in front of her.

"You best take the next one, lady," Tyrell said to her. "There's been an accident on this carpet, don't smell good in here."

Zach slipped the gun into his jeans back pocket. Hoped his jacket would conceal it.

"Thank you, young man," the woman said, clearly relieved of a decision. "I'll wait, as you suggest."

Tyrell didn't speak again until they reached the loading area of the basement. A dirty white van waited. No business name, no cute slogan painted on the side. Two bros stood alongside it, both sweating and jittery. One of them opened the rear doors. Zach and Tyrell dropped the carpet inside, slammed the doors behind it.

"You know where to take this?" Tyrell asked them.

One of them nodded.

"Don't keep the carpet either, is all I'm saying. Hand everything over to the Iron Man. No souvenirs. You don't, your asses is gonna be flaming instead."

The other one nodded, more convincingly than the first one.

"Next I see you, I'll have a bunch of pipes ready, okay?"

They scrambled into the cab and drove up the exit ramp.

"They going to burn it?" Zach asked as they waited for the elevator.

"More than burn it, man." Tyrell was watching the elevator lights edge downwards. "Iron Man is a specialist. Got a metal workshop, furnace going all day. When the body is only a bunch of ashes, he takes a hammer and smashes any bone parts to crumbs. No ID left, no DNA either. Adds some other shit and sells it off as garden fertilizer."

"This a steady business for him?"

Tyrell cocked his head. "Why don't you ask him yourself? Oh, I forgot, you be dead and all by then."

"Yeah, right. And you'll be explaining to the cops why you brought the two of us here after we disappeared. Why you and me carried a rug to the basement and gave it to a couple of kids, their license plate visible to the security cameras. You always do your dirty stuff in front of an audience?"

The elevator arrived empty.

"Cameras?" Tyrell hit the button for their floor. "Those things that get switched off every time Ritchie arrives here? Hmm. Must check with the concierge that he's doing what he paid for."

"All the cameras?" The fuckers were ahead of him.

"Just the right ones."

The rest of the ride was silent until Tyrell said, "I think you know who done Dash."

"Sorry, I don't," Zach replied. "I'm not in the killing business, hardly know anyone in that line. Reckon you'd be a lot closer to a bunch of killers than I am. Ask them."

"We will, we will." Tyrell jerked his chin upward. "Think that was Virgil before?"

Zach said, "Looked like his work. He did the same shit to my apartment. Left the furniture all over and upside down, jumbled up. I wasn't there at the time. I guess it was a warning."

"Think he'll come back?"

"I get the unmistakable feeling he wants all of you on the dead side."

"What about you?"

"Pretty sure he wants me there, too," Zach said. This was a no lie. Virgil, so far targeting only Ritchie and his crowd. Saving a pesky reporter for last.

"You don't look worried."

"I have the gift of the gab, figure I can talk my way out of it."

The elevator stopped. "What you have," Tyrell said, "is not a gift."

Keera was still on the couch when they returned, her demeanor telling him she wasn't worried, either—yet. Giving off the air of an anthropologist who had stumbled on a fascinating branch of the human race.

"All good?" Ritchie asked Tyrell.

"Sweet."

Ritchie swept a glance over Zach and Keera and back to Tyrell. Zach knew what that meant. What do we do with these two now? Didn't need psychic powers for this. It was a good time to take the initiative, give Ritchie stuff to think about, hope he'd make the wrong call. He wondered if the safety on the gun was on or off. Made a note to check, the first instant he drew it out. If he had time.

"So, Frankie," Zach said. "What's next? Got a fresh plan?"

"Leave the planning to me," Ritchie replied. "You just practice any prayers you haven't used since Sunday School."

"Your ideas haven't worked out too good if you don't mind me saying so. Let's listen to one of mine. We walk out of here and forget about you. You disappear forever."

Ritchie cocked his head as though he hadn't heard right. "You saying I take your word that you stay quiet, not write about me no more?" He felt behind him for his beer. "I could make sure of it, not rely on your nice nature."

"It'll be easy if you're not around. No bad guy, no bad guy story."

"No reporter, no bad guy story either."

Zach switched tactics. "What are you going to do about Virgil? You saw what he did to Melvin, and he hates you even more."

Tyrell said. "He don't like you a lot either, from what you said."

Ritchie said to him. "He tell you this, when?"

"Just now, coming back."

Ritchie said to Zach, "What did Virgil do to you?"

Zach waved his hand around the room. "Moved stuff. Stacked furniture and shit. Didn't attack, not like here. I passed the news onto Dash. He not tell you?"

Ritchie's face said: no, the fucker didn't.

Zach lost interest in talking. Adrenaline and anger within flamed up, his heart rate jumped a million notches, and his breathing grew ragged and jumpy. His legs lost sureness, and a fog descended, leaving him barely aware of his surroundings. Only Ritchie remained in strong focus.

Keera jumped up. Agitated.

"You feeling poorly?" Ritchie asked. "You want a calming pill? A knock on the head I can do for free, give you something new to think about—"

"I want you," Zach heard someone say. His voice, but guttural and croaky. He drew Melvin's gun from his back pocket, his arm heavy as a steel beam and Novocain numb.

"Shit," Ritchie said, fumbled around his waist.

Zach, his hand quivering, raised his weapon, thumbed the

safety off like he'd done it a million times before and fired. The blast shocked him. Not him, he didn't do this, somebody else.

"No!" Keera coming at him.

Ritchie slid down the counter, one side of his face bloody, some of it missing; his eyes dulled as he completed the descent to a motionless heap on the floor.

Zach's gun hand swung to Tyrell, who hadn't moved, his face a stupefied mask.

"No," Keera shouted. "Go, go from here. You do not belong."

His finger tightened on the trigger, not his, somebody else's. Somebody using his body. He fought back, tried to drop the gun. A cold shroud gripped him, squeezed him.

"Get out!" She struck him on the shoulder.

He felt the muffled thud of it. Her voice a million miles away. The fog in his head lessened. His limbs regained feeling, regained their strength. The cold withdrew, the anger within dissipated.

"Get out of Zach," she shouted, striking him again and again. "Get out, now!"

Each impact stronger than the one before. Why was she shouting at him? The tightness in his throat vanished, his heart slowed, and he looked at the gun still in his hand.

"Go, Virgil," Keera said, more quietly but still insistent. "Go away from here."

Ritchie on the floor.

Tyrell reached for something behind him, and Zach raised the gun again. Instinctively. Tyrell dropped his hand back, in front of him, where everybody could see it.

"No call for that," Tyrell said.

300

Zach had no quick answer; he struggled to make sense of himself. What was going on? He knew one thing: Tyrell was armed and ready to pull his gun.

"No call for Ritchie to order our deaths either," he said, slowly, having to take his time, put the words in the right order. "When you've got nothing, you've got nothing to lose."

"Who that poet?" Tyrell asked. "Must look him up. He writes stuff easy to remember."

Zach stared at the gun in his hand. "I don't remember grabbing this."

"It was Virgil," Keera said, her arm around him. "He channeled into you, caught you by surprise. I should've guessed it sooner, done something."

Zach contemplated Ritchie. "Good outcome, though."

"You think?" she said, astonished. "You've murdered somebody. Virgil got you to do his work."

He lacked sharpness, fuzzy all over, his mind reeling, wheeling while it sorted the facts from the fantastical. He'd shot and killed Ritchie. The murder weapon still in his hand. Tyrell's hand creeping towards his own weapon again.

Zach raised the gun at Tyrell, who again lowered his hand. "You face the wall with your hands high up." The first time he'd held a gun on a person, and he felt the power it brought. Transformed a man into a giant. Understood why others got so addicted to this.

"You gonna shoot me in the back?"

"I didn't shoot anybody." Zach removed Tyrell's gun from the guy's waistband and jammed into his back pocket. "You heard the lady; it was Virgil."

"Yeah, sure it was."

"Believe what you want but here's the thing: it's time to write a nice story that everyone wants to believe."

"Means what?"

"Means shut the fuck up, listen and you might, just might, avoid major jail time."

◆ ◆ ◆

Zach knelt next to Ritchie's body. Ran his hands around the massive waist and thighs. His fingers touched metal in the waistband, and he lifted the shirt. The glossy wooden butt of a small-caliber revolver showed.

"I still feel weird," he said to Keera. "But we can't waste time. We have to do some editing."

"You what?" Tyrell asked.

Zach stood and pulled open the kitchen cupboard doors with the outside of his thumb, avoiding any fingerprint problems later. Under the sink, he found what he wanted next to the bottles of dish detergent: a half-empty pack of latex gloves left by the cleaners. He pulled out two and slipped them on. Knelt down beside Ritchie, removed his gun and shoved it partway into Ritchie's right hand, smearing dead fingers over his own prints. The unresponsive fingers making his stomach turn.

Tyrell looked over his shoulder. "Realistic as shit. You should get a job arranging store window displays."

"What are you doing, Zach?" Keera asked.

"I'm organizing the narrative. Here's what's happened: Ritchie shot Melvin after an argument and made me and Tyrell take the body to the basement. I found Melvin's gun in the carpet and on my return, I pulled it out to secure our release."

Tyrell said, "That where you got the gun—?"

"Don't interrupt a good story; it makes the narrator angry. And believe me, I'm highly stressed right now." He stopped to gather his thoughts again. "Ritchie didn't believe I'd shoot and drew his gun. I fired in self-defense, I had no choice."

Keera said, "What did Ritchie and Melvin argue about?" Getting into it. Understanding the need for a clear and believable storyline.

Zach looked at Tyrell, who said, "Your story, man. Make up your own details."

"I can change it. I can say you shot Melvin."

Tyrell lowered his hands, turned around and folded his arms. "Melvin made Frankie mad when he knocked Dash around one night."

"I saw Dash's face; that was Melvin's work?"

"May I continue?" Tyrell said, getting all huffy. "Frankie asked if Melvin followed up by finishing Dash off and dumping his body like we saw on TV. Melvin was downright unconvincing when Frankie asked him about it. Like he didn't care what Frankie thought. Frankie, he's been strange since Dash was found. Musta crossed some line in his head, know what I mean. Pulled out that dinky thing and did Melvin. How's that?" Tyrell cocked his head like he was waiting for applause.

"You showing creative talent there, Tyrell. Look me up when you get released. Just joking. You sure this little gun could kill a big man like Melvin. With one shot?"

"Through the eye."

"Yuuck," Keera said.

"Frankie loved that li'l ol' twenty-two peashooter." Tyrell getting sentimental. "Said it came with a lifetime warranty."

"We all admire a man who knows value when he sees it," Zach said. "That's the way to go: one shot, one lucky shot through the eye."

Tyrell looked left and right, came to the point. "You tell 'em I tried to stop Frankie, right? Didn't want no deaths."

"Didn't see you protesting when you got told to take us to a concrete mixer."

"Told him not to snatch you and your girl in the first place."

"You didn't have much influence, did you?"

"There gotta be something in this for me, you know what I mean?" Tyrell was half pleading, half threatening.

"I hear you." Zach glanced at Keera, back to Tyrell. "Which part of the story do you want me to rewrite?"

"Like, say I was all the time trying to stop him hurting you. Against the whole thing."

"Words, Tyrell, I need actual words. Otherwise, what you say to the authorities won't match what I say I heard you say."

"I'm down with that. Gimme a second."

Zach said to Keera, "Looks like we've got ourselves sorted out. You have anything to add?"

"Won't the police sniff Ritchie's gun to see if it's been fired? They do that in the movies."

"Shit. Of course. And gunshot residue on his fingers." He looked around the room, a knee-high round tub in a corner. A fat, bulbous vase of a thing with a waxy fern stuck out of it. He went over and tilted it. Heavy, full of packed earth. Wet earth. Rolled it on its rim right up to Ritchie.

Tipped it over carefully on its side, the planter resting at around thirty degrees and pointing at Ritchie. The soil stayed put, too compacted to move. He lifted Ritchie's gun hand, holding the gun in place, worked his fingers under Ritchie's so the residue would leave a normal pattern. He fired into the earth. The smaller caliber produced a sharp crack compared to the boom of Melvin's gun. A handful of potting mix spattered loose, but no bullet emerged from the base of the planter.

"It couldn't have penetrated far," Zach said and plunged his hand into the mix. The spent bullet wasn't six inches in. He retrieved it and placed it in the sink. He rolled the tub back, rummaged under the kitchen sink, found a dustpan and brush, swept up the scattered dirt and tipped it back into the tub. "Any other loose ends?" he asked.

"You're suspiciously adept at this," Keera said. "I wonder where you learned such things."

"I mix with some of the interesting minds in the world," he said, stripping off the gloves. "We compare notes." He dropped the gloves into the sink. Reached for the disposal switch.

"Don't," Keera said.

"Don't what?"

"I tried that once, and the gloves just jammed up the unit."

"I got it," Tyrell said. "How about I say, 'Frankie said, Tyrell, you go out and lose them in some concrete,' and I said, 'No Frankie, it ain't right.' And he gets mad and draws his little toy, and you draw this gun from nowhere and blam, blam. That's all I have to remember, 'No Frankie, it ain't right.'" He nodded, satisfied. "Don't want to make it complicated. What do you think?"

"There was only one blam."

"Okay, I got it."

"What happened after that blam?'

"Your girl, she was yelling at Virgil—"

"No, dammit, leave all that out. There is no Virgil. After I shot Ritchie, I held the gun on you and called the cops. We never spoke after that. Got it?"

"Okay, I got it good, now."

Keera said, "Is anybody going to clean up the couch leg?"

"Jesus. I forgot about that." Zach grabbed more gloves, ripped several squares of paper towel from a dispenser on the kitchen wall and crouched beside the couch. Wiped everything he could think of. Threw his gloves and paper into the sink to join the first gloves.

"There's no reason for them to look at the couch leg. They'll figure all the stuff that came out of Melvin stayed on the rug we took out."

"Please," Keera said. "Enough of the details." She came over to the sink and removed the bullet, gloves and paper shreds. Took them to the bathroom where a toilet flushed.

"You dumped the bullet down the toilet?" Zach asked her when she returned. "It won't flush; it's too heavy."

"The bullet, wiped clean, went out the window to the alley below," she said. "The rest disappeared down the toilet."

"You're getting good at this."

"I see no other way." She didn't look pleased.

Zach to Tyrell. "You good now? Remember, the more details you provide, the more they have to trip you up with."

"I'm fly with that," Tyrell said. Waited a couple of beats. "This is what I'm doing for you, what are you doing for me?"

"I never saw you before today. I know nothing about you except that you are a kind, caring person who tried to stop Ritchie killing us."

"Sounds good. Sounds like me."

"You nail Ritchie for organizing Virgil's death, the cops will like you a little. You say Melvin killed Dash; they'll love you lots more. You'll be helping them clear their cases." He remembered Warren's last call. "You know a kid called Elon?"

Tyrell said nothing.

"He was found dead in a junkyard. If you know who did it, the cops will be nicer to you."

Keera said to Tyrell, "You're still a worm, though. Always."

Tyrell stared out the window at the gray waters of Lake Michigan. "You forgot something. The gunshots. Somebody's gonna report them."

Keera said. "They won't." She pointed to each wall of the apartment. "That way is the Lake; over there is the alley. Against that wall is the fire stairs and the woman who lives on the other side isn't home."

"How you know about the woman?" Tyrell acting suspicious about this new information.

"I just do."

"That's good enough for me," Zach said. He picked his cell off the counter and switched it on.

"Detective Warren?" he said. "Have I got news for you."

CHAPTER 33

Keera waited in the CPD reception for Zach. Close to midnight, he joined her, his aura perky as a sunbeam.

"How did it go?" she asked as they held each other.

"Fine. Let's not talk here."

They stepped outside and Zach hailed a cab.

"Where to?" the cabbie asked, sticking his head out the window. "I hope you're gonna say someplace north. That's home, and that's where I should be."

His neck chain carried a gold crucifix and a Star of David. Somebody was backing up his Christianity with an extra touch of Judaism. Keera caught a sharp vision of a woman and two sub-teen daughters eating at a table for four. An empty chair completed the group. She picked up an ache in his heart: he had worked late, had missed his family meal.

"Old Town," she said.

"Best two words I've heard all night," the cabbie responded. "Been waiting for a fare to take me home for hours."

"A win-win, how good is that?" Zach said as he climbed in behind Keera.

The cabbie twisted around in his seat. "You again? Another

press conference? This time of night?"

"And you again?" he said. "Still playing two religions at once, like they were Vegas slots?"

"Sure. You done a bad thing to be in the copshop this late?"

"No, I was helping the police with their inquiries. Took longer than expected."

"Never neglect your sleep, young fella," the cabbie said. "Look at me, hardly seen my wife and kids since I took this shift. Never see them. I'm sleeping when I'm home, and when they around I'm off to work."

"You should change shifts," Zach said.

"Yep, yep, but I told the boss I'd stick it out for three months. I always do what I say. I'm like that."

"Good to hear."

The driver, shielded from them by the closed glass partition between front and back seats, pulled away.

Zach took Keera's hand. "I'm glad you waited."

"You think I'm going to leave you alone after all that?" she said. "I had no idea you were open enough to get channeled so easily." Could Virgil return and take control of Zach again? Please, no.

"I didn't either. What do I do if he comes back?"

Good question. "You resist, Zach, you resist. Tell him to get out of you, to go. Be firm."

"Be firm? I'll be more than firm;, I'll be downright unmannerly about it." His breeziness was intact, a good sign. The experience hadn't shaken him too much.

"I hope so. What took so long, anyway? I was done in just over two hours. You stayed with Detective Warren for three."

"Warren made me account for nearly every minute of my time after I left the *Post* building. He was methodical, careful to reconstruct the scene. It's the way they work. Once the situation is clarified, it's easier to spot the strange stuff. The stuff that doesn't make sense and makes them come and collect me for more questioning."

"You think he saw holes in your story?"

"He shouldn't be able to. Not right away. It's the forensics guys who are more likely to find something that doesn't fit."

"What's the chance of that?"

"Who knows?" Zach jerked his chin at the closed glass partition, not wanting to talk further.

But she knew what he was thinking. His version and the real thing differed mostly in the interpretation. Nobody would believe Melvin died at Virgil's hands; that made Ritchie the natural suspect, with Zach and Tyrell corroborating.

That left only the worst problem—Virgil himself.

She settled back in the seat and asked Bardo if Virgil was gone now. Silly question.

Of course not. His power is greatly enhanced. He will not stay his hand, as they say.

Do we have a chance against him?

Yes.

If I fail?

The struggle continues on the other side.

The answer rocked her. He was saying that she might die and be forced to renew the fight against Virgil in the next life.

What about Zach?

Please be more precise.

Will Zach die?

This answer was worse than the previous one.

If he dies, he will be chained to Virgil until you defeat him.

Holy God. When will Virgil appear again?

He's already here.

The cabbie rocked back and forth, clutching the wheel, looking like he was trying to shake off some internal demon. When he turned to look back at them, she knew why.

He wasn't driving.

Virgil was.

She shouted. "Virgil's taken over the cabbie."

Zach leaped at the partition, scrabbling, straining to open the slider wider. It didn't move. There was no way to reach the handle.

The cab lurched away from the curb, speeding up, the driver twisting wildly as he fought for the controls with a force he couldn't identify. Virgil was winning. The cab shot across the center line and barreled down the wrong side of the road.

Midnight, the traffic sparse but not completely gone. Distant headlights approaching, the drivers unlikely to react quickly to a crazy cab coming right at them.

I never expected to die like this, she said to herself.

The cab drifted farther left as if lining up one particular set of headlights.

"Jesus, no," Zach said.

A flatbed truck ahead, backing out of a driveway into their lane. Virgil and the cabbie gripped the wheel in a mad struggle. The cab veered away from the flatbed milliseconds before the collision that would have decapitated them all. It sideswiped an oncoming car and spun out. Tires squealing. Keera tensed for a bone-breaking impact.

The cab spun once, twice, then skidded to a rocking halt.

Zach threw himself across her and wrenched her door open.

"Out, out," he shouted, pushing her, not giving her time to think. She tumbled to the ground, the tarmac scraping her hands, Zach falling on top of her. The cab was moving again. Zach on his feet first, dragged her upright and pulled her to the curb.

The cab, its rear door open, attempted to circle, but more cars pulled up, hemming it in. It reversed a few yards, stopped again.

The driver slumped over the wheel.

Virgil had abandoned his body.

A babble of voices grew louder as drivers emerged from cars and gathered around. "What the fuck happened?" one accusatory voice asked Zach.

"It was horrible," he said. "I think the driver had a seizure. Nobody hurt, I hope."

A damaged car door opened in squealing protest. "Damn cabbies," another voice shouted. "He was fucking crazy." This from the guy who was sideswiped. "Can't believe I'm alive."

Keera's cargo pants were ripped at one knee. She wiped the dirt off her palms and inspected the grazes. Nothing a splash of antiseptic couldn't fix.

She needed something stronger for Virgil.

A distant howl of sirens, a cluster of flashing blue and red lights reflected off store windows, drawing closer. The cab's driver door was open, but the driver hadn't moved. The way the crowd stayed back, not helping, told her he was dead. Must have hit his head somehow. Zach with them, probably taking mental notes for a later write-up if required. She scanned the area to see if the cabbie had remained on the scene. A quick, violent death often resulted in souls staying around, not understanding they were dead.

He was one of those.

Standing on the other side of the road, still a cabbie, gazing at the damaged car, looking around for something. Or someone.

He found him.

The cabbie strode across the road not yet knowing he could simply think himself to his destination. He shouted at an onlooker.

It was no onlooker.

Virgil. Blending in like a preppy passerby, but not fooling the cabbie.

"You took me out of my life," he yelled at Virgil.

Virgil sneered at the cabbie. "What kind of life you call that? You were just a cabbie."

"I had a life, a family, wife and two beautiful daughters. And now we're split up." His auric energy pulsed a violent black and red, the colors of anger.

"Get yourself a soapbox, find yourself a crowd. I'm not listening." Virgil fixed on her, was about to say something.

The cabbie flew at him like a lightning bolt. Passed through in a snap-crackle of electric energy. Stopped on the other side and turned around again. Virgil faced him, obviously surprised at encountering a force as strong as this.

The cabbie attacked again. The collision was more violent this time, the energy exchange whip-crack loud.

Virgil vanished and reappeared ten yards away. "Maybe you ought to find a warm, sleepy lagoon, lie down and relax," he said to the cabbie. "Chill. Find out how sweet life is on this side."

The cabbie wasn't chilling. She saw he was deliberately stoking his anger, not wanting to stop, giving into his rage in front of him, the callous cause of his death.

"I'm not going anywhere," he said. He launched himself at Virgil again, but Virgil vanished. The cabbie spotted her staring right at him.

"You see me?" he asked. Puzzled but not frightened.

"Yes," she said, silently. "And I'm truly sorry to get you involved in this. He was after us, not you."

"He was a devil's child. I knew it as soon as he pushed into me. He was too strong, laughed when I prayed." He watched the paramedics lifting his body out of the cab. "Can you get a word to my wife and kids?" he asked her.

"I can't," she said. "I won't be treated warmly if I arrive and say I have a message from a dead husband. She'll throw me out. Wait until your wife sees a good medium."

"She'll never do that, not the type." He thought for a second. "Tell her you heard my dying words. That I said I loved her, and our children, and that I'll look after them for the rest of their lives. How's that sound?"

"It sounds fine." Unexpected tears prickled. "I'll pass your words on."

Zach walked back to her as a couple of patrol cars arrived.

"The cabbie's dead. Looks like he's sleeping but the medics couldn't find a pulse." He searched her face. "You need any treatment?"

"The scratches I've got," she said, "I can treat myself." She scanned Zach, saw his aura was thin, his energy down to it's lowest levels but not totally extinguished. His ingrained persistence was working to carry him through his worst nightmares.

"You see Virgil?" Zach said. "He still about? Shit, he's so fucking inventive when it comes to killing people."

"He's gone. He just made his first mistake."

"How so?"

"He killed the cab driver: not you or me."

"Collateral damage, I suppose, the poor guy." Zach not getting that Virgil would have known the cabbie would likely die.

"He's still here."

"Oh, like in spirit?"

"Yes, and he's not happy."

Her earlier vision came back to her. The family and the empty chair. The vision wasn't of the cabbie's present, as she'd assumed, it was of the future. That chair would always be empty.

"Does he understand what happened?" Zach asked.

"He knows what Virgil did and he's angry; attacked him while I watched."

"You're kidding. You know what this means?" He lit up, his aura pulsing with joy.

"That Virgil makes enemies regularly?"

"And his enemies could become our friends." He grew even more animated.

"Ritchie didn't."

"The cabbie might."

Where was he going with this?

"I know what he means." The cabbie burst in on her thoughts. "He wants me to keep chasing that demon."

Keera asked Zach, "You think this poor man can keep Virgil away from us? You want to drag him into our conflict?"

"It'd change everything," Zach said. "Why don't you ask nicely?"

"What conflict?" the cabbie asked.

"Virgil, the spirit that took over your body, is trying to kill us," she explained. "You were an innocent bystander, an accident."

"The hell I was, he used me. I want the bastard, so tell me what to do."

"What are you thinking?" Zach asked her.

"Wait a minute, our driver is asking questions."

"How do I find that devil again?" The cabbie was jiggling with impatience. "He's not getting away with this shit."

She was trembling, the delayed shock of the car chase and crash setting in. It felt wrong to involve the dead cabbie like this, but he would figure out how to find Virgil soon enough, without her help. And Zach was right. Virgil would be far less a problem to them if he were continually pursued by the cabbie.

"You simply think of him," she said, "and you're taken to him. Be careful, he's relentless when he's after something."

"So am I, lady," the cabbie said, "so am I." He folded his arms and furrowed his brow.

"You don't need to try so hard. Let his image float in your mind and ask to be taken there."

"Ask who?"

"Your guide. He'll show himself soon."

The cabbie relaxed and, still looking at her, faded away.

Keera linked her arm with Zach's, and her trembling stopped.

"So," Zach said. "Are we reaching some deal here?'"

"He's gone. I didn't need to convince him; he was desperate to find Virgil."

The medics closed the rear ambulance doors and drove away. No flashing lights, no siren, no rushing for a dead man.

Zach asked, "You think he'll keep after Virgil?"

"He's very motivated, isn't he? I guess he won't stop for ages."

"How long have we got?"

"Quite a while. Time doesn't exist where they are."

"Which means what?"

It means we're free of him she realized. Virgil's power had grown immensely in a short time; it was evident that he would have made life unbearable for Zach. Worse than unbearable—totally unlivable. Virgil had come so close to killing; he wouldn't fail next time.

But tonight's callous act had linked him irretrievably to the angry cabbie—a bond he'd never escape. His time in the afterlife would be spent on the run, with no respite from his pursuer.

Not ever.

Am I right she asked Bardo silently.

Virgil's pursuit of Zach blinded him to the consequences of his actions. Had he paused to consider the situation he would have recognized in the cabdriver an obsessive soul like his own.

We'll never see him again? She had to be sure there were no hidden riders to Bardo's pronouncement.

I'm being as plain as I can. If you don't call him, he won't come. He will lose interest in the physical plane; there'll be more pressing matters to occupy him.

Bardo was gone again. Not for him the uplifting of the soul after a happy conclusion, nor the cheering and the backslapping. That was for humans only. For Bardo, there was no good or evil: only consequences.

Zach was waiting for her to finish her private conversation; her body language had alerted him to it.

Now, he asked again. "How long have we got?"

She wrapped her arms around him and pulled him closer. "Forever and a day." He resisted, placing his hands on her shoulders. Still wanting words instead of allowing their souls to mingle.

"Such poetry," he said, "but what does it mean?"

"A long time, Zach, a very long time."

"Years?"

She pulled him closer still. "For God's sake, I'm talking eternity."

THE END

ACKNOWLEDGEMENT

As always in the process of fiction creation there are others who labor to make the author appear better than he thought he was.

My thanks go to Arlene Robinson for editing an early draft and for suggesting that I needed a writers' group at that stage much more than a proofreader.

I joined the Internet Writing Workshop and dozens of writers jumped at the chance of shredding a chapter or two. I have to thank especially Charles Cox, Bill Bartlett and Francene Stanley for staying with the whole book as it was posted a piece each week. All your comments were invaluable.

John Hutt, Lari Ferguson and Robin Cain also offered excellent suggestions on many chapters. Thank you all.

Also thanks to Michael Cunningham who provided a critical read through before publication and to Anita Saunders for the final proofing.

Cover design by Olatunji Olawale Iyiola.

ABOUT THE AUTHOR

Parker Rimes

Parker Rimes has spent his life in Europe, Australia, the UK and the US. When not writing, he reads four or five books a week. Well, the first fifty pages at least. He blames that on a short attention span.

In the course of his journalist life, he has interviewed over a thousand people who claim paranormal experiences have occurred in their homes. Some of these stories seem truthful.

He enjoys discovering new verbs and wishing he'd thought of them first. He likes animals but prefers that most of them stay in their place of origin. His favorite wines are those sold close to wherever he lives.

Diligent research for his novels led him to enrol in a school for mediums, where he failed nearly every psychic test. But he can now predict where to find a good parking space slightly better than the average person.

BOOKS BY THIS AUTHOR

The Backward Time Traveler

Keera Miles, a psychic, has a most unusual quest. To travel back 200 years and rescue a sacred stone from a Sioux tribe before it's lost forever. She teams up with an annoying, cynical reporter Zach Bones.

Not that he believes her story, but, because he's hiding from a loan shark, because he needs a good story and because Keera is so gorgeous, he agrees to help her.

The ingenious, twisty plot follows the pair as they adapt to Indian bodies, and become trapped in a ferocious Crow raid. Their plan to snatch the stone from the wily and ruthless Red Leaf grows increasingly desperate.

When they flee back to the present, they find they have swapped one nightmare for a worse one.

The Upside Of Death

What happens when a psychic gets kidnapped? When psychic abilities are the only defense against physical violence. What if you know more about your kidnappers than they know about each other? What if access to the afterlife is all you have to keep you alive?

Never Show Them Money

When too much money is not nearly enough. Zach Bones, a reporter on the Chicago Post, has liberated three million dollars from a Russian kidnappers' bank account. Now he's offering the money to a rival syndicate in grateful payment for them eliminating his psychic girlfriend's kidnappers.

Trouble is, these Russians believe that if he took money out of one bank account, he could do it again. For them. And forever. Even worse, the hot-headed Olga arrives in town determined to avenge her father's past death at the hands of these Russians. While Zach searches for a solution, his girlfriend Keera enlists the aid of her spirit guide Bardo, whose enigmatic advice is hardly better than no advice at all.

The Darker You Get

Reporter Zach Bones still has Russian mob money. He'd like to keep it; his psychic girlfriend Keera says give it away—it's dirty.

A hitman Lev wants it also and uses a sniper rifle to make his point. The cops can't understand why a hitman would target an ordinary reporter, and grow suspicious of Zach's lack of explanation.

He can't find a solution that leaves him with a life worth living. And Keera's abilities can only do so much to protect both of them. Especially when Lev is steadily losing his grip on reality.

Eye Of The Beholder, A Novella

Zia checks out a dating website. It lets her view her prospective soulmate's world through his eyes. She sees blue skies. Leafy trees. A car interior. And a pair of feet—chained together. Puzzled and concerned, Zia searches for the truth in the glossy world of people-matching, and uncovers disturbing surgical procedures.

Worse, her bestie is involved...

Catch Your Death, A Novella

There's weird, and there's seriously weird. One of them can really wreck a girl's evening. And every evening after that.
Reporter Ruby Moskewitz is interviewing a famous Professor of Biology when he vanishes during a meal break. Just like that. Has this anything to do with his new drug that accelerates brain?
When she contacts his university she's told the professor has a contagious condition and had to be isolated urgently. This is a lie, she knows it, and she investigates.
Her one advantage? She's in sole possession of the drug that gifts normal people with abnormal powers.